RECLAIMING BRAVE

THE KANE BROTHERS BOOK THREE

GINA AZZI

Reclaiming Brave

Cover Design by: Regina Wamba of MaeIDesign.com

PROLOGUE

Ring. Ring.

"Hello?"

"Hey."

"Sierra?"

Pause. A stifled sigh. "Yeah. So, listen, I know you're like, living your best life in Georgia, but I'm pregnant."

1

DENVER

Three Weeks Earlier
End of August

"You all packed up?" I knock lightly against Jax's doorframe, noting the taped-up boxes and zipped suitcases.

"Pretty much," he responds on his knees, his voice muffled as his upper half is somewhere in his closet, digging around. "You think Marco will want these?" He appears suddenly, holding up a few baseball T-shirts—the ones that are white in the center with the three-quarter sleeves in red or green, or in this case, yellow.

I shrug, thinking about the kid my other brother, Carter, was partnered up with through the Big Brothers and Big Sisters of Georgia program. "I'm sure Carter will pass them along."

"Yeah," Jax agrees, dipping back into the closet.

A pang hits me in the chest as I watch him pack up his room. Jax has only been back a few months, and he's already taking off again. Not that I blame him. If I reconnected with the love of my life, hell, if I even had a love of my life, I would follow her to the ends of the earth if I could. Jax and Evie are moving to San

Antonio on Sunday, and this is their last weekend in town. My other brother, Carter, is going on a date tonight with the first woman who makes him really smile.

I groan inwardly. *Stop sounding like such a sap.*

But I can't help but wish I had something, someone, like that. Someone who makes me look forward to tomorrow. Soon, it will just be Daisy and me, and then she'll get some hotshot job somewhere and leave, and it will just be me. Denver Kane, all alone in his childhood home with no real career prospects and no genuine options. This is it. I look at the chipping paint on Jax's bedroom walls and the old comforter on his bed. This is as good as it's gonna get for me.

"Den." Jax's voice pulls me from my thoughts.

"Hmm?" I look up.

He stares at me strangely, as if he's studying me. "You okay, man? I called you like three times."

"Yeah. Fine."

He continues to watch me for several seconds before shrugging. "I asked if you want to grab a few beers at Raf's tonight."

"Oh, yeah, sure."

"It's mine and Evie's last Friday night."

"I know."

"And Carter will be there with Taylor."

"Yeah."

"And Sierra is in town to see Daisy."

"What?" I glance up sharply, an image of my sister's college roommate flooding my mind: long, dark hair that curls slightly at the ends, big, soulful chocolate eyes, and a wicked grin. Sierra Begay is the most intriguing woman I've ever met. And she's completely off limits.

"Daisy invited Sierra to visit," Jax repeats.

"Oh, cool," I say, trying to keep my voice even. Inside, my head spins. Sierra will be here, under the same roof as me. For an *entire* weekend.

* * *

I spit a loud curse as the wrench slips from my hand, catching the edge of my finger. Straightening from under the hood of the Toyota Camry, I hold an old bandana to the cut, stemming the light bleeding. My head is all over the place today.

"All good, Den?" Dean hollers over.

"Yeah, man." I duck back under the hood, keeping the bandana pressed to my hand as I try to clear my mind from thoughts of her.

Ever since I found out she's coming this weekend, she's all I can think about. Worming her way into my head and sabotaging my thoughts, she's suddenly everywhere, and I don't like it. In fact, I fucking hate it.

"Owner's picking up in an hour," Dean reminds me.

"Yep. It'll be finished." I've been working at Benny's Auto Repair for almost a month. I tried working for myself but wasn't earning enough money and was grateful when an old buddy from high school vouched for me at Benny's. It's all right money, no issues with my background, and Benny doesn't give a shit that I still do jobs on the side to make extra dough.

For a guy like me, it's a consistent paycheck and legit work, so I have no complaints.

Turning the wrench another half an inch, I tighten the bolt until sweat beads on my forehead. Blowing out a deep breath, I drop the wrench next to the tools I'm working with and walk over to a side table to grab my water bottle.

Guzzling back the cool liquid, I squeeze my eyes shut and shake my head, trying to clear the thoughts of Sierra from my mind. The smooth, rich undertones of her skin, her large, dark eyes, and the long, thick sheet of black hair falling like a curtain down her back. Damn it.

I need to forget her. Forget she's going to be under the same roof as me for the entire weekend and finish this job, so I can go home and crack a cold beer.

I just have to get through the rest of today.

Easier said than done.

2

SIERRA

"I'm so happy you're here." My best friend Daisy wraps me up in a warm hug the second I clear baggage claim.

I hug her back, my fingers almost clenching at the fabric of her tank top. God, I've missed her. Four years spent as roommates and best friends, and suddenly it's like she's been ripped from my life. Only now, back in her presence, am I able to find my footing. "You have no idea."

She pulls back, her nose wrinkling. "Is it that bad?"

I sigh, gesturing toward the airport exit as I roll my small suitcase behind me. "It's not bad. It's just...it's different. Being on my own without you is really like being on my own. The apartment is too quiet. You should have come to New York this summer like I begged you to a million times. How're you adjusting?"

Daisy fiddles with the ends of her hair as she glances at me from the corner of her eye. "You know I would have come if I could afford it."

"Daisy, you don't need –"

"Stop. I'm not going to mooch off of you. Or technically, James." She raises her eyebrows at me, referencing my generous stepdad who still bankrolls my life. And hasn't said a thing about my credit card bills this summer. “I still haven't found a job. No interviews. No prospects. Nothing. And until that happens, I’ll be right here in Ashby County."

"You will find a job, Dais. Trust me, you are crazy qualified for so many awesome positions. Any company would be lucky to have you. Anderson Marketing and PR -"

But Daisy holds up a hand and shakes her head before I can bring up my stepfather’s marketing company again. I’ve been offering to pass along her resume for weeks but she keeps shutting down the option.

I bite my tongue. Whatever else I say will make me look like a spoiled little brat. Daisy and I graduated together in May, and while she's been actively job searching and seeking, reaching out to alumni and writing a bazillion cover letters, I've been circumventing my mom and stepdad's attempts to pull me into the family business. They own a public relations and marketing conglomerate based in London, with offices throughout the UK, slowly expanding into mainland Europe. A company all my brothers—blood, half, and step—work at. Plus, my cousins. A company promising me financial stability and security, and the kicker is I wouldn't even start at the bottom. Nope, I could work under one of my brothers, or two cousins for that matter, and within a year, be an associate.

But I don't want it. I never have. But how the hell could I openly admit that to Daisy Kane, my hardworking, dedicated, determined, and stupidly driven best friend?

I can't, so I forgo the topic completely. "What are we doing tonight?"

She smiles, her whole face opening like sunshine blocking out a momentary storm cloud. "Raf's."

I snort, nodding in agreement. Raf's is seriously a dive, but it's a frequent hotspot in Daisy's tiny hometown. And while I'd never want it to be my hangout, there is something charming about it. Especially in comparison to the nightclubs in New York I danced at all summer. Sometimes, a girl just wants a piece of familiarity and small-town love.

"It gets better."

"What does?"

"Carter has a date tonight," Daisy practically squeals, clasping her hands together as we step through the airport doors, and the humidity hits me full on.

"Your brother? A date?"

"I know. It's insane that he convinced someone to go out with him."

I snort, rolling my eyes. Carter Kane is smoking hot. All Daisy's brothers are. I'm sure there are girls a mile long lining up to even get a smile from Carter. No, the surprising thing is that Carter doesn't do dates. He does hookups. So, this girl, she must be special.

"Are we going to tease him relentlessly before he picks her up?" I guess, as that's exactly what I'd do to any of my brothers.

"Even better."

I raise my eyebrows.

"We're going to crash his date!"

I lean my head back and laugh, throwing my arm around Daisy. God, I've really missed my best friend. How could I possibly move to the UK and leave my best girl behind? Why won't she just come with me? It's bad enough I'm in New York, and she's in Georgia, but a two-hour flight definitely beats a time zone change.

* * *

"Brain freeze." I cringe, swallowing a massive gulp of my cherry Slurpee.

Daisy snorts beside me, passing me a napkin from the cup holder of the white Jetta she's driving.

"I like your ride," I comment, wiping up the Slurpee drops falling from my mouth.

She shrugs. "Den's fixing cars up these days, so it's a loaner."

"It's a sweet loaner."

"Says the girl who drives a Benz."

I roll my eyes. "It was meant to bribe me, not help me out. And I don't even have it anymore since I'm in the city."

She laughs. "Sierra, take the job."

I look out the window, noting the lush green of the passing trees and shrubbery. It would be so easy to say yes, to just take the job. But it's not what I want. I want to pursue my art, I always have. I'm not going to give up on my passion, on my dream, for a job in a field I'm not interested in.

"How much longer is Jax home?" I ask instead, referencing Daisy's brother who is getting ready to move to Texas with his girlfriend. Out of all of the Kanes, Jax is the one I know the least, in terms of time spent in his company, but Denver's the toughest one to figure out. I may not have spent a lot of time with Jax, but he's easygoing and open, whereas Denver's always been a murky shadow in the background. He's tough to read, impossible to make smile, and sometimes I think he can't stand me.

"This is his last weekend."

"No way!"

"I know." Daisy turns to me, taking her eyes off the road to give me puppy eyes. "I'm going to miss him like crazy. It's been so great having him around for the whole summer and getting to spend so much time with him. But I'm happy for him and Evie. Plus, now we have an excuse to visit San Antonio."

"There is that," I agree.

"Want to grab a late lunch in Savannah? Raf's won't pick up 'til tenish, and we don't have any other plans."

"And we can't annoy Carter all day if we're crashing his date tonight."

"True. Lunch?"

"Done." I smile at my bestie as she makes a left and heads toward downtown Savannah.

Sometimes, the best things are just being with the people who get you.

Now, that is a real luxury.

* * *

It's early evening when Daisy and I enter the Kane home. The living room is empty, and I leave my suitcase by the stairs, flopping onto the couch with Daisy dropping down beside me. She kicks her feet up on the coffee table and toes off her sandals, letting them fall to the floor.

I love being at the Kanes. It's warm and comfortable and reminds me a lot of how Lach and I grew up, especially in the first years after Mom left Dad, before she met James. Lach and I relied on each other for everything and spent most of our afternoons hanging on the living room couch, waiting for friends to come over, playing video games or watching movies.

I glance at Daisy as she scrolls through messages and emails on her phone, the frown between her eyebrows deepening. She gives a heavy sigh, and I want to hug her. I've offered several times to put her in contact with Lachlan or my cousin Finn but she refused, saying she doesn't want to leave the US. Given her resigned expression and the dejection that weighs on her shoulders, I'll offer again in a few weeks. If she doesn't have any job bites by then, she may be open to other options.

"Job hunt?" I ask softly.

"More like job fail."

"You're going to find a job you love, Daisy. A few months one way or the other won't make much of a difference."

She mumbles under her breath, and I don't press her since it sounds like "easy for you to say."

"Let's go out and have some serious fun tonight. Me and you.

Like old times." I raise my eyebrows at her as she turns to look at me.

"Want to start the party early?" She tilts her head toward the kitchen and what I presume is waiting alcohol.

"As if I'd ever say no to that."

She giggles and dashes into the kitchen, returning with a bottle of wine and two glasses. The bottle is already opened, and she pulls out the cork and pours two glasses, handing me one.

"To being unemployed." She raises a glass in my direction.

"But still hot," I counter.

She snorts and we clink glasses. I take a tentative sip of the wine and feel my nose wrinkle, mirroring Daisy's expression. "What is this?"

She shrugs. "Never trust my brothers to buy wine. Ever. It's probably something Den cooks with."

"Whatever." I take another sip. "It's not bad after you get used to the taste."

Footsteps sound on the staircase, and Carter's frame comes into view.

"Ow-oo, ow-oo!" Daisy catcalls him, whistling obnoxiously.

He gives her the middle finger, and I laugh, suddenly missing the easy camaraderie I have with my own brothers. I've barely seen them this summer. Daisy and I walk toward the bottom of the staircase to give Carter hell.

"Sierra Grace." He turns to me, smiling.

"Hi, Carter." I breathe him in. "You even smell good. A shower and cologne? This must be one lucky lady."

"Shut it." He waves me away, and the familiarity I have with him warms my heart. It's nice to feel like I belong somewhere every once in a while, especially since my entire family is currently in the UK, and I'm here, alone.

Daisy stares at Carter with wide, shiny eyes. A bubble of laughter falls from her mouth.

"What are you staring at?" he asks her curiously.

"This is the best."

"What is?" A flash of annoyance crosses Carter's face, and I bite the inside of my cheek to keep from grinning. He really likes this woman. And Daisy is dying to give him hell for it.

"You. Actually getting bent out of a shape over a girl. Who would have thought we'd see the day?"

"Not me," a low voice says, and my shoulders tense as goosebumps break out over my skin.

Denver Kane.

I'd recognize his voice anywhere, and the sound of it crashes over me like a cresting wave. I could literally drown in Denver, and he wouldn't have a clue. His eyes cut to me, unnerving me and keeping me rooted with the intensity flaring around his irises, darkening his eyes to black.

"Hey, Denver," I manage to say, lifting my hand in a wave. I hope my voice isn't wavering.

He nods at me, businesslike, and then looks to his sister and brother, completely dismissing me. Like usual. My cheeks blaze at his rejection, but I shouldn't be surprised. I've pined for Denver since I met him during my sophomore year of college. Unnerved by how ridiculously hot he was, I was also drawn to his quiet intensity. The entire time I stayed with Daisy, I barely heard him speak but his eyes, his black eyes saw everything, even me. Although I never had a conversation with him, I knew, just knew, that if he spoke to me, it would be easy between us, natural. Instead, he remained a mystery.

Denver exudes confidence, an unapologetic boldness that shifts the entire dynamic of a room the moment he enters. His presence could fill a solar system and here I am, one tiny moon, desperate to be sucked into his orbit. I've attempted for years to get to know him better, or at least be friendly, but he's shut me down each time.

That doesn't mean I've moved on though. Nope, my stupid, desperate heart still beats faster at the sight of Denver.

"Have fun tonight," he tells Carter before turning around and walking back into the kitchen, the swinging door swaying in his wake.

"Weird," Carter murmurs.

"I know, right?" Daisy agrees, staring at the space where Denver disappeared moments before.

I take a small step back, studying my hands. Denver can't stand me. I don't know why exactly, but he glares at me like he's angry I'm in his space, frustrated he even has to waste a breath greeting me. A burn blazes through my veins, and I take a fortifying breath.

"Seriously, is something up with you and my brother?" Daisy asks me, her eyebrows arching.

A blush burns up my neck, bleeding into my cheeks in embarrassment. "I don't think he likes me much." I admit. Flicking my wrist dismissively, I change the subject. "It doesn't matter. So, you're taking her to Raf's?" I direct my question toward Carter and Daisy's laughter escapes, picking back up with her teasing.

"I'm leaving." Carter raises his hands in surrender. "Whatever you girls get into tonight, be safe."

I look at Daisy, and she rolls her eyes and we both laugh, knowing that we're getting into his date tonight.

"See you later." Carter pushes through the front door, and we wait until we hear the door close behind him.

"He has no idea, does he?" I ask Daisy.

She shakes her head. "None whatsoever. I never thought I'd see the day Carter would actually fall for someone."

I walk back to the coffee table and down half the contents of my wine glass. A breath of relief escapes me, grateful that it's Carter and not Denver. The relief is quickly followed by a pang of longing, of knowing. One day Denver Kane will fall in love, and my heart will break. He'll just never know it. No one will.

3

DENVER

Storming into the kitchen after seeing her, my hands clench into fists. She's here in my living room. Laughing with Daisy and joking with Carter like she's part of the family. Because she is. Kind of.

But she shouldn't be. No, Sierra Begay should definitely not be part of my family.

Wicked curves, long black hair I could fist in my hands and wrap around my wrists. I see it splayed around the colorful ink decorating my arms. Her mischievous smirk pisses me off as much as it turns me on; Sierra forces me to the brink with just one word, one look, one irritating eye roll.

Her laughter follows me into the kitchen, as if in mockery, and I feel a wave of anger mixed with a flicker of desire heat my blood. Shaking my head, I pull a Coke from the fridge and walk out to the back porch, letting the door slam shut behind me.

Breathing in the heavy, humid air, I hold it in my lungs, trying to calm the racing of my heart. Kicking back in one of the deck chairs, I close my eyes, the sweet Cola quieting my mind and easing my nerves. She's the one girl I can't pursue. I can't mess with the girl that my sister considers a sister because even if

Sierra and I did hookup, that's all it would be. A hookup. One night. Fine, it'd be a smoking hot, passionate as all hell, perfect fucking night. But then the morning would come, and I'd be forced to leave her bed, leave her behind, not get all kinds of tangled up in her life when I have my own shit to worry about.

And I can't do that to my sister's best friend. It would create a wedge in their friendship that Daisy may never forgive me for. Hell, I can't forgive myself for, and I have too many goddamn sins to start adding to the list now.

Draining the Coke and soaking in the silence of night, I feel better. Calmer. More in control of my emotions and more in control of how things are going to play out tonight. I'm gonna hit Raf's with Evie and Jax. See Carter and Taylor. Watch over Daisy and Sierra as they undoubtedly consume too many sugary drinks with umbrellas from the bartender, Lenny. And then I'm going to come home, sleep off the night and my own frustrations, and work like hell for the rest of the weekend, avoiding all signs of Sierra Begay until she's gone.

I blow out a deep breath.

Just get through this weekend, Den. Then it'll be months until you have to see her again. By then, things could be completely different.

I crush the Coke can in my hand.

Who am I kidding? The only thing that could be different is if Sierra is seeing someone. And even then, just a glimpse of her would be the same type of sweet torture for me.

* * *

She's reckless. Wild. Her dark hair slides over her shoulders as she tosses her head back, her arms reaching out to the ceiling as she bumps and grinds to the beat. Her eyes are closed, the delicate curve of her neck on full display, and the ridiculous jangle of bangle bracelets slides down nearly to her elbows as she waves her arms.

I close my eyes, needing to rip my gaze away from her. She's dangerous.

A guy I recognize as a hang-around to the Devil's Shadows MC comes up behind her and places a hand possessively on her hip, and I take a menacing step forward from my perch against the bar.

She turns in his arms and smiles but shakes her head, stepping out of his grasp, and a shock of relief rocks through my system, surprising me in its intensity. What is wrong with me? She's Daisy's best friend. I'm just looking out for her, making sure she's okay since the rest of my siblings are caught up in their own fun.

If only I believed that's all it is. But I know my interest is deeper than just keeping an eye out for my sister's friend.

I want her. I've wanted her since she appeared on our doorstep for a visit Daisy's second year of college. She was just a kid then, nineteen, and I was keeping my head down after completing my bullshit prison sentence. She was all big eyes and a contagious laugh. She spoke of art and textures, or colors and lighting. Her idealism and zest for life pissed me off in its naivete and yet, I wanted to listen to her speak for hours, learn more about the way her mind worked, see the world the way she did, if only for a moment.

Damn it. Desire thrums through my veins, turning my blood hot, and I bang a fist down on the top of the bar, irritated with myself.

Get it together, Kane. She's off limits. She's not for you.

"Den!" Daisy looks up from her spot on the dance floor, her golden-brown hair sticking to her neck with sweat. "Come dance and join the party." She spreads her arms out wide, encompassing the makeshift dance floor at Raf's Bar and Grill. A local hangout, the place is a complete hole-in-the-wall, and yet to us Kane kids, it's practically home.

I shake my head, raising my lukewarm bottle of beer to my lips and continuing to glare at anyone who steps up to Sierra. Everyone here knows better than to step to Daisy. Especially with Carter, Jax, and me present.

Out on the dance floor, my brother Carter is wrapped up with his new girl, Taylor. Their heads are bent together, his hands gripping her hips. My other brother, Jax, whispers into his girl Evie's ear, and her laugh echoes around me.

And I'm just standing here, watching my brothers tangle up with women who love them, or at least are falling in love with them, and care about them. Beautiful, intelligent, kindhearted women.

And all I can do is stare at the one girl in the world I can't have, and who I want more than I've wanted any woman in a long, long time.

* * *

The night seems to drag on as Sierra loses herself to whisky and music. What kind of girl drinks whisky, anyway? I mean, except for the girls who would be perfect for me.

My sister is sloshed off of Lenny's fruity cocktails complete with tiny umbrellas, Evie is gulping water to stay hydrated, and Taylor is being spread out across the bar, a bottle of tequila pushed into Carter's hand for a body shot.

And Sierra is drinking whisky—not just any whisky, Glenlivet 18.

Just another reminder why she's different than any woman I've ever met—one more reason to desire her more than my next breath.

4

SIERRA

The soft snores whistling in and out of Daisy's nose are the loudest sound I hear as I lay next to her in her childhood bedroom. It's funny, really, Daisy and me. We couldn't be more different, our upbringings completely opposite, yet she's like my sister.

I guess college living does that. You meet when you're at one of the most vulnerable times in your life, trying to figure out who you are, and what you're going to do with the rest of your life. At the same time, you're learning how to do laundry, attempting not to substitute cereal—or Cheetos—for dinner, and pretending you're not gaining the freshman fifteen. It's exhausting without being paired up with a roommate from hell.

Luckily, I got my best friend.

As Daisy's snores even out, other sounds from the house begin to infiltrate my consciousness: Evie's laughter as she Face-Time's with her brother, Jax and Denver's voices mingling in the background, and nothing from Carter, which makes sense as Taylor was practically sleeping while walking home from Raf's.

Within moments, I hear another bedroom door close, and a hush settles over the house. At first, I think it's Denver who's gone to sleep, but after several minutes pass without Evie and Jax's playful bickering, I know, just know, that the creaking floorboards and flipping of the television channels means Denver is awake.

And so am I.

Excitement bubbles in my stomach quickly followed by nerves. Should I go down? Feign I need a glass of water? Turning to my side, I take in Daisy's peaceful expression. No, this is stupid. What if he ignores me?

But what if he doesn't?

I roll my eyes at myself, turning onto my back. I stare up at Daisy's ceiling fan, the spinning blades churning out a soft hum.

Hooking up with Denver will make things awkward. And the last thing I need in my life right now is to have a strain on my friendship with Daisy.

He coughs, the sound seeming to echo around me.

I am thirsty. Kind of.

Ugh.

I bounce my head back against my pillow, hating my own indecision. From the first time I laid eyes on Denver Kane, I wanted to make him smile. Laugh. Trade a bit of his ever-present severity for a spark of mischief.

That was years ago.

And still every time our paths cross, my body tingles with an awareness that I have only experienced in his presence. I can feel his eyes, black as coal, tracking my movements. The low, sharp intake of his breath when I pass by him, my arm just brushing against his chest or bicep. From that first encounter nearly three years ago, everything between Denver and me has been tense, bordering on strained. And yet, just below that tightness is a thread of flirtation, of awareness, of palpable excitement. An energy runs through my body like a live wire, heightening my senses and amplifying my perception as I strain my ears for any sound of Denver.

I hear him clear his throat, a chuckle hovering in the space between us like a homing beacon.

I squeeze my eyes shut tight, my mind already made up.

Throwing the covers back and swinging my legs to the side of the bed, I listen to make sure there is no change in Daisy's breathing.

Confident that she is out for the count, I stand up on shaky legs, although I'm not sure if my unsteadiness is from the whisky still coursing through my veins or my own anticipation of being face to face with Denver.

Alone.

Just the two of us.

Gah!

I sneak into the bathroom to brush my teeth again and fluff the roots of my straight black hair for volume. Swiping my fingers across my eyebrows and adding a coat of lip balm to my lips, I take a deep breath and bite back the swell of nervous laughter that wants to burst forth.

Get it together, Sierra. You can do this. You are *doing this.*

Clad in my pajamas consisting of a pair of tiny, grey sweat shorts, and a simple, black tank top, I walk down the stairs with care, grimacing as the third step creaks loudly. Denver pauses the TV, effectively silencing the space between us with the exception of our combined breathing.

My foot clears the last step, and I brace my arm on the stair post, biting my lower lip. "Hey."

He nods at me, his eyes darkening to midnight from his seat on the couch. Behind him, a comedian walks across stage on the television, spewing jokes, but nothing is funny or amusing between Denver and me.

No. Like usual, everything between us is stiflingly serious.

"Can't sleep?" His voice is low and gruff and grazes across my skin like sandpaper, causing goosebumps to rush up my arms.

I shake my head, blinking slowly.

"You, um, hungry?"

My stomach clenches at the question, but it's a different kind of hunger than a physical need for food. It's a need for him.

Whatever he reads in my face causes his eyes to flash—a quick dash of danger, and a sharp intake of breath.

"Can I sit with you for a while?" I ask instead, my voice breathy, my footing unsure.

He nods once, and I walk over to the couch, sitting down next to him and leaning into the cushions.

He un-mutes the TV and sound resumes, laughter from the crowd and the fast talking of the comedian echoing around us. I can't focus on the jokes. I can't focus on anything except the heat radiating off of Denver's body, seeping into my skin.

God, it's torturous.

Everything with him is.

With Carter, I can say whatever I'm thinking and joke around until I'm blue in the face. With Jax, I can drink a beer and discuss current events or my favorite book. With Denver, I can hardly freaking breathe.

He shifts in his seat, and I'm incredibly aware that the movement causes the couch cushion to dip, bringing our bodies closer together, as if we're magnets. His knee brushes against my thigh, and I swallow thickly, turning to look at his profile.

When I turn my head just a fraction of an inch, Denver's dark gaze bores straight into my eyes, and my mouth simultaneously dries and waters. How the hell is that even possible?

"Sierra?" His voice is gruff and pained. Raw.

I place my hand over his knee, and even though I'm nervous, my fingers are sure, steady. He's changed into basketball shorts, and the heat from his skin warms my palm. I brush my fingers across the soft hairs curling on his leg and he exhales, causing me to look away from my hand and back to his face.

"Sierra."

I shake my head, inching my fingers up his leg, shifting closer until our shoulders bump, and I fight the urge to melt into him.

Denver's eyes close for a beat too long; a second that stretches like eternity as I wait for him to make up his mind, to decide one way or the other. My heart stutters in my chest and anxiety threatens to cloud my mind. What if he shuts me down? The embarrassment alone may kill me; how could I ever face him again? My fingers clench as hysteria threatens to consume me when his eyes finally snap open.

His gaze is like steel, his jaw resolute, a tiny muscle twitching under his left eye.

"Fuck it," he says.

And then his lips crash over mine, his fingers tangling in my hair, knotting at the base of my neck to hold my head steady against the onslaught of his kiss.

I meet him kiss for kiss, moaning when his tongue sweeps into my mouth. The scruff marking his cheeks and chin scrapes over my neck, and I reach up, tugging on his messy man-bun and pulling him closer.

His eyes blaze, fierce and wild, as I lose myself in his touch. He nips at my lower lip and I groan, shifting so I'm lying on the couch with Denver hovering over me.

He pauses for a moment, his dark eyes searching mine and scanning my face. He rakes his teeth across his lower lip and I hiss, my fingers tangled in the collar of his T-shirt.

"Sierra."

"Don't."

"We shouldn't. This is—"

"A long time coming."

He grins, a low chuckle working its way up from his belly and my heart freaking stops. Finally, a Denver Kane smile, an acknowledgment of some sort. My fingers clench his shirt tighter, trying to pull him closer before he changes his mind or stops completely. "Still. If we do this, we can't go back."

"I know."

"You're making it fucking impossible for me to walk away."

"Then don't."

"Sierra." My name is like a plea on his lips, and I'm unsure if it's said in surrender or rejection.

"I want this. Den, I want you."

His biceps flex when I say the name everyone calls him, everyone except me, as it's always seemed too familiar for the strained relationship we danced around.

He nods once, the lines of his face shifting as he dips his head gently and captures my mouth once more, this time sweetly and with reverence. Denver moves over me, his hands grazing every inch of my skin as he undresses me. I shiver from his touch and then from the lack of his heat as he pulls back to glance at my naked body, splayed out beneath him on the couch.

"You're perfect. Too goddamn good for me." His lip quirks in jest, but his tone is serious.

Before I can respond or disagree or consider the fact that anyone could walk downstairs and see us on the couch, he pounces, building me up and working me over like a professional. And I shatter beneath him, over and over. And again.

5

DENVER

It's early when I wake the next morning, the stillness of the house too quiet, in sharp contrast to my immediate restlessness.

Sierra is gone, and I think I dreamed the entire thing. The searing kisses, the hot touches, the languid build between us that reached a frenzied pitch before we crashed, again and again.

Fuck.

Except I can still taste her skin on my lips, can still smell her perfume wrapped around the discarded basketball shorts I pull off the floor. No, I didn't imagine last night. It was real. Every single moment of it burned into my mind forever, like some type of sweet torture.

Sierra has disappeared, and my house is too damn quiet for the thoughts ping-ponging around my brain. What the hell was I thinking? Losing myself in Sierra, God, it was perfect. But taking her on the freaking couch in the family room? That was something I would have done at seventeen, not thirty. It was stupid, reckless, a moment of desperation that blocked out my ability to think clearly. I never take girls to my home, ever. But I've never tried so hard to stay away from anyone like I have Sierra. Last night, all of my restraint snapped, my mind clicked off, and I allowed myself to be consumed by her vibrancy, her sweet uncertainty, her passionate surrender to the moment. How can one woman be everything at once?

I sigh, sitting up and hunching forward on the couch. Scraping my hands across my face, I rub my eyes and stand, making my way into the kitchen. Pouring a large glass of water, I down it in three gulps before flipping the switch for the coffee maker. I decide that eggs Benedict will keep me busy—my hands at least—until everyone finds their way to the kitchen for breakfast.

But the entire time I'm whisking the hollandaise sauce, I'm thinking of her. The melting chocolate of her eyes as they flashed in anticipation, the fullness of her mouth as she captured my bottom lip, sucking softly, and the wicked curves of her body as she moved, almost danced, under my touch.

"You're up early," Daisy quips as she pushes into the kitchen, the door swinging behind her as she beelines for the refrigerator.

I jump at my sister's intrusion to my thoughts and look away, suddenly ashamed for my actions last night. Actions that brought me so much pleasure, but are going to undoubtedly cause pain. Embarrassment, an emotion I'm not used to feeling, skitters along my nerves as I realize that just ten minutes earlier, Daisy would have caught me in my birthday suit on the couch and I may as well have broadcasted the fact that Sierra and I hooked up.

Jesus.

"You okay?" Daisy asks me over her glass of orange juice. "Oh, thank God, coffee." She nods toward the full coffee pot and pours three mugs, placing one next to me on the counter as she rummages in the fridge for cream.

"Yeah. You're not too hungover, are you?"

She shakes her head, leaning against the closed refrigerator door and crosses her feet at the ankles, regarding me.

"Nope. But I was definitely drunker than I thought. Those fruity drinks go straight to my head."

"Yeah, can't taste the alcohol. Glad you're not wrecked today, and that you can hold your liquor."

"Uh-huh."

I turn back to whisking, adding the melted butter slowly to the bowl.

"So, strange thing happened last night," Daisy pauses, and I can feel her gaze pinning me right between my shoulder blades.

Even though I don't turn around, my shoulders tense at the words, and I hear her sigh behind me.

"What's that?" I ask anyway.

"I woke up in the middle of the night to pee and Sierra was gone."

I don't say anything, but my hand turns the whisk faster, beating the egg yolks harder.

"She's my best friend, Denver. And you're my brother." Daisy voice dips, an edge of anger I'm not used to having directed at me infused in her tone. "We all know who's gonna end up hurt if last night's sexcapade turns into a thing before crashing and burning. If you ruin my friendship, I'll never forgive you."

I nod, letting her know I hear her. The clink of a spoon hitting the inside of the sink dings out behind me.

"I'm going to bring Sierra a coffee," she says before retreating from the kitchen.

I grab the steaming mug of coffee and take a large gulp, glad for the burn along the roof of my mouth. Jesus. It's already starting.

* * *

I'm literally pacing along the back porch as I try to sort out everything I want to say to Sierra before she leaves. Because suddenly, and out of nowhere, she's heading out early, and I know it has something to do with the mind-blowing sex we had on the couch last night.

Jax and Evie are moving to San Antonio tomorrow morning, and right now I can't think about anything except clearing the charged air between Sierra and me.

"Whoa, don't give yourself an aneurysm." Her honeyed voice breaks through my thoughts and I turn, my steps faltering at the sight of her.

Tall and graceful, bright, amused eyes, and a cocky grin slashing her mouth, Sierra is all playful confidence this morning. As if everything is cool between us. As if she isn't getting the hell out of dodge to put some space between her and the obvious mistake she made last night when she decided to go slumming with me.

"What?"

"Thinking that hard." She laughs easily, tapping the side of her head. "I just wanted to come say 'bye. And thanks for breakfast. I was hoping for a Denver omelette but the eggs benedict was really good."

I nod, not even registering her joke as I search her expression for signs of...what? "Why're you leaving early?" I ask, my heart thumping in my chest.

She sighs, and there it is, a flash of uncertainty, a falter in the bravado act she's trying on. I reach out, my fingers circling her wrist as she looks up at me, her confidence from earlier slipping into uneasiness.

"Truth?" She asks, clearing her throat.

I nod.

"My brother and cousin are unexpectedly flying in to meet me in New York."

"Why?"

"Because they're trying to convince me to take a job at James's business."

"James?" I cringe at the hard edge in my tone. Who the hell is James?

"My stepdad."

Stupid. "Oh."

"Yeah, so, I've gotta leave early. But listen, last night," Sierra pauses and I lean closer, as if straining for her words, "it was freaking incredible." She smiles shyly, shifting her weight from foot to foot.

I chuckle, relief flooding through me at her words. "Yeah?"

"Yeah. Thanks Den. For...everything. We're cool, right?"

I nod again, apparently incapable of speaking. What else is new? I drop her wrist, my fingers reaching up to brush against her cheekbone as she blushes a delicate pink.

Reaching up on her toes, Sierra brushes a quick kiss against my cheek before turning, waving to me over her shoulder before disappearing inside.

What the hell is with this girl? Everything about her gets under my skin. She's fun and playful, flirty and easygoing. She's sweet and shy, vulnerable and unsure. She's colorful and passionate and so goddamn naive and trusting and understanding that she infuriates me almost more than I want her.

And did she just give me the talk? The easy, brush off after sex? The "we're cool" so things are all good? The two words I yearn to hear from every woman after sex. Every woman except her.

My chest feels hollow as I stare at the closed back door. Clenching my hands into fists, I shake my head at myself.

Where has my manhood gone?

* * *

The house seems to relax the moment Sierra leaves, but I know it's just me who feels that way. To be honest, even though I'm relieved she's gone, her presence wreaking havoc on my thoughts and causing all of these unexpected emotions to overwhelm me, a part of me is disappointed. I was hoping we'd hookup again tonight or at least get to spend more time together than her giving me the brush off talk on her way out the door.

That was definitely a first.

And not a first I ever anticipated having with Sierra.

I lose myself in a couple of side jobs I picked up for the weekend while Daisy pouts in her room over her friend's sudden departure, shooting me death glares whenever our paths cross. Carter is wrapped up in Taylor, literally, and Jax and Evie are saying goodbye to a few friends before their departure tomorrow morning.

Things are definitely changing for the Kane kids, with a lot of uncertainty and new beginnings on the horizon—at least for everyone except me.

I crank the socket wrench another quarter of an inch, sweat beading on my forehead as I peer under the hood of an old Chevrolet. It's hot as balls outside, and still I prefer the quiet solitude of the garage to the emptiness of my house.

It seems like everyone is moving forward except me.

And all I have to hang on to are memories of a beautiful woman who knows better than to really tangle up with me. A woman who haunts my waking hours and lingers in my dreams but will never be part of my reality.

6

SIERRA

"Absolutely not," I shoot down Lachlan and Finlay before the words are even out of their mouths.

"Come on, Sierra." Lach blows out an exasperated breath, leaning forward onto the table, his elbows seeming to support his entire body weight. "You're wasting your time. And for what? Parties and painting?"

I glare at him, narrowing my eyes. "Don't belittle my passion just because you don't have one."

He sighs again and looks to my cousin, Finn, for direction.

"What Lach's trying to say is—"

"That I should jump on the family bandwagon and accept a job I have no desire in doing because it's the easy way out, and I'll make a decent salary."

"Well, yes." Finn smiles, an easy grin that stretches across his face and lightens the mood. "And the salary is better than decent."

"You guys." I groan, signaling to the waitress that I need another cucumber martini. "I like my life here. I like my painting." I stick my tongue out at my brother, but Lachlan just rolls his eyes in return.

"You're twenty-three-years-old, Sisi. You have to grow up sometime." Lachlan uses his stern voice, and I flip him the middle finger.

Only two years older than me, Lachlan acts like my dad half the time, which makes sense since he stepped into the role easily enough when Mom and Dad split. Still, it pisses me off because I still have a father. Whether he's in the picture or not is another story.

"James isn't going to bankroll your lifestyle forever." My brother tries again.

I thank the waitress for my martini and take a big gulp before turning back to my brother and cousin. "That's fine. I can support myself."

Lachlan laughs, running a hand down his face. "On what money? What are you going to do? Find a roommate in a walkup in Brooklyn and waitress?"

"If I have to." I shrug, irritated that Lachlan thinks having a roommate and waitressing are so far beneath him. And that *I* wouldn't be able to do it. Does he forget where we came from? Did he tune out the years that Mom worked two jobs and struggled to make mortgage payments?

"Sisi," Finn says, his Scottish brogue comforting as he reaches out and gently wraps his fingers around my wrist, "we all just want what's best for you. That's all. James is offering you an opportunity to join the family business, gain a lot of experience, build your resume, and earn a shit-ton of money. Marketing and PR is necessary in the art world, too."

I nod, letting him know I hear his message loud and clear. Gain experience, find your footing, learn, and grow. That's what James pitched to my brothers and cousins before they joined the family company, and then they never left. Why? Because the salaries are too good and the lifestyles too glamorous.

I just want to paint. I'm not cut out for corporate bullshit and dress codes or learning about email etiquette and the hierarchy of office dynamics. I'm a free spirit. Like my dad.

"Don't worry too much. I'm sure James will bankroll your life for a bit longer yet," Finn adds to take the sting out of the conversation.

Lachlan heaves a massive sigh, and I take another gulp of my martini.

"Is that why you guys flew here at the last minute?"

Lach and Finn exchange a look before turning back to me. "The position needs to be filled. You've got three more months to decide if you want it before James moves someone up internally."

"Seems fair."

Lach pulls at the collar of his shirt, as if it's suddenly suffocating him and Finn snorts. "It is what it is."

"Enough talk about the family business." I change the subject as our waitress moves closer to our table on the outdoor patio. "Let's order, and then figure out what we want to do tonight."

* * *

The club is pulsing: bodies gyrating, lights flashing, music pounding. Shots are being tossed back, cocaine cut, disregard and disobedience easily strumming through the partygoers' veins.

I watch my cousin and brother make their way to the bar while I sit in a VIP booth, suddenly feeling out of place. I've been doing the City party scene all summer and while it was fun at the time, it feels different tonight. Instead of losing myself to the music, my thoughts are caught on Denver. What was I thinking, giving him the brush off? I didn't mean it. I mean, I did mean that things are cool between us, because they are, but I didn't mean it to sound so blasé when I said it.

I was so nervous to face him the following day. What if he gave me the brush off? What if he acted like nothing even happened between us? So many what-if's and given our strained history, I was desperate to settle things between us on my own terms. Still, I watched the way his eyes narrowed when I tried to act flippant, the small muscle under his left eye twitching subtly.

But then he reached out and touched me and my pretense slipped. I knew the moment he saw through me because his shoulders relaxed and the severe line of his mouth softened. But what does that mean?

Did he want to acknowledge that there is something between us? Did I blow any chance of that something developing by trying to shut it down before it could even begin? Sighing, I rest my head back against the plush padding of the booth and take another sip of my whiskey.

"Hey gorgeous." A guy smirks at me, his green eyes blazing, his light hair perfectly styled in a casual, I-don't-give-a-fuck kind of way.

Three nights ago, I would have found him delicious. Hell, three nights ago I would have gone home with him.

But not now. Not when all I can think of are a pair of eyes dark like midnight, the scrape of scruff against my skin, and my fingers clutching tightly to thick forearms stained with ink. The presence of Denver Kane shadows me, and I can't shake him.

Not yet.

Maybe not ever.

I give a light smile and flip my chin at the guy in greeting before turning back to my drink and pulling out my cell phone.

Tapping out a quick text to my dad, I ask him if he wants to chat tomorrow about the paintings he's working on. It's a long shot; he rarely, if ever, responds to my messages. But that doesn't mean I've stopped trying. At least, not yet.

* * *

Lach and Finn are gone as quickly as they came. Their trips are always like this, speedy turnarounds and twenty-four hours of fun. Then back to the grind, to work, to clocking hours, and gazing out at the world from corner offices.

I miss them the moment they're gone. Sitting alone in my bedroom at James's penthouse, I blow out a deep breath and realize that I'm alone. Three days ago, I was hanging out with my best friend. Two nights ago, I was with Denver Kane.

Was that only two nights ago? I touch my lips at the memory, remembering his kiss. Flopping back against my mattress, I close my eyes and let the moments between Denver and me flood my mind. It was perfect. It was more than I imagined and hoped for, more than I ever thought possible. I wish we had more time together, or that there was some type of chance of a relationship developing between us. But now I'm just being greedy.

Denver Kane doesn't date women like me. I don't know who the hell he dates but I do know, via Daisy, that his only serious relationships were with quiet, homegrown girls. Girls who knew how to knit and bake. Girls who were tamer, sweeter.

Still, that was before he went to jail. Maybe things are different now? The truth is, I don't know much about Denver's past. But I do know that when he turns his gaze on me, he sees the part of me I try to keep hidden. The unsure, uneasy portion that's so worried I'm going to sell-out and get sucked into the monotonous routine of life. The part of me that would forsake my art for stability. The piece of me I like the least. He sees it, or senses it, and still, there's no judgement in his eyes.

I bang my head against my mattress, trying to clear my thoughts of Denver. He was a one-time thing, a one-night encounter. It's done. I need to move on. Figure out what I'm going to do with the rest of my life. I have three months to sort out my future.

That thought is so depressing, I dismiss it immediately. Today, I will lose myself in my art.

Ignoring that stab in my chest from my dad's unanswered text message, I leave my bedroom and step into the room that James converted into a studio for me years ago. Opening the Sonos app on my phone, the tension in my neck dissipates as soon as Lana del Rey's voice fills the space. I take out my paints and brushes, running my fingertips over them lovingly as I sit in front of a blank canvas. I ignore my racing mind and overwhelming thoughts in favor of my passion—my painting.

Hours later I step back, pausing the music as I study my work. The strokes of the blues and purples are strong and bold, vividly jumping from the canvas. The greys and greens are subtler, fading into the shadows. The woman's face materializes slowly and gains definition the longer I stare. A strong nose, graceful neck, and eyes that see everything, my grandmother stares back at me. A simple beaded necklace with a feather dangles from her neck, her wrists adorned with leather cuffs. Her hands are cupped before her, reaching out, as though gifting an offering, bequeathing me something.

I bite my lower lip, narrowing my gaze as I study her expression, but the shrill beep of my cell phone receiving a text breaks the spell of the moment. I startle, glancing down at the screen of my phone.

Denver.

He messaged me!

Denver: Hey. All work out okay with your family's surprise visit?

I smile, still gnawing on my lip at his thoughtfulness. That he even reached out to me at all. Does this mean he's thinking about me as much as I'm thinking of him? Probably not.

Plucking my phone from the small table, I flip off the lights and exit the studio, walking to the kitchen and pouring myself a glass of chilled Riesling as I tap out a reply.

Me: Hi! Yes, all good thanks. My brother and cousin came to bombard me with pleas to move closer to the family unit.

Small dots appear at the bottom of my screen immediately, and I relish the lick of excitement swiping low in my belly.

Denver: England?

Me: Scotland.

Denver: You moving?

Me: Undecided. I've got three months to sort out my life.

Several minutes pass before he replies.

Denver: Good luck.

Good luck? What's that supposed to mean? I sigh, draining my wine. Rereading our brief exchange, I'm desperate to keep the conversation going. But what do I say?

Me: Thanks. How's all by you?

Denver: All good. Heading to work now. Talk to you soon.

He will? Talk to me soon? I smile as I re-read the words, knowing that I would look like a complete idiot to anyone witnessing the roller coaster of emotions I'm dealing with from texting with Denver.

Me: Okay. Have a good day.

Heading into the living room, I collapse on the couch and flip on the TV, hopeful for a distraction when I know there isn't any when it comes to Denver Kane.

SEPTEMBER

7

SIERRA

After my getaway to Ashby County, Georgia, my life resumes in New York, although not quite like before. Instead of spending my nights at art galleries or clubs, I spend every second of my time painting. And thinking about Denver.

We've spoken a handful of times, via text messages, in the week following our night together. Our conversations are brief and friendly, just bordering on flirty. As they pick up in frequency, we start exchanging memes and random photos. And last night, he called me. I almost passed out when his name flashed across my screen but the moment I answered, an easiness stretched between us. I found myself joking and laughing with Denver, well, I did most of the laughing, as if we talk all the time.

We spoke about our days and a movie we both want to see. It wasn't anything spectacular and yet, my heart danced in my chest and I wore the goofiest grin for the next eighteen hours. The more Denver slips into my day-to-day, the more I avoid my brothers and cousins' messages to pull me into the family business.

Getting lost in my work, I give myself up to my own feelings of excitement and giddiness. I paint vivid, striking portraits with bold colors and sharp angles. The techniques I'm applying are new and I attribute the shift in my painting to my budding relationship with Denver. Most of my paintings feature my grandmother, but two are of my father, dressed in the traditional clothing of our tribe, the Navajo, a headdress adorning his thick, black hair.

A long time ago, he was considered a prominent member of our community. But the outside world was too alluring for a free spirit like him, and he shunned traditional values, opting to marry my mother, a White woman, relocate away from his family's reservation in Arizona, and adopt a Western appreciation for materialistic goods. Slowly, his painting ceased and his presence at various poker tables filled the void. It wasn't long before he gambled away my parent's savings and my mother left him, taking Lachlan and I with her to the East Coast.

When Mom married James, a successful Scottish businessman with the largest marketing and PR company in the UK, our lives shifted once again, as we were suddenly thrust into seemingly endless wealth, bustling lives in both New York and London, and family stability.

Unlike Lachlan, I didn't completely succumb to this new lifestyle, opting to attend college in Arizona where I could reconnect with my dad, the free spirit, the painter. We never reconnected the way I hoped or imagined we would, but I did develop a relationship with my grandmother, which I'm incredibly grateful for. In that aspect alone, it was all worth it.

Except now, Tota haunts my paintings, making constant appearances in my dreams. She's trying to tell me something, forewarn me. A change is coming. I just have no clue what that change is or what any of it means.

* * *

It's not until two days later when I pop into a Duane Reade to buy

Q-tips and deodorant that it hits me. I'm late. Like, really late. Stopping abruptly in front of the feminine hygiene products, I calculate nearly a week late!

My period has been regular, like clockwork, since I first got it at age twelve. I've never been late. Ever. I feel the blood drain from my face, working its way down my body, and pooling in my feet until my shoes feel like cement bricks, and I'm unable to move. Literally.

Tears prick the corners of my eyes in a sudden surge of emotion, and I hastily pick up three different brands of pregnancy tests and toss them into my basket, beelining for the register, Q-tips forgotten.

The moment I'm home, I rip into the first box and glance at the directions. My fingers are shaking, and my stomach roils in panic. Is that nausea or nerves? Oh, my God. I could be pregnant.

Grabbing my cell phone, my thumb hovers above the call button for Daisy, but what the heck am I going to say to her? I think your brother knocked me up? No, I shake my head, dismissing the idea. I'm a big girl. I can do this.

Disappearing into the bathroom, I pee on the stick and then wait.

The longest two minutes of my freaking life.

And when two pink lines greet me, I almost vomit.

8

DENVER

Sierra's name lights up my screen and I smile, biting it back before it has the chance to spread across my face like some whipped teenager. But God, even the chance to talk to her affects me. I never thought we'd keep anything going since she left Georgia but the past two weeks have been cool, easy, and natural between us.

Ring. Ring. My phone screeches again.

"Hello?"

"Hey." Her voice sounds different, husky, as though she's been crying.

"Sierra?" I clench the phone tighter, concerned.

Pause. A stifled sigh. "Yeah. So, listen, I know you're like, living your best life in Georgia, but I'm pregnant."

Huh? What the hell? My throat dries and my heart beats furiously in my chest. Pregnant? Me, a father? I open my mouth, but no sound escapes and Sierra's loud breathing through the line clogs my eardrums.

"It's yours," she says on a huff, but I hear the emotion, the swell of tears in her voice, and I mentally curse myself.

"I, uh, of course I know it's mine," I manage to mutter, working a thick swallow. "I'm just, Jesus, I'm processing."

"Oh." Her voice is quiet, but I can hear the uncertainty and confusion she's not sharing, and my heart squeezes into my throat, making it difficult to swallow, never mind speak.

Jesus. I'm going to have a baby. I shake my head at the thought as an image of my own father pops into my head. I can't raise a kid. Look at how my dad messed me up, fucked with Carter's head, and messed with Jax and Daisy's futures. I'm not cut out to play hero to some little boy. Or girl. Oh God. What if it's a girl?

"Denver?"

"Yeah. Sorry. I'm, uh, I'm here." I slide onto one of the island barstools and clench the water bottle I discarded hours ago. "Are you sure?"

Sierra snorts, the sound delicate coming from her. The easy-going, relaxed friendship we've forged over the past two weeks is gone. In its place is a stifled, tense awkwardness. "Yes, I'm sure. I'm late, like a week late. And I took three different pregnancy tests. My doctor confirmed it this morning."

Oh. "Oh."

"Look, I'm not asking you for anything or expecting anything from you. I just thought you should know. So, I guess I'll just—"

"Wait a minute." Her words slam into me, searing through me and blazing a trail of anger in their wake. She's not asking me for anything? She doesn't expect anything from me? Screw that. The second her words collided with the image of my father, clarity ripped through me. I don't want to be like *him*. I won't be like *him*. Not a shot in hell. Which means she should ask me for anything she needs and expect me to be just as present in this process as she is. That's exactly what I'm going to tell her. Except when I open my mouth, I don't know how to explain all of those thoughts. I don't know the right way to say anything bouncing around in my head. "Don't do that. Don't brush me off like I don't care about you. About...the baby." I sigh, rubbing the space between my forehead and trying to make some sense of my own thoughts. "When's your next appointment?"

Sierra's even breathing fills the line for several seconds. "I have an ultrasound on October 12."

"Okay. I'll be there."

"What?" She laughs, but it's nervous and forced. "You don't have to do that."

"I want to. Send me the details, okay?"

"Um, yeah. Okay."

"Shit. Sierra, I'm late for work. I'll call you later. We should, I don't know, talk about things."

She breathes out a laugh that sounds more like her. "Yeah. All right. I'll talk to you later."

I nod before realizing she can't see me. Then I hang up the phone and exhale, a whoosh of air that lasts several seconds.

I'm going to be a father. A parent.

I'm having a baby...with Sierra.

Closing my eyes, I drop my head, the scenes flooding my mind even though I don't want them to. Sierra and I laughing and watching over our baby. Taking a family trip to the beach and teaching the little guy how to boogie board. And fish. Ordering ice cream and tasting all the flavors. Sierra rocking our baby at nighttime, singing a lullaby.

It's a yearning so strong, it stabs me. A hope I have no right wishing for. A dream that will never come true. I may be becoming a father but there's no way in hell a woman like Sierra would want to create a family with me. The nuclear kind. She'd be selling herself short and I'd be selfish as hell if I allowed that to happen.

Tossing the phone down on the butcher block island, I blow out a deep breath and rake my fingers through my hair. Jesus. I'm having a baby. A coldness settles in my shoulders, sweeping throughout my body as panic grips me. I can't raise a kid. I mean, look at me. An ex-convict with no future and no real prospects.

How am I going to afford to give a kid the type of lifestyle Sierra is used to? Just last year, my sister spent Thanksgiving with her family in St. Barth's. An island! The closest thing I've ever experienced to being on an island was solitary confinement. What a joke.

But wow. A baby. With Sierra. I swallow thickly, already knowing I can't—won't—walk away from my own blood. Not the way my dad did. I never want to be anything like him. Can I be a decent father? I don't have to be the dad of the year or anything crazy, but can I be enough for my own kid to not think I screwed him or her up?

Sierra is going to be an amazing mother. She's all giving and nurturing and caring. She's tough though, won't let our kid get out of line too much. She'll be a natural while I'll be stumbling along every single step of the way.

Still, I'll be there. I have to be.

How will that work? A guy at Benny's co-parents with his baby's mama. Is that what Sierra and I will do? Or could we try for something more? Is it even possible? Or would I ruin her the way I seem to ruin everything good my life touches?

Will the baby have my last name? My panic spikes at the thought. Probably. I mean, yes, he will, unless Sierra doesn't want him to. Can I do that to my kid? Let him carry around all of my sins, the weight of the Kane name hanging heavily on his neck? His friends will know me as the dad who went to jail.

My stomach sinks at the thought, settling somewhere around my toes, and I suddenly feel sick. Like I could puke this lukewarm water up right now. Anger simmers in my veins, and my hands tighten into fists. A wave of hate for my own father surges forward, overwhelming in its intensity.

For the first time in a long time, I think about clearing my name.

Could it even be done? I've maintained that I'm innocent from the moment the cops threw me in the back of their car, the red and blue lights whirling. A part of me wanted to fall on the sword for my dad but not after I realized how he set me up to take his fall. He always talked about loyalty, trust, and family. When I realized he was willing to let me pay for his actions, I learned that those values mean very different things to us. But still, they're values I want to live by.

They've just taken on a different meaning now.

Now that I'm not an MC hang around searching for my dad's approval, I know that the entire code only works if everyone follows it. And my dad never put me or my best interest before his own.

What kind of a dad does that?

My baby is probably the size of a blueberry or something, and I already know I won't let him sacrifice himself and his future for my own bad choices.

I need to clear my name.

Tossing the water bottle in recycling, I check the time on my phone and curse, knowing I'm going to be late. My head is all over the place and I can't even think straight. Swiping my keys off the kitchen table, I hustle to the front door and slam the door closed. I take the steps to my SUV quickly and back out of the driveway, glancing at the clock. I can't mess up my only source of income, especially when another mouth is going to be relying on it.

* * *

It's late when I call her. The ringing in my ear as I wait for her to pick up the phone kicks my adrenaline up a notch, and I'm desperate for her to pick up.

"Hey," she answers just as I'm considering disconnecting the call.

"Hey."

"How was work?"

I sigh, almost grinning to myself as she asks me the most normal, mundane question. A casual question friends would ask each other without thinking about it. Is that what we are? Friends? Jesus. Why am I so bad at this?

"Denver?'

"Yeah. Sorry. It was fine. Just work."

"Oh."

Pause.

Think Denver. Say something.

"So, are you feeling okay?" I ask finally, frowning as my words come out harsh instead of curious.

"For the most part." Sierra pauses, and I wish I could see her, wish I could read her expression to understand the thoughts she's not voicing. "A little nauseated. Exhausted."

I nod before remembering she can't see me. A quick Google search during my break informed me that all of these symptoms are normal in early pregnancy. But she already knows that, right?

"Honestly, I wish I could tell Daisy," she admits, her words a whisper.

Panic and shame flare through me. I scrub my hand over my face, my fingers scraping against the three-day old scruff I desperately need to shave. Of course, she wants to tell Daisy. She's her best friend. If I had a best friend, maybe I'd tell him, too. But my brothers are my best friends, and I can't tell them this. Not yet. Not now.

How much more of a screw-up can I possibly be? Hanging around my old man, dealing with his bullshit, and facing jail time all meant leaving Jax, Carter, and Dais on their own, to fend for themselves. It meant Carter raising Daisy when it should have been me. It meant him making choices he never should have had to make to keep the rest of us unburdened. It meant Jax cutting from town and Daisy growing up in constant instability. Now, I knocked up her best friend from a one-night stand? Even if that's not how I view Sierra, even though I'd want nothing more than for her to be my girl, for us to be having a baby that we plan to raise together, there's no way my family will understand that. How could they? I know what people will think when they see Sierra, promising artist and jetsetter, with Denver, ex-convict and struggling mechanic.

How can I make my siblings understand that?

But keeping our baby a secret isn't fair to Sierra. I know it the second she whispers the words about telling Daisy. She needs support; she must be reeling from the shock of this news. And here I am, the only person she's confiding in.

That's laughable.

"Denver?"

I squeeze my eyes shut and mentally slap myself. *Get your shit together, Den.* "I'd never tell you what to do, Sierra. Of course, if you want to tell Daisy, you should."

Sierra sighs loudly. "I don't know how she'll take the news. I honestly, I don't know what to do."

"I know. It's a lot to process," I admit, wishing I was more like Carter or Jax and could just put my thoughts and feelings into fucking words. But I've always been like this, incapable of expressing myself.

"I don't know if I should even keep the baby." Her voice is small and quiet, her words said on a breath of air.

But they stop my blood all the same.

Not keep the baby?

"You wanna have an abortion?" I wince at my bluntness, and my fingers clench the phone that much harder.

"No," she says immediately, and I hear the tears in her voice. "I just, I don't know what to do. I mean, adoption is something I could consider or—"

"No."

"No?"

"No. This baby, he or she, is mine and yours, and we're going to figure all this shit out. Jesus, do you have any idea how lucky a kid would be to have you as a mama?" I bite my lip hard until I draw blood to try to take the bitterness from my words. But is she crazy? She's all color and passion and life. Who could possibly be better at raising our baby?

"I'm scared, Den. I'm confused and overwhelmed and I'm... I'm all alone."

"I know. I can't imagine how you feel. But you're not alone. Sierra, I'm here. And I'll be in New York next week. Just...just give me a chance. Me and you, we're going to figure all of this out, okay?"

She's silent for several seconds, and I swear I can hear the thud of my heartbeat in my eardrums. When the hell did this become so important to me?

The moment I learned Sierra is having my baby.

"Okay."

I give a sharp nod. "Okay. I'm going to shuffle a few things around here, and then I'm coming to New York. Give me a few days?"

"Yeah."

"And if you need anything, absolutely anything, you'll call me."

"Okay."

"'Kay, babe. Get some sleep. I'll talk to you in the morning."

"'Night, Den."

"Goodnight, Sierra."

I toss the phone down on the island and exhale a large breath, releasing the heaviness of our conversation like air leaking from a balloon. I've got a lot of shit to sort out and a short amount of time to do it.

OCTOBER

9

SIERRA

He's both comfortable and at odds in the crowded streets of Manhattan. I see him before he sees me, standing outside of Grand Central Station, his worn leather jacket hugging his biceps, and his hair pulled back in a messy man-bun. Women's heads turn as they pass him, their eyes raking over his body, their mouths parting at the bad boy vibe Denver Kane emits like potpourri gives off perfume. It's ridiculous really. But what's even crazier is he doesn't seem to notice. Glancing up at the skyscrapers with a duffle bag slung over his shoulder, Denver seems oblivious to all the extra attention he's earning.

I bite my lip as I study him, wondering how things will be between us. Will he kiss me hello? Sleep in my bed? Hold me at night like he did in Georgia, even after he fell asleep? The weight of Denver's hand on my lower back was grounding and comforting in a way I never anticipated. The scent of his cologne, the scrape of his stubble against my cheek, the warmth of his chest beneath my ear, it rushes back as I watch him and my anxiety spikes, knowing these next few moments are a lot more important than two "friends" meeting up in New York.

"Denver!" I call out when I'm a quarter of a block away from him.

He turns toward me expectantly, his lips twitching when his eyes find mine. He begins walking in my direction and when we meet, standing just inches from each other, he wraps his arms around me and pulls me into the warmest, strongest hug I've ever been swept up in.

"You okay?" His low voice rumbles in my ear.

I nod into his shoulder, my hands gripping at the leather of his jacket as tears well in my eyes, burning behind my nose.

Goddamn pregnancy hormones.

But if I'm honest, I think it may be more than that. The entire past week, I've felt like a shipwrecked hot mess deserted on an island. With nothing but my painting and the desperate, searching eyes of my grandmother staring at me, watching me, on canvas after canvas, I've felt helpless. And now, Denver Kane strides over, pulls me into his warmth, and shoulders some of the weight that's been crushing me like it's the most natural thing in the world and I'm...relieved.

"Hey." He pulls back, his eyebrows dipping and a frown twisting his perfect lips. "What's wrong?"

"It's nothing." I snort, wiping the backs of my hands over my eyes. "Ignore me. I'm super emotional. Pregnancy hormones."

Den watches me closely for a long moment before nodding slowly. "It's going to be okay, Sierra."

"Okay."

"I mean it." His eyes are black as coal, somber as midnight. Serious.

"I know," I say and I mean it. Now that he's here, standing before me, I know he's telling me the truth. My reality shifts, and it seems like for the first time since I peed on the stick, things may actually turn out all right.

He rakes his teeth over his lower lip and watches me for a

long moment. Then the corner of his mouth ticks up and he dips his head to mine, pressing a sweet kiss against my lips.

I close my eyes, melting into him. I'm not even embarrassed when a groan falls from my mouth and I feel Denver's chest rumble with a chuckle I never hear. His tongue swipes across my lips, gaining access to my mouth and I lose myself in the moment, not caring that we're on a crowded street in Manhattan, not paying any attention to the hordes of people shuffling around us. Right now, I can't focus on anything except Denver and the way his presence simultaneously excites and steadies me.

After a moment he pulls back, his gaze heated, his expression almost tender. "I promise." He says the words earnestly and I step into him, resting my head against his leather-clad shoulder.

"I know." I repeat. And I do.

* * *

As much as I want to show Denver around the city, tiredness slams into me like a freight train, and I struggle to keep my eyes open.

"You tired?" Denver asks me, popping a French fry into his mouth.

I nod, smiling sheepishly, as I pick at my sandwich. My appetite has all but left me the past few days, until it suddenly surges forth with a vengeance I've never experienced. Not even after smoking a joint and getting the munchies.

"Let's grab the check and get you home. You should rest," Denver says, his eyes scanning the restaurant for our server.

We're at a casual place I frequent, about two blocks from James's penthouse and I nod in agreement, knowing I'm not going to be able to stay awake for much longer.

Denver signals for the check and when our server approaches our table, he hands her his credit card.

"Den, you don't have to—"

He holds up a hand, cutting me off, and nods to our server who hurries away to close out our table. "Don't do that."

"Do what?" I ask, my fingers clutching my wallet.

"I'm never, and I mean never, going to be able to provide you or our baby with the type of life you're used to, Sierra."

"That's not—"

"But I can feed you. And make sure you sleep when you're tired. And be here for you. For our baby. So, let me take care of you, yeah?"

I give a slow nod, a lump forming in my throat at his words, at the earnest, almost tender expression on his face. I wish I could tell him that this gesture, his truth, means more to me than a brand-new car or custom closet, but I know he wouldn't believe me. "Thank you," I say instead.

He nods, slipping his credit card back into his wallet once the server drops it at our table. "Come on." He holds his hand out to me, and I take it, lacing my fingers with his.

He holds my hand the entire time to James's apartment, and while I'm sure the presence of the doorman and the size of the penthouse must have been a shock to him, I'm too tired to gage his reaction.

In fact, I'm too tired to do much of anything except let Denver tuck me into my bed.

And smile when I feel his lips brush against my forehead.

* * *

"I feel you, man. I know it won't be easy. Or cheap. But I just need to know what I'm up against. Understand the process."

Pause.

"Yeah, I know. It's just things are different now. So, if you were me, where would you start?"

The sound of Denver's voice and the one side of the conversation I catch wake me God only knows how many hours later. I squint into the dusk of my bedroom, my walls darker than they were when Denver pulled my comforter up over my shoulders earlier. Squinting, I pull my cell phone off my bedside table and nearly drop it as the time glares at me.

6:07 PM.

Crap! I've been sleeping for more than four hours. Groaning, I drop my head back against my pillow and scroll down the long list of notifications I've received while playing Sleeping Beauty.

One missed call from Daisy. Three from Lachlan. One from Finlay.

Ninety-seven new likes on Facebook.

Forty-three comments on the new painting I posted on Instagram.

One email from my grandmother.

Nothing from my father.

A stupid amount of text messages, the most important ones:

Daisy: Miss your face. What's going on these days? I've barely heard from you. Call me.

Lachlan: Stop screening your calls. It's weird. Just call me already, so we can talk.

Mom: Hi Sisi. It's Mom. Lachlan says you're not answering your phone, but we really need to speak with you. Let's FaceTime?

James: Sierra, give me a call. I want to discuss your new position.

Lachlan: Seriously, stop acting like a child and call me.

Finlay: Lachlan is drinking Scotch and being a total wanker to the hot birds at the pub. Call him already before I curse you for ruining any chance I have of getting laid tonight.

Lachlan: Sierra??? R u OK? Tlk 2 me.

Finlay: You're ruining my life.

I close my eyes and feel my iPhone slide from my fingers, landing with a soft thud next to me on the bed. I've never avoided my family like this before, not even when I first contacted Dad and was nervous about how my mom and Lachlan would receive the news. Of course, they were supportive and understanding of my desire to build a relationship with my father. Mom more so than Lachlan. But this, dropping a pregnancy bomb, is completely different.

Will they be disappointed? Will they judge me for being so careless, becoming pregnant after one night with a man I'm not even really dating? Will they be hurt? Cut me off financially? Revoke the offer to work at the PR company?

My hands grow clammy at the thoughts swirling in my mind, creating a dark vortex that I know if I fall into, I'll have to claw my way out of. I shake my head, deciding that for now, ignorance is bliss and it's best that I continue to avoid the world. Like the adult I am.

Yawning, I stretch and force myself to sit up. My stomach grumbles, and suddenly I'm ravenous. Like starving for carbohydrates.

Shoving my feet into my slippers, I slip into the bathroom to sort myself out and make sure I look, well, somewhat presentable, before pushing out of my bedroom and stubbing my toe as I stop short.

Pacing back in forth in front of the television is Denver, his phone pressed against his ear, his face twisted by anger and pain.

But the aroma stops me short. Oh God. The delicious, heavenly scent of food. Garlic and basil and bread. A bubbling pot of pasta sauce simmering on the stove. An unopened box of penne sitting off to the side. A can of Coke, the tab popped, next to the sink.

I breathe in deeply, enjoying the scent of deliciousness until my stomach revolts wildly, and I clench my abdomen, leaning forward at the waist.

Holy crap. I'm going to—

"Sierra! I'll call you back." Denver's footsteps move closer as I drop to my knees and vomit, just missing his bare feet.

"Oh God," I murmur, my eyes squeezing shut as I feel dizzy and mortified and... hungry. What the hell?

"It's okay, babe." Denver drops to his knees by my side, pulling me into his frame and lifting me off my feet like I'm a feather. Ha! Let's see if he can do that seven months from now.

"Denver, I'm so sorry."

"Shh," he quiets me, placing me on the couch before disappearing. I hear the clink of ice and the faucet being turned on. Then he's back, wiping my mouth gently with a wet cloth and pressing a cold glass of water into my hands. "Take small sips. Want some crackers? I didn't even think that the smell..." He shakes his head, his eyes wide and wild. "I'm so sorry."

My stomach grumbles again. "Don't be. I don't know what happened. But I'm actually starving."

He eyes me skeptically and I laugh. "I'm serious. I'm really hungry."

"For pasta?"

I nod again. "I just need to brush my teeth first."

"Okay. Well, sit tight, and I'll have a plate for you in about ten minutes." He stands up from the couch. "Do you need anything?" He gestures toward the remote control on a side table as I stand and walk back toward my bathroom.

"Nope, I'm all good." I answer honestly as I escape into the bathroom to brush my teeth. Taking a few cleansing breaths, I rest my hand on my abdomen and glance down at my stomach, confused as to how I could feel so ill one moment and fine the next. Weird.

Making my way back to the living room, I collapse on the soft cushions of the couch and flip on the TV.

Denver's hard at work in the kitchen, the sounds of someone else being here, of being with me, is comforting in a way I never anticipated.

Smiling to myself, I let Denver take care of me. Of us. And God, does it feel good.

10

DENVER

"Who were you talking to before?" Sierra asks me as the pasta cooks.

I stall, gazing across the massive penthouse, my eyes lingering on the built-in ovens, that's right, ovens, and wine cooler. I'm way out of my league here. I could never give this, provide this, with a record hanging over my head. But can I tell her the truth?

A truth that no one except me, my sorry excuse for a father, and Griller, the President of the Devil's Shadows MC, knows.

"Denver?"

I blink, forcing my gaze to meet hers.

Sierra stands before me, her fingers twisting together nervously, chewing the corner of her mouth. She sighs, "Look, you don't have to tell me. It's just, I don't know. It sounded important and like you were upset, so if you want to talk about it, I'm here."

"I want to clear my name," I blurt, wincing as soon as the words are in the space between us.

"Clear your name?"

I nod, swallowing, trying to sort out the mess of thoughts ping-ponging around my brain. "The baby, you think he or she will take my last name? Be a Kane?" I swipe my palms against my jeans, suddenly nervous for her response. Why would she want the baby to be a Kane? To be associated with me and the Devil's Shadows MC and all the stupid shit I've done over the years? Why would she want any of that when our baby could have a name connected to a family with built-in ovens and penthouses in Manhattan?

"Of course, the baby will be a Kane. You're the father."

I nod again, curt and brisk. My head swims with new thoughts and an endless maze of questions.

"What's going on?" she asks, taking a step closer.

I walk over to the massive dining table and pull out a chair for Sierra before sliding onto the seat across from her. This is a serious conversation, and I want to treat it that way.

"About eight years ago, I got out of prison. I served two years."

She nods again, eyeing me curiously. Of course, she knows I've been locked up; Daisy would have told her that. But she doesn't know the full story. She can't. Because no one does, not even Daisy.

"I was charged with a simple robbery of a gas station. The clerk was also assaulted."

Sierra inhales sharply, her eyes never leaving mine, although they seem to widen and darken, a flash of nerves rippling through them.

I lean forward on the table, reaching for one of her hands, and I'm relieved when she doesn't pull away or flinch.

"I didn't do it. I swear to you, I didn't do it."

"Then why did you go to jail?" she asks after a few beats of silence.

I blow out a deep breath, kicking back in my chair again.

"My dad. He set me up. Sort of. He and Griller, the president of the Devil's Shadows MC, would have been implicated and the whole MC would have taken a huge hit if Griller landed in prison. Especially with all of his priors. The gas station, it was a robbery in a series of robberies, and while the police couldn't prove that I was involved with all of them, if they dug for more information, they could have started linking the MC and putting the pieces together. But the MC has a lot of cops in their pocket, throughout the state and beyond. Dad and Griller pegged me, set me up as the one to take the pinch."

"And you agreed to that?"

I shake my head, a bark of laughter dying on my lips. "No. I've maintained my innocence from the beginning. At the time, I was confused, bulldozed really, by my own father's betrayal. I never anticipated I'd be sentenced to serve time. But my dad and Griller offered the police a few anonymous tips, paid some witnesses off to corroborate the story they wanted. The video footage from the gas station mysteriously went missing." I shrug, reaching up to tug on my hair. "In the absence of evidence and coupled with my shitty reputation of being an MC hang around, desperate for Club access, the jury found me guilty."

Sierra swallows and watches me curiously. I can tell there are a million questions running through her mind but when she opens her mouth, she asks, "Why now? Why is it important to clear your name now? Hasn't it bothered you all of this time?"

"Of course it's bothered me all this time." I lean forward again in my chair, exasperated at my inability to explain the swirl of anger and failure bubbling in my chest. "I just, fuck it's stupid, but I figured what's the point? I live in a small town where perceptions are the reality. My reputation is my reputation now and I doubt clearing my name would change that. But ever since you told me you're pregnant, everything changed. There's gonna be a kid running around with that association, with the Kane name. I don't want that for him or her. Do you?"

"Not really." She tilts her head to the left, as if considering something. "But I do want the baby to have your name, whatever the outcome of clearing it. Because you're the father, and our baby will be proud of you no matter what."

I bite down on my tongue, hard, to keep the swell of emotion clogging my chest at bay. I didn't expect Sierra to say that. Hell, I didn't expect her to even feel that way. But it means a lot, more than I thought it would, and more than she probably realizes. Jesus, could we make this work? My heartrate picks up at her compassion, her empathy, further solidifying that she's too damn good for me and making me want her even more than I already do.

"Thank you."

She reaches out and squeezes my fingers with hers. "We'll figure it out, Den. All of it."

"Yeah."

"Thanks for telling me."

"I haven't told anyone."

"What about your brothers and Daisy?"

"Nah."

Her grip on my fingers intensifies, forcing me to look up. "Why not? That's, I mean, you let them believe that—"

I shrug, cutting her off. "Easier that way."

"Wow. All these years, I just thought Daisy didn't want to talk about it or dwell on her old man, but turns out she really doesn't know much of the story, does she?"

"We kept her out of things as much as we could. She was just a little girl when Mom passed. I made a lot of mistakes with her, with my brothers. But I don't want to repeat them. I don't want to do that with our kid. So, I'm here, yeah? And I'm going to clear this mess up."

"I know you will."

"How? How do you know that?"

"Because you're a good man, Denver Kane. Better than you think or believe."

I don't say anything. I can't because this girl is leveling me without even trying to. "You hungry?"

She nods, a shy smile on her lips. "Starving."

"Stay here. I'll fix us some plates."

* * *

I finish drying the last dish as Sierra snoozes on the couch. I'm relieved she ate a good bit of dinner, but moments after eating her eyelids grew heavy. She shook her head, smiling at me, embarrassed. I told her to take a rest while I cleaned up, and it took a lot of convincing on my part for her to finally collapse on the couch, pulling a blanket over her legs.

Checking out the fancy kitchen, I have no clue how to even use the dishwasher. Used to hand washing dishes, I straightened up the kitchen quickly, dividing the remaining pasta and sauce into glass containers for Sierra to heat up as leftovers.

Now standing in the kitchen, bracing my arms against the countertop, and watching the top of her head peeking up over the back of the sofa, I can't believe how comfortable things are between us. I didn't know what to expect, but it wasn't this—this natural ease and lack of awkwardness. It's like we've known each other for years and while that's technically true, we've never really spent time together, barely speaking until the last month or so. Guilt floods my chest as I remember all of the time I brushed off her friendly attempts at conversation. But I couldn't give in to her persistent questions and flirty smile, because I knew I wouldn't be able to let her go with just a chat and a laugh. I've always wanted Sierra and now I've had her, we're having a baby, and I don't want to let her go.

But would she really want to take a stab at a relationship with me if she wasn't pregnant with my baby? If the answer is no, which it's gotta be, then what's the point of trying something now?

Because she's having your baby. Because you care about her. Because she's the only woman you could ever see yourself being committed to, having a family with, growing old next to.

I close my eyes as the thoughts assault my brain. I hate that stupid, irritating voice that always reminds you of the truths you try to bury away.

Sierra snores lightly and I smile, remembering the first time I met her. She was nineteen years-old and came to visit my sister over Christmas Break their sophomore year. I had been out of prison for several years and was trying really hard not to mix up with any trouble.

The moment I saw that jet-black hair hanging to her waist, the amusement flashing in her big eyes, and heard her laugh, uninhibited and sexy as hell, I knew she was trouble. Wild curves, long legs, and a sway to her hips that could tempt a priest, Sierra walks around like sin. But then she opened her mouth, and everything that fell out of it irked the shit out of me.

Because she was smart.

And funny.

And witty.

She was quick, had a great sense of humor, and was chill in a way that the girls I ran with weren't.

She spoke of ideas and art, of painting and colors. She liked to run her hands over things like the table or couch, as if she was connecting with the texture. She was so in tune, so present, so overwhelming, and God, I was so tempted.

I think she made it her personal mission to get me to speak or laugh the whole four days she stayed with us. But I shut her down, never giving more than the basic politeness required of a civil person. My mama would be so disappointed in me if she could see how I treated Sierra in our home. Even Daisy and Carter shot me weird looks from time to time. But I stuck to it, never giving Sierra more than was absolutely required. And she backed off.

Over the years, I ran into her randomly when she would come home with Daisy or pop up for a visit. But I never had a friendship with her. I never had the easygoing, natural relationship that

Carter managed. Probably because I never thought of her like another sister the way Carter did. Nope. I always thought of Sierra as so much more. Being in close proximity to her and not being able to react was painful. And it pissed me off. No one got under my skin like this girl.

Until she did.

And now, I don't want her to go anywhere else.

Sierra clears her throat from the couch, turning to find me staring at her and I shift, embarrassed at being caught.

"What are you thinking about?" she asks, her voice shy.

I bite the corner of my mouth, unsure of how much to reveal. But what's the use in trying to stay away now? We're having a baby together. We will be connected and bound in the most significant way for the rest of our lives. I confessed my darkest secret. In this moment, Sierra probably knows more about me than anyone else in the world.

"The first time we met."

Her eyebrows arch in surprise, and she twists on the couch until she's kneeling on the cushions, her arms hanging over the back of the couch. "You were such a jerk."

I laugh, the sound loud and unexpected and Sierra's eyes widen.

"Finally," she exclaims, clasping her hands together. "Jesus. It's been my goal for the past however many years to get the great, stoic, moody Denver Kane to laugh. Really laugh. Just once. And now, I call you a jerk and you laugh." She tilts her head at me, a teasing grin spreading across her face.

"Don't tell anyone," I deadpan, walking over to the couch. She laughs, turning to face me and leaning back against the corner throw pillows.

"Swear it." She runs her fingers over her lips like a zipper and tosses the imaginary key.

I shake my head, bending forward and before I can overthink it, I kiss her locked lips, conversation forgotten. Her mouth is soft and sweet and she shifts under me, tugging me closer until I'm straddling her. Lacing my fingers in her hair, I slant my mouth over hers, anxious to pour all of the thoughts I can't voice into this moment, this connection. Does she have any idea how much I want her? Want all of it with her? The baby and the family and the future? But can I go there? Is it fair to her?

She moans lightly and leans forward, her gestures growing hurried as her fingers nip under my T-shirt, working it up my chest and over my head.

I glance at her, take in the fevered flush of her cheeks, the heat in her eyes, the fullness of her lips. "You're beautiful. So unbelievably beautiful." I tell her before shielding her body with mine once more.

She squirms beneath me, her fingers popping the button on my jeans as I pull off her shirt, pausing to kiss the space above her naval, resting my cheek against the smooth skin of her stomach. I hear the soft sigh that falls from her lips and feel her fingers tug in my hair. I enjoy this moment, exposing a side of myself that I rarely show anyone but feel comfortable showing Sierra. After a minute, the stroking of her fingers in my hair has my mind fixated on other things and I continue to explore her body, vowing to never take one minute with her for granted ever again.

So caught up in the moment, I have no idea how much time passes when Sierra and I finally settle against the couch cushions, random pieces of clothing skewed across our bodies, other articles strewn on the floor.

I wipe my hand across my face, looking over at her from the corner of my eye. The moment I see her hesitant expression transform into one of confidence, I know that our encounter affected her as much as it did me, she's just not going to admit it.

"So, are couches like your thing?" She quips, lifting an eyebrow at me.

"What?" I chuckle, trying to understand her thought process.

She raises her eyebrows at me and widens her eyes.

“Oh.” I laugh, biting my lip as I realize I haven’t ever laughed as much as I do in Sierra’s presence. “No. I’m not sure what’s going on. I can barely think straight around you; you make me lose my mind.” I shake my head to clear it so I follow our conversation.

Sierra beams at me. Literally. Her smile brightens her whole face until it’s like sunshine and I pull her closer until she rests her cheek against my chest. Rubbing my fingers up and down her arm, I kick my feet up on an ottoman and cuddle the woman I think I’ve fallen for without even trying. That’s right. I cuddle her.

“So, why were you so nasty?” She shifts her weight, snuggling deeper under the blanket and turning her head up to look at me.

Huh? What is she talking about? Once again, I try to focus on the conversation but I’m having a tough time following her thoughts. “Nasty?”

“When we first met?”

I grin at her, tugging on the ends of her hair. “I wasn’t nasty. I was...”

"Sullen, moody, unfriendly, broody—"

"All right, all right, take it easy." I hold the hand that isn’t wrapped around her up in surrender. "I could have been nicer."

"You think?"

"You just...you pissed me off."

Her mouth falls open, shocked. "How did I manage that by being my sweet, polite, charming self?"

"Oh, you're sweet all right."

She waggles her eyebrows at me, and I tug her close again, dropping a kiss to the top of her head. "I wanted you," I admit, the words rolling off my tongue in a rare showing of truth, which seems to be the new norm around Sierra. "Jesus, I wanted you. But you were off limits, and I knew it, so I just—"

"Tried to push me away?" Her voice is soft, her expression unreadable.

"Something like that."

She nods, chewing the corner of her lip. "That makes sense. Kind of. Not that it made it any easier; I thought, I don't know, that you hated me or something. That I was just your sister's annoying, stupid little friend."

"Nah." My fingers draw lazy eights over her shoulder. "I definitely never hated you, although yeah, you used to annoy the crap out of me. You used to show up and be charming and funny and wear your tight jeans and little shirts and my blood would boil because I knew you were unattainable."

She snorts, a small smile passing over her lips. “Until now.”

“Now I just feel like I won the lottery.” I admit.

She looks up at me, her big eyes serious. “Really? You’re not upset at all about the baby?”

I shake my head slowly, trying to sort out my thoughts so I can explain them. I rub my hand over the stubble on my chin before tucking a piece of hair behind Sierra’s ear. “I’m not upset at all. To be honest, I’m really happy that I’m having a baby with you and not someone else. I know this isn’t what you or I planned and maybe we wouldn’t be here,” I gesture to the apartment, “if you weren’t pregnant. But I’m okay with that. I just worry that you’re not.”

She watches me quietly, as if searching for the truth in my eyes, the sincerity in my words. “I’m scared.”

I hold her closer, my chest constricting at the emotion in her words.

“But I’m not unhappy.” She moves her hand to cover her stomach. “I’m already in love with this little peanut.”

I drop my hand to cover hers and squeeze her fingers lightly. “I know what you mean.”

“When I first called you –”

“I freaked out.”

“Kind of.”

I drop my head back against the cushions and blow out a deep breath. “That was less about you being pregnant and more about my relationship with my dad, clearing my name, a bunch of random thoughts that collided in that moment. I never meant to make you feel like I wasn't happy about the baby."

"And you're happy it's with me?"

I nod, leaning forward to kiss her.

She sighs, snuggling into my side and we sit in a comfortable silence for several minutes.

"Hey, you still paint and stuff?" I ask her suddenly, remembering how passionate she was about art.

"What?"

"Painting and art. You were always into that, talking about colors and shadows and lighting. You still do it?"

"You actually listened when I talked?

"Every now and then. Don't get a big head about it or anything."

She smiles, the simple gesture lighting up her face like summertime. "Yeah. I do. Come on, I want to show you something." She pushes herself off of me, standing from the couch.

Reaching down, she offers me her hand and I take it, the gesture meaning more than a simple help up from the couch. She squeezes my fingers lightly, I squeeze back, a silent understanding passing between us.

We're in this, whatever this is, together.

11

SIERRA

I'm nervous, my hands growing clammy and my heartrate ticking up with each step we take toward the studio. It's not that I've never shown my art to anyone before. I have. But with Denver, now, it's just different. I want him to like it, to feel it, to see me and understand me through my painting, so yeah, I'm nervous. Because what if he doesn't get it? What if he just thinks it's, I don't know, meh? Then what? Painting is my soul, it's who I am, and it's something I hope to share with my children. If Denver doesn't understand how important it is to me, how my brushes are practically an extension of my fingers, I know I'll look at him differently.

And I don't want to.

Because when I look at Denver, really look at him, past the sexy man-bun and the intriguing scrolls of ink that line his arms, I like what I see. And the more that he opens up to me, really talks to me and confides in me, the more I feel myself start to freefall past like into love.

"What's this?" he asks, just before I push open the studio door.

"James, my stepdad, had this studio made for me years ago. It's where I create," I say for lack of a better term. Opening the door, I flip on the lights and step inside, Denver close behind me.

He doesn't say anything for several seconds, and my heart dips dangerously low to the ground. Just before it crashes at my feet, a gasp, a sharp inhale of breath tickling the back of my neck sounds behind me, and my heart hovers, waiting for his words.

"This is...wow. You're incredible, Sierra," he whispers, awe and shock lacing his tone.

And my heart, my stupid, passionate, romantic heart, swoops and soars until it's higher than the Empire State Building.

"You did these? All of them?" Denver drops my fingers, turning in a slow circle, his eyes scanning over canvas after canvas lining the studio, in some places stacked three or four deep.

"Yeah."

"You're really talented." He looks at me sharply, as if seeing me for the first time, as if *seeing* me.

I bite back my smile and manage to tame the happy dance that is desperate to break free. Opting for casual, I shrug. "Thanks. I love painting. Like I *love* it. It's just, I don't even know how to explain it."

"Try."

"It's who I am. It's my purpose. My passion. When I'm having a shitty day or upset about something, it's how I cope. When I'm happy and excited, energy literally tingles my fingertips until I have a brush in my hand. It's an extension of who I am."

He watches me as I talk, his eyes curious, his face smooth. After a moment, he nods, as if to himself, confirming a thought or a belief. "I had no idea you were this good. That it was for, I don't know, real."

I laugh. "It's seriously my life."

"It should be. You shouldn't waste a talent like this. How'd you even get into painting? Is your family a bunch of, I don't know, famous artists or something?" He gestures around the studio, his eyes trailing to the door and the rest of the penthouse as if to make his point.

"Hardly. My family is, well, we're kind of a hot mess."

His gaze swings back to me, and a bark of laughter echoes in the space. "What do you mean?"

I nod toward a couch lining one wall of the studio, and we walk over to it. Clearing off a pile of blank canvases and a box of paints, we sit down. I tuck my knees up under my chin and hug my knees into my chest, choosing my words carefully.

"My mom is Scottish. My dad is an American Indian."

"Like a Native American?"

"Yeah. We're part of the Navajo tribe. Our people live mostly in Arizona. My dad's family is large and intricate and quite high up in the hierarchy. At one time, he was in a position to play an important role in our society. But then, he met Mom. She was doing an exchange program at a college in Arizona and they met at a bar."

A sigh falls from Denver's mouth, and I shift my gaze to him. He's watching me intently, hanging on to my words as if my family history is somehow interesting and not a series of mistakes and desperate choices.

"They fell in love, and Dad left the reservation, pretty much turned his back on our people, and married Mom. She finished her degree and they settled outside of Phoenix. They were happy for a few years, had Lachlan and me. But after a while, Dad hated the mundane routine of being a family man. He was a free spirit, always had been. It's probably why Mom was attracted to him in the first place, if I'm being honest. He wanted to paint and create and dream and inspire. To be inspired. Mom wanted him to get a reliable job that would, in addition to her salary, ensure consistent mortgage payments and start saving for my and Lach's college funds."

"Makes sense."

"Yeah, well, Dad didn't see it that way. He started gambling, getting mixed up in poker games and big betting. I guess he was really unhappy, maybe even depressed. Anyway, he grew more and more unreliable, and Mom become exasperated and felt like she was raising us on her own. Eventually, he split. Went back to the reservation. Except by that time, his favor with the community had fallen. Before he left the reservation, he advocated for decreasing the presence of alcohol and wanted to crack down on bootlegging. He wanted to ensure that the reservation school lunches were well balanced, and kids had extracurricular activities to join in order to curtail the rise in obesity among the younger generations. And then he shows up years later, overweight, incredibly unhealthy, and a gambler. It was bad."

Den squeezes my fingers lightly, and I offer him a small smile.

"After Dad left, Mom moved us to the East Coast, to New Jersey. She found a job in New York through one of her college friends and began commuting in and out of the city. At night, she worked as a seamstress, doing the work from home so she was with Lachlan and me but still earning money. She went to a conference in New York one day for her job and met James. I mean, years passed in between with us making it work but when she met James, everything changed. James is Scottish, too, and owns a massive PR and marketing company, the biggest in the UK with offices in Ireland, Scotland, and England. He lived in London, so suddenly we began spending loads of time there. Mom and he fell in love quickly but took their relationship slowly because of us kids. Mom had me and Lach to think about, and James had his son, Callum, to consider. But we all hit it off. To be honest, Callum and I are nearly as close as Lach and me. After Mom and James married, James bought the penthouse in New York, so Lach and I would always have a home in the States. We moved to London, and I finished high school there. But for college, I wanted to be closer to Dad, to get to know his side of the family, meet my grandmother, so I applied to ASU."

"Ah." Den nods, as if starting to understand the connection.

"And I did get to know her, which I'm so grateful for. She's amazing." I point to the various canvases showing her face, hidden by shadows or open in the natural light, her hands always stretched out before her as if offering a gift. "But Dad and I never really connected the way I hoped." I shrug, as if to ward off the chill I feel by my father's consistent rejection. Den must feel it, too, because he shifts closer to me, his arm snaking around my shoulders. "Anyway, I'm glad I came back to the US. I only lived in London for three years and it was great but I missed the States. Going back to Arizona really helped with my painting, understanding who I am, where I come from. Does that make sense?"

"Yeah, a lot of sense. Do you always paint, I don't know what it's called, faces?"

"Portraits. Usually. Sometimes landscapes."

"You're really amazing. I had no idea."

"Thanks. I wish my family saw it that way."

"They don't think you're good?"

"No, it's not that. They do. They love my art, but they don't think it's a stable career choice. Probably because it's not."

"But it's what you love." His tone is harsh, as if he's trying to convince me.

"Yeah." I smile at him. "It is. But Mom worries I'm going to end up drifting and unsettled like Dad. My brother Lachlan and my step-brother Callum both work for James. So do my cousins Finlay and Aaron. And I'm sure when my other brother, he's actually my half-brother, Liam, graduates, he'll work there, too. He's already interning there during the summers and on holiday breaks."

"Wow. That's, I mean, it's cool to have an opportunity like that."

"I know." I nod in agreement because it is. "But it's not what I want. I want—"

"To create?"

"Yeah." I smile up at him.

Denver's eyes warm, the black shifting from midnight to whisky, and I want to melt into them. "Then do you," he says seriously. "You're an adult; you don't actually have to do whatever your parents tell you."

"Is that how you're going to be with our baby?" I ask, teasing, but my question causes Den to pause as he considers it.

"Not with everything. Not when he or she is small and needs to be told what to do. Like no running in the street or playing by the stove. But when he or she is all grown up? Yeah. If our kid is half as talented as you and wants to pursue a dream, I'd encourage him or her to do it. And to do it right, give one hundred percent. There's no shame in failing. None at all. Loads of people wait for someone to mess up, so they can point and talk about how the person didn't make it. But you gotta keep going, keep at it. Because there is shame in wasting talent, in purposely missing opportunities out of fear, in giving up because you think you're supposed to pick the safest choice. You're not. You're supposed to always pick the option that causes something to blaze inside of you, something that keeps you up at night. That is, if you're lucky enough to find it."

I bite my bottom lip, surprised by his admission, surprised that he even spoke so many consecutive sentences. "I like that. A lot," I tell him, snuggling deeper into his side. "What keeps you up at night?"

His fingers brush against my arm as he hugs me into him, his fingers playing over the ends of my hair. "I haven't found it yet. I've been stuck for a long time now and kind of forgot what it feels like to be excited by something, to be challenged."

"Well don't give up on it."

"I won't." His chest rumbles under my ear as he speaks, the sound comforting. "I can't, especially now that we're going to have a kid. Kids learn more by what they see then what they're told. That's probably the one good thing I learned from watching my dad. I know this isn't what you planned or expected. But me and you, we're going to be a good team, Sierra. We're going to be good parents to our baby."

"I know."

"Good."

I try to swallow back my yawn, but Denver catches it and chuckles lightly, the sound rolling through his chest. "Let's get you back to bed. I hear rest is important when you're creating a human."

I giggle as he pulls me into his chest and stands easily, carrying me out of the studio and depositing me into my bed like I'm a pillow. Pulling my comforter up, he tucks me in and smiles down at me. "Sleep tight."

I gesture toward the space next to me. "You'll be back, right? I mean, there's five other bedrooms here that you can choose from but –"

"I'll definitely be sleeping in here with you, babe." Den brushes his lips against mine, lingering for a beat too long, and I close my eyes as I breathe him in. Soap and basil and leather and something distinctly Denver, purely male. Already, I want him again. Need him. "I'm going to make a few calls but I'll be in in a little while. You sleep now."

"Okay," I whisper, my eyes already closing as sleep pulls me under.

"Okay."

12

DENVER

Sierra's appointment is the next morning, and I can tell she's nervous. Unsure. She's jittery and hoppy and keeps flipping her hair over her shoulder, a habit I recently noticed.

"You all set?" I ask, tugging on my black, scuffed up boots.

"Think so," she says, flipping through the papers in her hand again.

"What's all that?"

"Insurance stuff, some questions, a copy of my most recent bloodwork."

"You have questions?"

She shrugs, her eyes darting to the door, and I can tell she wants to get moving.

I open the door for her, and she locks up behind us. We wait for the elevator in silence, a strange tension forming around us. We're both on edge, unsure and expectant. We're both way out of our element. The elevator dings and we step inside. I press the button for the lobby and the silence continues.

Sighing, I reach out and take her hand in mine.

Her neck jerks up at the contact, and her eyes scan over me, but I don't turn to stare back. Instead, I squeeze her fingers until she slowly relaxes, and I'm able to lace her fingers with mine.

We got this. We're in it together.

Then we're out on the street, swept up in the insane hustle of New York City, walking the three blocks and two avenues to Sierra's doctor's office.

The office is...unlike any doctor's office I've ever been inside. Not that that's saying much since all of my experiences were with small town doctors in Georgia. But this, this is something else. Sleek furnishings and a calming waterfall greet us when we enter. Around the waiting room are framed black and white pictures of newborn babies or women in various stages of pregnancy. The room is inviting yet sterile. It's a far cry from the worn chairs and fading carpet and one receptionist at Dr. Green's back in Ashby County.

"Sierra Begay," Sierra says as she steps up to the receptionist. The receptionist is seated behind a long, white desk that is elevated just above the rest of the waiting room. There is no glass, just wide-open space. Weird.

"Take a seat, Sierra. Dr. Leona will be with you shortly."

"Great, thanks." Sierra gestures to a pair of chairs and we sit down.

I can't help but scan the other couples present. There are only two, but they're about as different from me as possible. One man is dressed in a pressed charcoal suit, his shoes so shiny I can see my reflection in them. He's scrolling through his phone, his fingers replying to messages and emails at a furious pace. Next to him, his wife sits, a pinched look on her face. Wearing a bright red dress with a colorful scarf tied around her neck, she clutches the straps of her handbag as if someone is about to rip it away from her.

On the other side of the room, another couple—two women —sits talking in hushed whispers and laughing quietly to each other. One of them is wearing tailored khaki pants and a white button down. She looks crisp, professional, and businesslike. The other woman sports a long, flowy skirt with sunflowers splashed throughout. It's so big and swooshy, it looks like it could swallow her. Her hair is long and wild, curling in a million different directions, and green, cat eye glasses are perched on the edge of her nose.

I glance from the corner of my eye to Sierra. She's sitting straight as a board, her hands clenching the armrests, her nails digging into the fabric.

Reaching out, I drop my open palm on her thigh, and she jumps slightly before shooting me a grateful smile and slowly, slowly she relaxes once more under my touch.

"Sierra Begay?" a voice calls from an opening door.

Sierra and I both stand and make our way toward the nurse who smiles brightly and escorts us to a room.

"You both can take a seat here." She gestures to two chairs in front of the organized desk. "Dr. Leona will be in in a few minutes."

"Thank you," Sierra and I both murmur.

The nurse leaves, and we look at each other. A million unsaid, unshared things seem to pass between us before we both smile.

And then we meet Dr. Leona.

Dr. Leona is a small, sweet woman with wild red hair and freckles spread across her nose and cheekbones.

"Hello and welcome. Congratulations on your new miracle!" she greets us warmly, gesturing for us to sit back down. "I'm Dr. Leona, and I will be caring for you and your baby during your pregnancy."

"Thanks. Hi. I'm Sierra and this is my...this is Denver."

"Very nice to meet you both."

Sierra sits down and looks up at me expectantly until I drop into the chair next to her, suddenly anxious. I have no clue what to expect, and the realization slams into me. I'm about to be a dad. A father. And I have no idea how to do that.

I look at Dr. Leona, the panic obvious in my expression because her smile softens.

"I'm going to answer all of your questions. I know this can be a scary time, but I'm here to support you through this process and ensure that the health of your child and Sierra are handled with the utmost care. Now, Sierra, when was your last period?"

Sierra blushes at the question, a soft pink blooming on her cheeks, which somehow calms me. This is awkward for her too. We're not like a normal couple. This wasn't planned, and we're not in a real...anything. But sitting here across from Dr. Leona, watching Sierra fidget next to me, I realize that needs to change. We're having a baby, we're connecting and sleeping together, we're...dating at least.

"August thirteenth."

Dr. Leona nods, marking something on the paper in front of her. "Okay." She picks up a spinning wheel and adjusts the different portions until she smiles up at us. "Then you should be about eight weeks along. You due date is May 20. Are you taking a prenatal vitamin?"

Next to me, Sierra's posture grows rigid, and her skin tone morphs from embarrassed to alarmed. "No." She shakes her head, her fingers curling into her hands.

I reach out and place my hand on her knee. Who knew anything about prenatal vitamins? I mean, is that something that people just know?

"Not a problem." Dr. Leona reaches into a drawer and hands Sierra a box with prenatal vitamins. "Start these today. You take one supplement each a day. One is a prenatal vitamin that contains the necessary amount of folic acid, and the other is an omega-3 fish oil supplement. These are to help aid your baby during his or her development."

Sierra nods.

"All right." Dr. Leona clasps her hands together. "How are you feeling, Sierra? Any nausea?"

Sierra nods again. "I feel mostly okay, just exhausted. Like completely worn out. And a bit nauseated. I threw up last night."

"Is the nausea manageable, or do you think you need medicine to help control it?"

"No, it's manageable. I'd rather not take any type of medicine that isn't absolutely necessary."

"I understand. And you, Denver, are the father?"

"Yes, ma'am."

"Excellent. Do you have any plans for how your roles will work during Sierra's pregnancy?"

"Um, roles?" I swallow the thick lump in my throat, a ball expanding in my chest and squeezing until I can't breathe.

"Yes. Will you be supporting Sierra throughout her pregnancy? Attending appointments? Maybe a prenatal class?"

"Dr. Leona, Denver and I aren't together. We're not, well, I'm not sure what we are. We're still sorting this all out, and the baby came as a surprise to us both." Sierra says, saving me.

But still, I hate the sound of her words hanging in the air between the doctor and us. They're heavy, disappointing words. They tell the story of a guy who knocked up a girl and now there's no plan, no cohesiveness, no family unit to raise this baby in. They're not the excited couple reminiscing of a wedding and a strong love and the desperate desire for a baby.

But I want them to be. I want this baby and I want Sierra and I want us to be a family.

Shame and guilt swirl in my stomach for not discussing this with Sierra earlier, for not learning about what she wants our roles to look like during her pregnancy. But screw that, I'm in this, I'm not going anywhere and –

"I'll be moving to New York. Sierra and I are still sorting out what our relationship will look like but as for roles, we're both committed to having our baby and I'm completely committed to her. Whatever she needs. Or wants."

Sierra's head whips to look at me but I just squeeze her hand in mine, letting her know I meant every word I said.

Across from me, Dr. Leona smiles, a pleased look passing over her features. "Excellent. I know this is a challenging time but Sierra is going to need a support system. Do either of you have family here?"

We both shake our heads.

"Then you'll need to rely on each other even more. Okay, let's examine you Sierra." Dr. Leona stands, gesturing for Sierra to hop up on the examination table.

I shuffle behind her, standing next to Sierra's shoulder as Dr. Leona picks up some gel. "This will feel a bit cold on your tummy."

Sierra lays back and folds her shirt back to below her bra as the doctor squirts some blue goo onto her stomach.

Dr. Leona takes a wand and runs it along Sierra's abdomen. Turning the ultrasound screen in our direction, a smile flickers across her face. "Here." She points to a small blob in a larger black circle. "This is your baby."

Sierra's hand flies up to cover her mouth and I grin, reaching blindly for her hand until I clasp it in mine. She laces our fingers together, turning to give me the brightest, sweetest smile I've ever seen as Dr. Leona fiddles with the controls. Then she's staring at the ultrasound monitor, fixated on our little peanut, her eyes shimmering with so much love I can't look away from her.

"That's your baby's heartbeat."

And then, I hear it.

The most beautiful sound, a rhythm so pure I want to memorize it for always, beats out, and my throat clogs with an unnamed emotion, my eyes stinging.

Tears dot the corners of Sierra's eyes and her expression blossoms into pure happiness, her smile genuine and true.

"Hi, little peanut," she whispers, her free hand cupping her flat stomach.

"Listen to that little hummingbird. Nice and strong. One-hundred-sixty beats per minute."

"Is that normal?" I ask, panic blazing through me. That's gotta be too fast, right?

"Perfectly normal at this stage," Dr. Leona reassures me. "Sierra, I'm going to take some measurements, and then I'll print out a photo for your fridge, and we'll discuss your medical history, as well as any concerns and questions you or Denver may have. And then, I'll see you in another four weeks, okay?"

"Okay," we say in unison, smiling at each other, suddenly lost in our own world.

Our baby's heartbeat.

It's the greatest moment of my life.

And it changes everything.

13

SIERRA

I clutch the black and white photo tightly in my hand. It's small and square and reminds me of a throwback polaroid, yet I'm in love with the tiny little peanut in the frame.

"You feeling okay?" Denver asks as we walk down the street, my eyes scanning the usual restaurants for a lunch spot.

"Yes. Hungry," I admit, my stomach growling as if on cue.

"Let's get you fed then." Den raises my hand to his lips and presses a sweet kiss to the back of it.

"Can you believe we heard the heartbeat?" I ask him, excitement still coursing through my veins.

"No." He shakes his head, grinning at me. "I wasn't expecting that at all. Best sound ever."

"I know, right?"

"What about this place?" Den points to a casual salad and sandwich shop.

"Yeah, this is great."

We take a seat inside, and I look at the ultrasound picture one more time before slipping it into my purse.

A server passes by, and we order a couple of sandwiches and coffees. I opt for a decaf.

I shuffle in my seat across from Denver and his eyes narrow, a frown twisting his features for a moment before smoothing out. I still can't believe he told Dr. Leona he's moving here. Is he moving here? For me? Or the baby? Or both of us?

His eyes blaze black, and I can tell he's got a lot on his mind just by how lost in thought he is. He rests his elbows on the table and drops his head into his hands, raking back flyaway pieces of hair and tucking them into the elastic that holds his hair in place. When he glances up, he tilts his head toward me, studying me. "You okay, Sierra?"

"Yeah. Are you?" I ask, suddenly nervous. What if this just became too much for him? Too real and he wants out? Oh God. Am I ready to care for and raise a baby on my own? Then I'd have to move back to the UK and accept the job at James's company. At least then I could properly support my baby, but what would I do for childcare? I wonder if Mom would watch the baby. I could ask her. But first, I'd have to tell her that I'm pregnant. That's going to be some conversation. Panic starts to build at the base of my neck, a slow and steady pressure that radiates upwards as my mind runs in a million different directions.

I'm totally screwed.

"Hey, where's your head at?" Denver reaches over, his fingers closing around my wrist.

"Are you really moving here?" I blurt out.

"Yeah. I told you, I'm in. All in. And I don't want to leave you tomorrow to fly back to Georgia." His voice breaks through the fog creeping in my mind, surprising me.

My head snaps up, so I can find his eyes, searching them for the truth. But it's there. Shining like diamonds in a pile of coal is an unrivaled sincerity. "You don't?"

"Of course not. I told Dr. Leona –"

"I thought you were having second thoughts."

Denver's eyes darken further, something I thought was impossible. "About the baby? Or you? Or us?"

"All of it." I admit, smiling at the server as she drops off our coffees. I pick up a creamer and rub it between my fingers just to have something to do with my hands.

"This is my fault." He shakes his head, his lips pressing into a thin line. He scrubs a hand down his face, exasperated. "I should have been more open with you. We should have talked about everything. I don't know, meeting the doctor just made everything...real, you know?"

I nod. Hell yeah I know. And I'm freaking out.

"I want to have our baby with you, Sierra. But more than that, I want this." He gestures between us. "I want to be with you, really be with you, and be a family. I want to come home to you after working all day and cook you dinner. I don't want to miss any of the baby's appointments or the prenatal class or whatever it is pregnant couples do. I'm all in. And not just because we're having a baby but because I'm, Jesus, it sounds so cliché but I don't know how else to explain it, I'm falling in love with you Sierra. And I'm already so in love with our little peanut."

"You're falling in love with me?" I whisper, my heart pounding in my chest, a reassurance and excitement building in my bloodstream.

Denver nods. "I'm pretty sure I've been falling for you for a long time, just resisting it."

My mouth drops open in shock and Denver chuckles, his fingertips tapping my inner wrist. Wait, is he nervous? "I want that too. All of it. Everything you said." I blurt out, suddenly incapable of explaining myself.

Denver grins and forces out a long exhale. "You were making me nervous. I've never, Jesus, I've never said that to a woman before."

"Good." I take a sip of my coffee, not even caring when it burns the roof of my mouth. "I've been hoping you'd say it to me since the first time I met you."

Now it's Denver's turn to stare at me in surprise, at a loss for words. "Seriously? Even though I was so "nasty" as you put it?"

I nod, wiping a napkin across my mouth. "Seriously. I used to love hearing Daisy talk about you and hate it at the same time, always wondering when she was going to tell me that you met someone."

He shakes his head, his eyes swirling with so many thoughts and emotions I can't pull one out. "Well I guess we have our little peanut to thank for bringing us together." He says finally and I smile. I couldn't agree more.

Our server drops off our sandwiches and Denver takes a gigantic bite of his Rueben, the coleslaw falling from his sandwich into the dish below. He chews thoughtfully and pops a French fry into his mouth.

"We need to figure out the logistics of my move. I'm sure I could find a job up here. I mean, I definitely could at an auto body shop. Maybe rent something in Queens or Brooklyn for the time being," he ponders out loud.

"Or you could just move in with me."

He looks up sharply, muttering a curse word under his breath. I giggle, slapping my hand over my mouth as his eyes darken and the small muscle under his eye twitches.

"I take it that's a no?" I ask, wondering if it's the money thing. "It doesn't have to be permanent. Just a temporary solution until we sort out a place here. I'm really focusing on the marketing aspect of my painting but in the meantime, I could get a job at a coffee house or something. And you'll need a few weeks to settle in and start a new job. At least this way, we're together."

He sighs, chewing another fry thoughtfully. "I get what you're saying but it doesn't feel right. Moving into a penthouse I could never afford and not being able to really take care of my girl, our baby," he shakes his head, "it seems like I'm taking advantage of your stepdad's generosity toward you. But he doesn't even know about us. Or that you're pregnant." Den raises his eyebrow at me.

I take another sip of my coffee, over his words. "I understand what you're saying. And I respect you for it, honestly. But we have to be smart about this. If our priority is to be together –"

"It is."

"Then we need to put that first. How about I talk to my mom and James and tell them everything and we take it from there? If James is cool with it, then you can move in with me for a few weeks until we can relocate to Brooklyn or Queens. By then I'll have another job sorted."

"I can take care of you." His tone is sharp, severe.

"I know you can but so can I. It's just, we'll both be working crazy hours just to cover basic necessities if we stay in Manhattan. A few weeks at James's will at least give us a bit of a cushion for a security deposit and a move. I have some money saved from summer jobs and random paintings that I've sold but we will burn through it if we aren't careful. To be honest, Mom and James supported me all through college. This summer is the first time I've even really thought about finances. And this is an expensive city."

"Do you want to come to Georgia?"

I scrunch up my nose at the thought. I could move in with Denver and being close to Daisy would be amazing. But Ashby County is a long cry from New York. How would I make connections in the art world? Do I shelve my painting for now? "That's an option. There's also the job offer in Scotland."

"You're still considering that?"

I sigh, my eyes closing. If I take the job in Edinburgh, I'd also be shelving my painting. And taking a job I really don't want to do in a field I'm not super interested in. But how do I explain to Denver, without hurting him, that without knowing if we're going to be able to make this work together, I have to be smart and make the best decisions for the baby?

"Not really. I mean, I don't want to move to Edinburgh, despite the obvious that I'd love to be closer to my family, I'd be giving up on my painting. And I'd also be taking a break from painting if I moved to Georgia. But all of my old reasons for staying in New York don't have that much merit when compared to having a baby. I just want to make sure we're being sensible about this. My brother told me a few weeks ago that I need to grow up and he's right. I can't exactly ask my mom and James to pay for my life and our baby's."

"I know that. You're supposed to ask me."

Cue the crickets. Awkward silence. Face palm. Yada, yada.

"But I don't want you to feel that you're shouldering all of this on your own. That's how my mom felt and look at what happened with her relationship with my dad. You keep telling me we're in this together and we are, so you have to count on me as being your partner in everything. Including the financial side."

Denver sighs heavily and I can tell he sees the merit in my explanation but doesn't like it. "I don't want you to give up your painting. If you think the best place to pursue your art is New York, then we make that work. Period."

"I just don't want to be one of those pipe dreamers who is so committed to my art, my dream, that I sacrifice all the other things."

"Like what?"

"Like you. Our family. Doing this the right way."

"There's no right way to do this other than together. And we're doing that. I'll go back to Georgia tomorrow, talk to my siblings. You talk to your mom and James. And in a week, we'll be back together. Sign us up for one of those baby classes. Or prenatal yoga. Or whatever you want to do. We're doing it all together."

"Okay." I smile, picking a fry off his place and popping it into my mouth, relieved that we're finally figuring out some of the logistics for our future. "But can I tell Daisy?"

His gaze softens and he reaches across the table to cup my cheek. "Of course, you should tell her, babe."

I smile, leaning into his touch just as the server passes with another tray of food. I inhale something that smells like bacon...a BLT? The moment the name of the sandwich registers in my mind, a bubble of nausea pops in my stomach. Oh God, I'm going to be sick again.

I stand quickly from the table, my eyes frantically searching out a sign for the bathroom. Placing the back of my hand over my mouth, I beeline for the restrooms, closing and locking the door before dropping to my knees in front of the toilet. When I finish cleaning up and rinsing out my mouth, I pull open the bathroom door and collide with Denver.

His hands grip my shoulders as he peers down at me, studying my face. "You okay, baby?"

I nod, his kindness and thoughtfulness unraveling me until tears well in my eyes. I drop my head, blinking furiously.

"What is it? Do you still feel sick? Is something wrong?" He works to gentle his tone but the way he holds onto my shoulders clues me in that I'm scaring him.

I shake my head, trying to regulate my breathing so I can talk without sounding like a train wreck. "I feel better. I'm just so, I don't know. I feel like I'm going to cry but I don't know why. I feel overwhelmed. Like, I'm so happy that you're going to move here." I nearly wail, burying my face in his shoulder.

I feel the soft rumble of the chuckle he doesn't let out as his arms wrap around me and hold me close. "You're all right, baby. We're going to be all right and figure everything out. We're together, yeah?"

I nod. We're definitely together.

14

DENVER

Leaving Sierra is hard. I hate kissing her forehead and breathing in her scent one last time even though I'll be back in New York in a week. I just need to go home, tell my siblings what's happening, let Dean at Benny's know what's up, and figure out a few things financially. But even a week seems too long; what if she needs me?

I stare at her sleeping form, listening to the sweet whistle that sounds with each of her inhales. I bend to pick up and fold the discarded clothing that I tugged off of her body last night. Mere hours ago, she was warm and naked in my arms and now I have to say good-bye.

It's bittersweet and I lean forward to kiss her shoulder one last time before I leave the apartment. I fixed her breakfast and wrote her a note earlier this morning but didn't have the heart to wake her. Not when I kept her awake for so many hours last night.

The ride to the airport is lonely, my thoughts still tangled up with Sierra. Heaviness hangs around my shoulders, and it's not the panic of impending fatherhood; it's the panic of being away from her. It's the overwhelming thought that I have no idea how to financially make my move to New York work but God, do I want to. I will, I know I will. I just wish I had it figured out yesterday so I didn't have to leave this morning.

My head throbs with different ideas and plans from the moment I enter the airport in New York until the wheels touch down in Georgia. By the time I'm waiting out front of Savannah's airport for Carter to pick me up, I've figured out a few things.

1. I need to find a job in New York.

2. I need to find an apartment to rent.

3. I need to tell my brothers and sister the truth.

I know the second I tell them, I'll feel better about confiding in them. I'm excited to gage their reactions about becoming uncles and an aunt. Sierra is going to call Daisy to fill her in. It's easier knowing that she and I are doing all of this together. But Jesus, a part of me is nervous to tell them about Sierra and me. About our peanut. Especially when things are so financially tight for all of us. I know my siblings; they'll do anything they can to help out. And it just seems unfair, as the oldest, to place a burden on them when I should already have a nest egg hidden away somewhere. I should be able to solve my problems on my own, not look to my little brothers and baby sister for help.

"Yo!" Carter pulls up beside me and taps his horn lightly.

I look up startled, so lost in my own thoughts that it takes me a minute to process why he's here, and why he's staring at me.

"Hey, how's it going?" I ask after a minute, opening the back door to his SUV and tossing in my duffle bag.

"Not bad. You? All good?" he asks, his eyebrows lifting over the top of his sunglasses. He peers at me as I snap in my seatbelt in the passenger seat.

"Yep."

Carter pulls away from the curb, tapping out a beat on the steering wheel. The silence between us is thick, and I know it's because he's waiting for me to speak. I'm waiting for him to ask, neither one of us wants to make the first move.

"How's Taylor?" I ask instead, referencing Carter's girlfriend whom he recently moved in with.

The smile stretching across his face is genuine and appears at just the mention of his girl. "She's doing great, man. Getting more modeling gigs now that her limp is gone."

"That's good."

He nods, taking a left on a side street.

The silence resumes.

"How was New York?" he starts.

"Okay."

"I didn't know you had a lot of friends there."

I shrug, turning to look out the window at the passing shrubbery.

"In fact, the only person I can think of who you know there is Sierra."

My head whips around and my eyes narrow, daring him to ask the question I know is on the tip of his tongue. I really want to tell Carter everything but I want to make sure Sierra has enough time to talk to Daisy first.

He chuckles, the sound easy and unaffected, as if we're discussing the weather. "I know y'all hooked up. Daisy told me back when it happened. Are you dating her or something?"

"Definitely more than something," I admit, looking away again.

Carter sighs and our silence resumes.

But as we near our house, I realize he's not going to let me off the hook so easily. The moment Carter makes a right when he should make a left it hits me that he's taking me to Raf's to feed me beers until I speak. I snort, the sound low and irritated, but Carter keeps driving without paying any attention to me.

Once we're parked at Raf's, he turns to me and tilts his head to the bar and grill. "I'm starving. Hope you don't mind that we're stopping for a quick bite."

I nod, knowing it's complete bullshit, but appreciating his concern anyway.

We enter Raf's, and several people holler out greetings.

"Hey y'all. Grab a seat anywhere. Mindy'll be right over," Lenny, the bartender calls out.

"Thanks, man." Carter lifts his hand in a half-wave and walks over to a corner booth, never bothering to turn around to make sure I'm following him. He knows I am.

I slide into the booth across from Carter, amused by how intent he is on learning the truth from me.

A small grin lifts the corner of his mouth, and he leans back in the booth, scanning Raf's.

"Hi guys. What can I get for you?" Mindy appears at our table a few moments later, a pen poised above a small notepad.

"Hey Mindy. How're you doing? How's your grandmother?" Carter asks warmly, his interest genuine.

I lift my hand in a casual wave to Mindy.

"Good, thanks. She has her good days and bad, but she'll be happy to know y'all popped in today."

"Tell her we say hello."

"Of course," Mindy pauses, expectantly.

"I'll take a burger and fries," I order the same thing I do every single time I come in here.

"I'll have the same, please, Mindy. And we'll also take two Heinekens and a couple of, hmm, let's do Glenlivet. Neat."

I can't contain my eye roll at the mention of the whiskey that Sierra drinks.

"You got it." Mindy smiles, completely unaware of the slight strain between Carter and me. Or really, just the tension I'm giving off because Carter is as unaffected as ever.

"Thanks." Carter smiles at her cheerfully as she walks over to Lenny to give him our drink orders.

"Glenlivet? Since when do you drink that?"

"Since I learned you have a preference for it," my brother replies easily.

I sigh, chuckling under my breath, and lean back in the booth.

I'm grateful as hell when Mindy drops off our drinks, and I take a long pull on the beer, prepared to tell Carter everything. I'll just make him swear not to tell Daisy. A tingle of nerves travels up my spine as I try to guess Carter's reaction. I don't know why I'm suddenly nervous. I guess it's my own shame of not having my life in the place I want it to be for Sierra and our peanut. But Carter will understand that. In fact, he'll probably tell me it's normal to want things to be more stable when bringing a baby into the world.

I grasp the glass of whisky and stare into the depths of the dark liquid, nearly the same shade as Sierra's eyes, and am hit with a pang of longing so sharp I wonder how I'm going to last an entire week away from my girl. My nerves dissipate and I know that Carter's going to be happy for me. Especially when he realizes he's going to be an uncle. And when he understands that I'm happy, really freaking happy, about everything except the part where I left Sierra sleeping in New York this morning and won't see her for a week.

"What gives, man?" Carter holds up his glass of whisky to me and I clink mine against his.

"You gotta swear not to tell Daisy."

My brother's face drops as he studies me. "I don't want to keep hiding things from her, Den. She's an adult now and –"

"Just for a day or two. You'll understand why once I explain everything."

Carter sighs and nods his agreement. "You in any trouble?"

"Not the kind you're thinking of."

A smirk curls the corners of his mouth. "All right. Enough with the stupid riddles. What's going on?"

"Sierra and I, we're together."

"No shit?" He asks, not as surprised as I thought he'd be.

"That's all you have to say?"

He shrugs. "Daisy already told me y'all hooked up the weekend Evie and Jax moved. You've always been so...strained around her, I figured you had a thing for her years ago."

I chuckle, taking another swig of beer. "And she's pregnant. We're having a baby."

This time, Carter chokes on his whisky, his face turning bright red and his eyes watering.

I smile. Finally, I got the reaction I was waiting for.

"What? Are you serious or joking?"

I stare at him, narrowing my gaze. "When do I really joke?"

"Good point. Wow. You're...you're going to be a father," he says this in pure wonderment, as if it's the best news he's ever heard. A large grin splits his face, and his eyes are suddenly wide. "I'm going to be an uncle. Hey, congratulations, man!"

"Thank you." I grin back at him, taking a long pull of the whiskey. "I'm really happy, Carter."

He nods, his smile growing as he realizes I'm serious. "I'm happy for you, Den."

"But Jesus, I'm overwhelmed," I tell him honestly before he gets carried away and tries to plan a baby shower or something. Because he would. "I want to be with her, in New York. I'm moving in a week. Everything's different now and I don't want to, I can't, be away from her and the baby. But I need to find a job and a place to live and I have no idea how I'm going to make that happen. I mean, can I even support myself and Sierra and a baby in New York on a mechanic's salary and with a record? I've been thinking about it since the second I left her this morning and I'm pissed at myself for being such an idiot for so long and not being in a better position to do this the way I want to."

Carter's face falls as the truth begins to worm its way through the happy cloud he's been existing in since he met Taylor this past summer.

"One week? I don't know if you're going to be able to figure all of that out in a week."

I nod, "I know. Sierra is talking to her mom and stepdad. I'm going to move in with her at first and then we'll move to a new place together but it feels wrong. I'm thirty-years-old and I'm moving into my girl's stepdad's apartment." I widen my eyes at my brother. "That's pathetic."

"So extend your time here until you have it all figured out." Carter says, logically.

I shake my head. "I can't be away from her, man. She's all on her own in the city. What if she needs me? No, the priority is that we're together. I just wish I didn't feel like a freeloader."

Carter shakes his head. "You're not a freeloader, Den. You work harder than anyone I know. Except for maybe Jax but don't tell him I said that. He already has the hero title. You're not taking a handout, you're accepting some help to start your life over in a new place. And you're doing it for the right reason, for your baby. It's not like you're going to show up to Sierra's stepdad's place and sit on the couch and play video games all day."

"I just don't know how I'm going to provide Sierra with the life she's used to."

"But Sierra's not like that. She doesn't care about money."

"Maybe. But things are different now. She's about to be a mother. I'm sure a little financial security is comforting when you're about to bring another life into the world."

Carter looks up to thank Mindy as she drops off our burgers and fries, but I can't even manage that. Now that I'm spilling my guts, my nerves ratchet up again, sending my panic into overdrive. How the hell am I going to pull this off?

"Okay," Carter drawls, picking up a French fry and holding it in the space between his plate and his mouth. "I see your point. This is tough. And unexpected. But Den, come on, man, you're a smart guy; you can figure it out."

I glare at him.

"What about opening up your own shop?"

"In Manhattan?"

Carter sighs. "We'll figure it out. If you need money or—"

"No."

"What?"

"I'm not taking anything from you or Jax or Daisy. Y'all are just starting your lives and shouldn't have to backtrack because I'm an idiot with no financial security." I toss back a large gulp of the Glenlivet, hissing as it hits my throat.

Carter chews his French fry and regards me thoughtfully. "When are you going to tell Jax?"

"As soon as Sierra tells Daisy. Tonight, tomorrow." I take a bite of my burger, unsure if I'm even hungry.

"Okay, then we'll all sit down and figure things out. Jax has a ton of Army contacts living in the New York area. I'm sure he can find a connection for a job. As for the finances," Carter says, shrugging and wiping a napkin across his mouth, "man, you're never going to provide Sierra with the lifestyle she has. At least not in the next year. No one could. Her step-dad built a business from when he was twenty. Her lifestyle is over thirty years in the making, and I'm sure she knows that, so don't be so hard on yourself."

I take another bite of my burger. I think I am hungry.

"This isn't the end of the world, Den. You're going to figure it out."

Swallowing, I nod. "I know, Carter. Honestly, I'm happy about the baby. Really happy. And being with Sierra is more than anything I ever thought possible. At the risk of sounding lame, I already miss her. I'm just, nervous about pulling everything off, and I don't want to disappoint Sierra. Or my kid."

"I hear you, man. Let Sierra talk to Daisy, tell Jax, and then we'll take it from there."

"Yeah," I agree, popping a fry into my mouth.

Carter grins. "So, you think it's a boy or a girl?"

I shake my head. “I have no idea. A boy, I guess. Could you even imagine me with a girl?”

Carter tilts his head to the side, studying me. “Yeah,” he says finally, “I can. In fact, I think I’d like to see you with a daughter. You’ll be even surlier than you are now.”

I snort, throwing a fry at his face. "Shut up."

Carter chuckles, picking up his beer bottle. "In all seriousness, I'm happy for you. And proud of you."

I nod, biting into my burger to save me from saying anything. Because Carter's words mean more than he'll ever know. And I should be saying them to him. Not the other way around.

15

SIERRA

Textured purples layered on top of each other swirl around the deep blue in her eyes. I take a step back, staring at my grandmother's face as it comes to life before me. I really need to call her. In this painting, she looks younger, her laugh lines not as pronounced, the wrinkles in her forehead barely noticeable. Her hair is long, black, and thick, hanging over her shoulder in a simple braid, tied at the end with a feather.

Narrowing my eyes, I focus on hers, dipping the tip of my brush in violet to lighten the outer ring of her irises when the shrill beep of an incoming message interrupts me.

Frowning, I place my brush down and turn to pick up my phone.

Denver: Hey baby. I miss you. How are you feeling? Sorry, can't call right now. Heading to work and running late. But I told Carter. Have you talked to Daisy yet?

Me: Not yet. I'll call her in a few. And my mom. And Tota, my grandmother. I have a lot of calls to make today.

Denver: You worried about talking to your mom?

I stare at the message before looking back up at Tota's painting. I don't know how I feel about telling my mom. I'm not sure what her reaction is going to be but I know the longer I wait to confide in her, the more hurt she's going to be.

Me: Not really worried. More like unsure of how she's going to react.

Denver: I hear you. Carter took the news great. He's already looking at sports memorabilia for the baby.

I laugh at this. I can see Carter taking his role as uncle very, very seriously.

Denver: Heading into the shop now. Miss you, babe. Let me know how it goes with your mom.

Me: I miss you, too. A lot. The bed was cold and lonely when I woke up this morning. Thank you for breakfast. Call after work?

Denver: Of course.

Me: Heart Emoji x Three

I pull myself off the couch and take one last look at my grandmother's face before storing my brushes and paints and flipping off the studio lights. Walking into the kitchen, I stop short. In the past, I would pour myself a glass of wine before starting a conversation like the one I'm about to have with Daisy. But that option is clearly off the table. Rummaging through a cupboard, I find a box of Tetley decaf tea. My mom loves Tetley tea and always makes sure there is an assortment of teas on hand. Putting the kettle on the stove, I sit at the island and wait for the water to boil.

Now that Denver messaged to tell me that Carter knows, I'm relieved to confide in my best friend. I've needed her so much over the past few weeks, and while I know she's going to be angry with me for keeping such a huge secret, I also know she's going to support me through everything. I just need to pick up my phone and call her.

The kettle whistles, and I hop off the barstool, fixing myself a tea and inhaling it deeply, calming my racing nerves. It's just Daisy. I can tell her this; I can tell her anything.

The ringing of my phone startles me and I jump, my mouth dropping open when Daisy's name flashes across the screen. Oh, my God. Did Carter accidently tell her? Does she know? Does she have ESP?

"Hello?" I answer, suddenly unsure.

"Hey! Finally, I got you. Jeez, you're like a ghost these days." Her voice is bubbly and normal. Weird.

"Yeah, sorry. I've been, uh, busy. Have some things going on. I was actually just going to call you."

"Good! Because I miss your life. What's going on?"

"I have pretty big news." I start.

"I'm sitting down. Lay it on me."

"I'm pregnant." I wince as soon as the words are out of my mouth, because obviously I could have said that in a million different ways.

"What?"

"I'm having a baby."

"Okay," Daisy draws out the word, concern and confusion in her tone.

"It's Denver's."

"Are you freaking kidding me?" Daisy's voice is sharp and angry.

I remain quiet, giving her a minute to process the bomb I just dropped.

"You're having a baby with my brother and you-you didn't tell me?" Now the anger has morphed into hurt, and I wince, hating that I made her feel betrayed by me. Or Denver. The both of us.

"I'm sorry. I know it was shitty of me, but I didn't know how to tell you. I needed to talk to Denver first, you know, because he's the father."

"And?"

"What do you mean?"

"Did you tell him?"

"He came up to see me in New York."

"He was staying with you?" Her voice is incredulous now, and I can imagine the red patches crawling up her neck.

"Yeah."

"Wow. I'm, uh, I'm surprised. And, I don't know. What are you guys going to do?"

"We're figuring it out. Together. Like a couple."

"You're dating Denver?"

"I know, it's crazy. But I've always –."

"Had a thing for him."

"You knew?"

"Of course I knew. Your eyes just about fell out of your head every time he entered a room."

I snort because it's a pretty accurate description. I guess I suck at hiding how I really feel.

"Are you okay?" Daisy's tone softens and a pang of roommate sickness hits me.

The tears are back, and I want to slap myself. I sniffle and Daisy sighs over the line.

"Yeah, I am. I'm sorry I didn't tell you. Honestly, I've wanted to a million different times. I have no clue what I'm doing, and I'm scared and worried and I'm crying all the time. I'm so tired and feel like crap and I have like, two weeks, to figure out where Denver and I are going to live in New York, tell my family I'm expecting, and turn down the job at James's company. I keep painting my grandmother's face. Over and over again. Like it's suddenly the only thing I'm capable of painting. I just, I have no clue what the hell I'm doing." I take a deep breath, already feeling better that I word vomited all of that to my best friend.

Daisy snorts on the other end of the line, and I'm relieved she's moving past the anger and hurt to acceptance and humor.

"All right, Jesus, I forgive you. I guess I can't stay mad at a pregnant woman. I'll take my anger of being excluded out on Den instead."

I laugh, the tears back in the corners of my eyes but this time for an entirely different reason. It feels good, normal, to laugh with Daisy again. "I'd appreciate that."

"Consider it done." She pauses for a moment before saying the words I've been waiting to hear, "Okay, let's take it one thing at a time. You didn't tell me because you wanted to sort things out with Denver first. Objectively, this is totally understandable. Because it's me and you, I wish you told me sooner but I get it. You're scared and crying all the time because you're having a baby! That's super normal from what I hear so don't even stress it. Just, welcome to the baby-making club. I'm sure there are a bazillion forums online where you can connect with a ton of other crazy first-time-moms-to-be and feel normal about yourself. Denver and you will figure out your living arrangements and if New York isn't in the cards, you can come here to Georgia, or y'all can head to the UK together. That's an easy one to figure out as long as you and Den are on the same page. We'll get to your family but honestly, they're going to understand why you're turning down the job once you tell them you're pregnant. We need to figure out how you can tell them so they're so excited that the happy news overshadows anything job-related."

I laugh at her logic, nodding my head in agreement even though she can't see me.

"And maybe you just need to call your grandmother and tell her what's happening so you can move on to other subjects. Or, maybe you can only paint her because some subconscious part of your brain thinks you need to reconnect more with your Navajo roots since you're having a baby? I'm not sure, I'll have to marinate on that further."

I sigh. "I'm seriously so happy I called you."

"I know. Now, tell me. How did my brother react to learning he's going to be a dad?"

I shake my head, grinning at the conversation Denver and I had when I told him I'm pregnant. "Well," I begin, settling back across the living room couch, relieved to be talking to Daisy and already feeling so much better. That's the thing with best friends, they can help you navigate anything. I know Daisy's going to help me sort out my thoughts and feelings until all of the big life changes happening right now aren't so overwhelming and scary, until they seem exciting and refreshing. Until I feel like I have some semblance of control over my future again.

* * *

After chatting with Daisy for over an hour, I call Tota. She doesn't answer but I leave a voicemail letting her know I've been thinking of her, painting her, and want to share some exciting news. Hopefully, she calls me back soon.

In the meantime, I have one more conversation I really need to have. Pulling out some of the frozen pasta sauce and meatballs Denver made the last time he was here, I pop the container into the microwave and hit the defrost option. I put a pot of water on the stove. While I wait for my dinner to be ready, I sit down at the table.

My fingertips tingle, and my knee bounces up and down under the table as I press the call button to FaceTime my mom.

"Sierra!" she answers, her beautiful face filling the screen.

"Hi Mom." I smile the moment I see her. She always calms me and comforts me without even knowing it. I hope I can be half the mom she is to my peanut.

"How are you, love? It's been a long time, Sierra. You could check in a little more often to let me know you're okay, what you're doing and—"

“I know, Mom. I'm sorry.”

Her eyes narrow as she looks at me. “Is everything okay, love? You look exhausted.”

At the genuine concern in her voice, my eyes fill with tears. “Oh Mom. I wish you were here.”

“Sierra? What is it, sweetheart? Don't cry. What happened?” Mom leans closer to the camera as if to close the distance between us.

I press my hand over my face and try to quiet my sobs.

"Sierra, whatever it is, you can tell me and we can sort it out, okay?" Mom tries again and I nod, wiping my tears with the backs of my knuckles.

"I need to tell you something. But you have to promise not to tell the boys. Please. I'm not ready for Lach or Callum or anyone to know."

"What about James?" Mom asks cautiously and I know she won't lie to her husband, not that I expect her to.

"Is James around?"

"No, he's still at work. Sierra, are you sick?"

"No, I'm not sick. Nothing like that. Of course you can tell James, I'm not trying to put you in an awkward position. Plus, I need to speak with him, too."

"Okay, love, you're scaring me. Out with it."

"Mom, I'm pregnant."

"Pregnant?" She repeats, her eyes widening, her hand coming up to cover her open mouth. Mom's expression flickers through a series of emotions: surprise, concern, excitement, uncertainty, and confusion. "Are you sure?"

I snort. "Very sure."

"Who's the, who's the father?" she asks cautiously.

"Denver Kane."

"Daisy's brother?" Her eyebrows shoot up into her hairline as her mouth falls open again.

I nod. "We're dating."

"Oh, well, I didn't know that. I mean, you never mentioned him. I mean, you did but not in that context. It was more in a hopeful, pining way then in an actual dating way." She rambles nervously, obviously overwhelmed by my news.

Jeez, did everyone know I had a thing for Denver? "It's still new."

"But you're having a baby?"

I nod again. "I'm nearly nine weeks."

"Oh, Sierra. Are you okay? How do you feel?" Her motherly instincts take over and she asks me the most important questions she could in this moment.

"I'm okay. I feel meh. All over the map emotionally. I cry over everything. I mean every. Single. Thing. And I'm simultaneously nauseous and hungry although that's getting better."

"But, how are you?" She asks, her concern for my state of mind winning out.

"I'm happy." I admit, smiling at her. "Really happy. Denver and I are figuring everything out. He's moving to New York. We're going to rent in Brooklyn or Queens and –"

"Why don't you stay where you are? Denver can move in." Mom's eyebrows dip over her nose in confusion.

"I told him that but he feels uncomfortable, as if he's taking advantage of you and James."

"Nonsense." Mom waves a hand dismissively.

"Think of it from his perspective."

She's quiet for a few moments before nodding reluctantly. "I can understand his desire to pave his own path. I respect him for it. He seems like a good man."

"He is. But still, I wanted to speak with you and James about our both living here temporarily. Just for a few weeks until we are able to secure a place to live and Denver finds a job."

"Of course. I will discuss it with James but it's not a problem."

"Thank you, Mom."

Mom's eyes well with tears as she watches me.

"Mom? Why're you crying?"

"I can't believe my baby is going to have a baby." She says, dabbing at the corners of her eyes with a tissue.

Of course, I tear up at her emotional display and soon, we're both crying with each other.

"Will you come, Mom? I miss you."

"Oh, sweet girl, I miss you, too. Of course I'll be there. I can come tomorrow."

I laugh, shaking my head. "How about in a few weeks? Let Denver get settled here."

"You let me know and I'll be on the first plane out."

"Thanks." I say gratefully. We talk awhile longer about the baby and my symptoms. Mom tells me about her pregnancy with me. We discuss nursery themes and prenatal classes. I tell her about Denver and how we plan to make things work between us. When my eyelids grow heavy, Mom reminds me to get some rest and call her in the morning.

"I will, Mom." I promise. "But please don't tell –"

"The boys. Sierra, I promise I won't. Honestly, I have no desire to spearhead that conversation."

I laugh, nodding in agreement. "It's going to be a tough one."

"Your brothers just want what's best for you."

"I know that."

"They worry about you."

"I know."

"I'll let you get some rest, love. Hey, did you speak with Daisy again about considering job options here? You should pass her CV to James or one of the boys."

"Oh, shoot. I've been meaning to bring it up again. I think she'll be more open to it now that more time has passed."

"Anytime, Sierra. Just send it along."

"Thanks, Mom."

Mom smiles at me sweetly and nods. "Go to bed. I love you."

"Love you too. Goodnight."

"Goodnight, Peanut."

I disconnect the call and walk over to the couch. Flipping on the TV, I stretch out and wait for Denver's call.

* * *

It's late when Denver calls; my eyelids are already dropping closed.

"Hey," I answer.

"Shit. Did I wake you, babe?" he asks, his voice gruff and low. I smile, loving it when he calls me babe, even though it's the most generic nickname in the world, and if any other guy said it, I'd think it was lame. Ugh. I'll blame that on the pregnancy hormones, too.

"No, I'm just dozing."

"You told Daisy."

"I told Daisy."

"She's pretty pissed."

I laugh, knowing she gave Denver an earful and a half since she spared me from it.

"What's so funny?"

"Nothing."

"So, now Daisy's making plans to come visit us in New York."

"She is?"

"She invited herself. Did you expect any less?"

I laugh again. "That sounds great. I'd love it if she came. I've been trying to get her to visit me in New York for the entire summer. If I knew I just had to get pregnant, jeez, I would have done it so much sooner."

The sound of Denver's low, rumbly chuckle warms me from the inside out. I love that I can finally make him smile and laugh about things. "You better not think about making babies with anyone else, babe."

I grin the goofiest smile of life and agree with him. "No worries there."

"Well, that's a relief."

"I spoke to my mom."

"And?"

"She's worried about me but also happy for us. She's honestly the best. I thought she'd be disappointed or upset or something but mostly she was just concerned."

"She sounds amazing."

"She is. You're going to love her."

"I have no doubt."

"I wish I could have known your mom." I tell him honestly and hear the catch in his breath.

Denver is quiet for several moments before he clears his throat. "Me too. She would have liked you, a lot. And you would have loved her."

I smile at the thought, my eyes closing.

"You tired, baby?" He asks after I don't say anything.

"Yeah. I think I'm dozing off."

"Go to sleep then."

"Okay. Mom is going to talk to James. It's fine if you move in while we figure everything out." I yawn.

"We'll talk about it tomorrow. Get some rest. I love you, Sierra." He says the words low, as if he couldn't help himself from saying them aloud.

I smile at the words, letting them wrap around me like a hug, and snuggle deeper into the couch cushions. "Love you too, Den."

And then, I'm fast asleep.

16

DENVER

"Okay, Den, what's going on?" Jax asks over FaceTime.

"How's Evie?" I stall.

He shakes his head at me, a grin shadowing his mouth. He knows I'm stalling, but he's going to play along like a good little brother. "She's fine. Great, actually. She's in class at the moment, so it's just me."

I breathe out in relief. I know I need to tell my family the truth, but it somehow seems easier without Evie and Taylor present. Not that they would judge me, but I just...I need my siblings to hear it first from me. And I don't know how much about the sordid past of the Kane family either of my brothers has confided in their women. I'm sure most of it, but who am I to blow up their spots?

"Good." I nod, looking up as Carter and Daisy walk into the kitchen from the living room.

"You summoned us?" Daisy asks, a sly grin on her face. She can't wait to see Jax's reaction to my baby news. And, I think she's secretly happy to not be the last Kane to learn about some big family announcement or drama.

"Gang's all here," Carter announces in a cheerful voice.

I position the laptop on the island, so Jax can see everyone. "Hey guys. How's the job hunt, Dais?"

She scowls at him, and he quickly asks Carter about Taylor.

Once the small talk winds down, all my siblings look at me expectantly, and I know this is it. The moment I tell them the truth. I've never really called a family meeting before, so I'm sure they're curious why I'm doing it now. Daisy and Carter think I'm going to tell Jax about the baby and I am, but there's so much more to this conversation than just Sierra and I trying to sort out a future.

"Okay." I rub my hands together, piercing each of my siblings with a look. "There's a lot I need to tell you guys and—"

"Oh God, this is becoming a theme," Jax interrupts, and Carter cracks a smile.

It's true. In the past few months, us Kane kids have been sharing a lot of family secrets, finally bringing them out into the light of day. I guess now it's my turn.

"What's going on, man?" Jax asks me directly.

"The first thing I need to tell you, Carter and Daisy already know. I confided in Carter and Sierra told Daisy just the other day."

Jax's mouth drops open before he grins wide, a laugh bursting out of his mouth. "Y'all are dating?"

"Yes, we are. But, we're also having a baby," I clarify.

"No shit!"

"I'm serious."

"When did this go down?"

"The weekend you and Evie moved to Texas," Daisy supplies helpfully.

"Wow, I didn't expect you to say that. Congratulations?" Jax says it like a question, and I scrub my hand over my face.

"It came as a surprise to me, too. Obviously. But it's definitely a good thing. I'm happy about the little peanut."

Jax's eyes widen in surprise but he takes it in stride. "How's

Sierra doing? Is she feeling okay? Does she have support in New York? Isn't her whole family in Europe?"

"The UK." Daisy again.

"Right." Jax nods.

I'm grateful for Jax's concern for Sierra. My brothers are always like that, worrying about everyone, and it makes my chest feel funny to know that they're looking out for Sierra, too. "She's doing all right. She doesn't really have any support in New York, which brings me to my second point."

"Which is?" Jax asks.

"I'm moving to New York." I turn toward the laptop. "I'm hoping to find a job at an auto body shop. Do you have any Army friends I can reach out to who—"

"Absolutely." Jax nods with enthusiasm. "Kenny Silva is up there and my man Migs. And so are a few guys I did my last tour with. No worries there, we can definitely find you a job."

My shoulders relax slightly at this good news. That's one corner puzzle piece falling into place right there. If Jax can hook me up with a few connections, I know I can land a job.

"That'd be great, Jax. Thanks."

"Yeah, you got it."

"Okay. So, the next thing I need to tell you all is—"

"There's more?" Carter asks, startled.

Him and Daisy look at me curiously and I nod, shifting my weight uncomfortably.

"So, the baby is going to have our last name. Kane."

"Of course, he or she is." Daisy's eyebrows dip low on her forehead as she watches me, obviously confused.

"And that got me to thinking about how I don't want my kid to be saddled with my past growing up, so I want to clear my name."

Silence. It's quiet and three startled and confused faces stare at me. One from a computer screen, but still Jax's expression is clear.

"Clear your name? How?" Carter drawls.

"I don't want to have my record anymore."

"Yeah, I get that, but you can't just be expunged for a crime you—"

"I didn't do it."

"What?" Jax's voice booms out of the computer speaker.

I sigh, massaging the center of my forehead, my thoughts a jumbled mess. How do I explain this so they understand? How could anyone understand how I served two years in prison while innocent? I mean, it obviously happens but it's not the norm.

"Den, what happened?" Daisy's fingers touch my wrist gently and when I glance up, her eyes hold all the compassion and love in the world.

"Dad set me up. Him and Griller. They were running a scam, hitting a lot of gas stations and corner stores. But this one job, it took a wrong turn. The clerk was assaulted. When it all came out, they paid a bunch of people off to say they saw a guy, a guy with my physical description. The surveillance footage went missing. You know how many of the cops around here are in the MC's pocket." I shrug. "Things just snowballed and I didn't have a chance in hell at being found innocent without all the doubt and perception that went with being arrested. I also shouldn't have been found guilty but you remember that year? It was an election year for the judges and they always take a harder stance on any type of crime before an election. With all the other gas stations and shops getting dinged, this was the judge's chance to put a face and a name to whoever was responsible for all the recent robberies."

"You pled guilty for a crime you didn't commit?" Jax asks, incredulous.

"I never pled guilty. I was found guilty by the jury. But I maintained that I was innocent the whole time. And that's why I served two years instead of one. I refused a plea deal because then you can never appeal. And I wouldn't agree to take the fall for something I didn't do, even though I ended up taking the fall for something I didn't do."

"So, you went to jail for a longer amount of time because of... integrity?" Daisy whispers, her eyes wide.

"Good for you, man." Carter says seriously, nodding at me.

"Good for me? I left you here, on your own, to look out for Daisy and Jax, for an entire extra year because –"

"Because you were being a role model. The type a kid could look up to and be proud of." Carter cuts me off, his green eyes dark with wisdom. Too much wisdom for someone his age.

I look down, studying my hands. "Griller used to visit me in lockup and tell me all this stupid shit about how I abandoned y'all, about how hard he was making things for you guys, especially..." My eyes cut to Daisy.

"Me again?" she asks.

I reach out and hook my arm around her neck, pulling her into my side and kissing the top of her head. "Obviously it was all crap but he wanted me to take a plea and name a bunch of guys in another MC as being the ones behind the robberies. He thought he could threaten me with you guys and I would take his offer, implicate other innocent guys, and never have a shot at clearing my name."

"But you didn't do it." Jax states the obvious.

"But was that the right call? You all were here on your own, Carter got sucked into the MC bullshit, Daisy could have –"

"It was the right call." Carter cuts me off again. "Trust me, you did the right thing."

Daisy and Jax nod in agreement and I sigh again, raking my fingers over my hair.

"I can't believe Dad set you up. I mean, I can. But I can't. It was two years," Carter says angrily, holding up two fingers. "Two fucking years and your whole future."

I nod, noting the anger in his eyes, but also knowing that it isn't directed at me. He's hurt. He was manipulated and betrayed by our father as well, and while he thought he was the only one taking the risks to keep the rest of us safe, he's now learning that we've all been affected in different ways by the man we call dad. "I know."

Jax grips the back of his neck as he stares at me from the laptop screen. His green eyes are narrowed in thought, and I can tell he's trying to make sense of everything. "Why're you telling us this now? Why didn't you tell us years ago? I always thought you pled guilty. Texas Ink said..." he trails off, his eyes widening as he mentions a member of the Devil's Shadows MC. The MC spread a lot of stories about me in the aftermath of my going to jail. I just never bothered to correct them because the damage to my reputation had already been done. And that's a really tough thing to restore in a small town like ours.

"I need your help." I finally get to my last point. "I need to clear my name before my baby is born, and I have no idea how to do that. I spoke to a guy I graduated high school with who's a lawyer now, and he gave me the names of a few lawyers to reach out to, but they're, Jesus, they're really expensive."

Carter begins, "We can figure out a way to—"

"I'm not taking money from any of you. I'm asking if you know anyone I can reach out to or have any other ideas about how I can go about this. Anyway, I figured it was time I just told y'all the truth."

"Ya think?" Jax asks, voice dripping with sarcasm.

"Did you tell Sierra?" Daisy asks me quietly, her big eyes peering up at me.

I nod, my gut sinking, as I know she's going to feel even more betrayed by me. How could I confide in her best friend about our family's past before I told her?

But instead of looking away like I expect, a small smile ghosts her lips. "Y'all are going to make it," she says in a soft voice. "You're both already in deeper than you think."

I kiss her head again and look at my brothers.

"I'll see what contacts I can come up with. Let me talk to Evie tonight," Jax offers.

"Thanks, man."

"I'm sure Taylor grew up with a bunch of lawyers that owe her family some type of favor or another." Carter cracks a small smile and I grin back.

"I appreciate it."

"Thanks for finally telling us the truth," Carter says.

"Anymore secrets? Anyone?" Jax asks loudly.

We all laugh.

"I'll keep you posted," Daisy says cryptically but when we all stare at her, she cracks up, holding her hands up surrender. "Just messing with you. I promise once I land a job, y'all will be the first to know."

* * *

I'm relieved when the cabin doors on the plane close and we are cleared for take-off. I've been away from Sierra for six days and it's been six days too long. I've never felt like this before. Ever. This antsy, jittery, unsettled feeling of being somewhere and having my thoughts fixated somewhere else. Of course, when Jax first deployed I worried about him constantly, but I still went about my day. Now, I can barely function without thinking about Sierra, picturing the curves of her body, imagining her carefree laugh. I'm just anxious to see her.

Dean was understanding when I told him I needed to leave Benny's. He even placed a call to a friend of his in New York and I start at Sal's Autobody in Queens next week. I didn't expect him to go above and beyond after I left so unexpectedly but he waved me off, saying something about putting your kids first. Either way, I'm grateful for the job.

The second the wheels touch down in New York, I power up my phone to see a string of text messages from Sierra. I can't stop the grin that cuts my face. When the hell did I ever smile so much? Shaking my head, I send her a quick reply that I'm on my way and exit the plane.

When I arrive at James's, I wave to Tom, the doorman, before beelining for the elevators. The ding of the elevator opening to the penthouse has the stress and tension from the past week flooding out of me, leaving me relaxed for the first time since I kissed my girl good-bye.

"You're here!" she squeals from the doorway.

"Hi baby." I grin, dropping my bag to lift her in my arms and kiss her. Her arms intertwine around my neck, her legs hooking around my hips. "Missed you." I tell her against an onslaught of kisses that has me backing her up until her back rests against the wall next to the open door to the apartment.

"Take me inside. I missed you more." She whispers, her hold on my hair tightening, her eyes dark.

I chuckle but immediately obey. Leaving my stuff in the hallway, I enter the apartment, kicking the door closed behind me. Walking intently toward Sierra's bedroom, an adorable pout crosses her face. "No couch?"

"Quit it." I kiss her nose. "I'm over the couch. I need to take my time with you. This week has been way too long."

"Tell me about it." She agrees, as I hitch her body higher and close my eyes as her lips connect with my neck and our bodies connect with her bed.

17

SIERRA

"So," I look over at Denver, lying next to me, his hair tangled, a lazy almost-smile on his lips. "I made you dinner. Sort of."

"Sort of?" he raises his eyebrows and turns from his side onto his stomach, crawling over me and pinning me to my pillow. "How did that happen?"

"I think I overcooked the pasta." I admit, trying to calculate how long we've been at it in my bed and knowing it is much, much longer than the eleven minute al dente cooking time on the box of penne.

Denver laughs, the corners of his eyes crinkling, his mouth pulling into a wide smile and I pause, my hands wrapped around his biceps, as I try to memorize this moment. God, he's so beautiful. Especially like this, when he isn't carrying the weight of the world on his shoulders, when he isn't brooding and sulking, when he allows himself to enjoy a moment and be present in it.

"What?" he asks, shaking his head at me. "I love that you made me dinner, babe. Thank you. I promise to eat it no matter what." He explains, misinterpreting my silence.

I smile at him. "It's just, I never really see you

laugh. I like it."

He grins at me, leaning down until our foreheads meet and pressing a kiss to my lips. "I promise to try it more often."

I run my hands from his biceps, up his strong shoulders, and around to rest on his broad back. His muscles bunch and shift under my touch and I moan, already wanting him again.

"How much do you care about the pasta?" I ask him, tugging his body closer to mine.

"Not as much as I care about you." He jokes, gathering me in his arms once more and kissing me senseless.

* * *

The penne is a blob. An actual blob of hardened mush, sticking to the bottom of the pot that I may or may not have burned. My mouth drops open in shock as the water has nearly boiled away.

Next to me, Denver is laughing again. Laughing!

"I love you, Sierra." He says, taking the pot from my hand and tossing the blob into a strainer. He picks at the mush and eats a bite. "Not bad, babe." He tries to say with a straight face but I swat at his hand.

"Oh, stop it. It's awful, even I know that."

He laughs again, the sound rich and wonderful and I swear I'd burn dinner every night if it meant getting to hear him laugh like this.

"We can make more pasta. Did you make sauce for it?" he asks, looking around for another pot.

It's then that I realize I forgot the most important part. The pasta sauce! I printed a recipe out earlier today and bought all of the ingredients and then I came home and took a nap and...forgot.

Denver's chuckling intensifies as the color drains from my face.

"Oh my God. I forgot." I admit. "I bought all the ingredients."

I add, pitifully.

Denver walks closer and fists my hair in his hands, pushing it away from my face and looping his arms around my shoulders. He hugs me to his chest where I can hear all the chuckles he's holding inside. He's really too sweet. My brothers would be broadcasting my cooking mishap from the rooftops to anyone who would listen. And Daisy would be sharing a live video on Instagram.

"It was a nice thought. And gesture." Den says seriously.

I look up into his dark eyes and they're no longer laughing.

"Thank you. No one's ever even tried to cook for me before." He explains.

"Ever?" I ask, my eyes widening at his admission.

He shakes his head. "Not since my mama passed."

I close my eyes and snuggle deeper into his embrace, vowing to at least learn how to cook one or two dinner recipes to make for Denver. I breathe in his scent and relax into his touch, so happy he's finally home. Who knew a week could feel like eternity?

"Come on, baby. Let's go out to dinner."

"Out?" I pull back, looking down at my disheveled self.

"Yeah. I want to take my girl on a date." He says, one side of his mouth pulling up. "I'll clean this up, you go get dressed, and we'll wander until we find a place we want to try."

My heart flutters in my chest as I grin at him. How the hell did I get so lucky? What guy laughs so hard that you ruined his meal and then offers to take you to dinner like it's the best thing in the world? Being with Denver, everything is new and fun and exciting. Everything makes me smile and I finally understand what it means to fall in love with someone. It truly is the greatest feeling in the world and it blocks out everything except your person. And my person is Denver Kane.

"Okay." I agree. "But leave the mess. I'll do it later. I'm serious."

Den waves me away and I duck back into my room, walking into my closet and flipping through racks, trying to find the perfect outfit for our impromptu date.

* * *

Clad in tight jeans, knee high boots, and a simple black sweater with a black leather bomber jacket, I turn in the mirror to check myself out. My jeans are definitely tighter than they were a few weeks ago but they still look good. I apply minimal make-up and run a brush through my hair. Adding some large gold hopes and a simple gold chain, I pick up my small cross-body bag and flip off my bedroom light.

Denver is waiting for me in the living room, his worn jeans riding low on his hips, his feet already jammed into his black motorcycle boots. His hair is pulled back neatly, a bun secured at the back of his head. He's wearing a dark grey button down, the sleeves rolled up on his forearms.

"New shirt?" I joke.

He looks down, his eyes flashing to mine uncertainly and I realize that it is indeed a new shirt. And he bought it...for me.

"I love it. You look hot in grey." I tell him truthfully.

He nods, his mouth barely moving and I walk toward him and kiss his shoulder, hugging his arm against me. "Come on. I'm starving."

"You or the peanut?" he asks, slipping an arm around my shoulder and steering us to the door.

"Both."

"Well then, we better not wander too long." He pulls the door closed behind us and locks up.

Slipping his hand in mine, we enter the elevator and walk out into the brisk cool of New York as a real couple, going on a real date. And I can't stop cheesing because damnit, it really is the best.

18

DENVER

Sierra and I duck into a small, Italian restaurant. My mouth is literally watering the moment the doors close behind us and I breathe in the fresh scents of garlic and basil and homemade pasta. The hostess settles us at a table and we're quiet, our eyes scanning the menu, our stomachs grumbling.

After we order, I reach over to take Sierra's hand in mine. "How's everything going with your art?"

She beams, her eyes brightening. "Really good. I have news, actually."

"What's that?"

"Well, over the past few months, I've been focusing a lot on my digital marketing and I've built a pretty substantial following on Facebook, Twitter, and most recently Instagram. My Instagram posts are definitely converting the best at bringing more attention to my work. Anyway, this past week, I reached out to a few people I know in the art industry, and I got a job!"

"A job?" I place down my fork, my attention solely focused on Sierra.

"Yes. I'm going to be managing the digital marketing for a small gallery nearby. Isn't that awesome? I'm going to gain a lot more exposure to the art world and connect with up-and-coming artists while also building my personal social media platform."

"Sierra, baby, congratulations. That's amazing." I raise my water glass to her and she clinks hers against mine, giggling.

"I'm really excited. I start on Monday."

"Wow. That's incredible. I don't know anything about social media other than it seems to be all people do these days."

She laughs harder, shaking her head at me. "I'm going to create you an Insta account yet. The handle will be @myboyfriendsmanbun and all the posts will be about your hair."

I pause, frowning as I try to understand what she's saying and decipher if she's serious or not. Sierra bursts out laughing, loud and uninhibited, drawing the attention of nearby tables until I just shake my head and congratulate her again. I'll have to ask Daisy to keep an eye out for any Insta-whatever posts about my hair.

"I definitely should have applied for a job like this sooner, like in May when I graduated. But I just feel so much more motivated to do everything now that we're having the peanut. Does that make sense?"

"Yeah. Definitely. It's like everything is for real now."

"Exactly. And my painting is going well. I'm still painting my grandmother's face but I feel like once I speak to her, I'll be able to move past it and paint other portraits as well."

"Why don't you call her?"

A frown twists Sierra's mouth. "I have. Twice. And I've sent three emails. She hasn't gotten back to me, which isn't unusual for her. She's not super into technology. But I'll try her again."

I nod, thanking the server as she drops off our entrees. Sierra's eyes slide closed across from me as she breathes in the delicious aroma of her dinner. She twirls some linguine around the tines of her fork and literally groans as she places the first bite in her mouth.

I sit and watch her eat, amused by how much she enjoys every single freaking thing she does. Every bite of food, every stroke of her paint brush, every dance move to a song that plays. Sierra lives with so much enthusiasm, such a zest for life.

"Do I have something on my face?" she asks, catching me staring at her.

"Nah," I shake my head. "I just hope our baby is exactly like you."

"What?" she laughs. "I hope he or she has your eyes."

I take a sip of my water, my eyes still locked on hers. I already know our baby will be perfect. I mean, come on, look at his or her mama.

* * *

Being in New York City is a completely different experience. It's so different than Ashby County, Georgia, I feel like I'm trying to find my footing every day with every single task that I do. The traffic, the noise, the constant commotion. The fast pace, the fast talking, the nonstop moving. It's exhausting. What happened to neighbors talking to neighbors? Sharing a glass of sweet tea or a conversation? Sierra doesn't know the names of anyone, except the doorman, in her building.

There's no chitchat while ordering a coffee or warm smiles at sweet babies or yapping dogs on the street. Everyone is focused on where they're going, and it always seems like if they don't get wherever their going in thirty seconds, the world is going to end.

I don't get it.

And I don't particularly like it.

But I'm hoping it grows on me because my life is here now, with Sierra and the peanut.

I settle into my work at Sal's Autobody easily. It's mostly the same work I did back in Georgia: tune-ups, oil changes, the occasional transmission change. It's not exciting or glamorous but it's a paycheck. Coupled with a bar-backing job I picked up for two nights a week, I've started saving for the first few months of rent once Sierra and I move to our own apartment.

Sierra began her new job at the art gallery and comes home every day exhausted. But her cheeks are flushed, her smile is bright, and her eyes are shining so I know she's enjoying the work. She chatters nonstop about both the artists and the clients she's meeting. I like hearing about the eccentricities, like one client who dresses up her poodle and carries the dog in a purse. A purse that apparently costs more than most people earn in half a year. Or a man she works with who always wears mismatched socks. The art industry is like a different world to me but I love how happy Sierra is immersed in it.

After our first week together in New York, we begin to settle into our own routine. Sierra made us a "bank" out of a shoebox. It's covered in different colored paper and decorated with cars and paintings and glitter and looks like a designer replica of a craft Daisy would make as a kid but Sierra got a kick out of it. It sits on our bedside table and each week, we drop our paychecks and spare money into it before going to the real bank and depositing our earnings in a joint bank account.

"Hey." Daisy smiles at me, holding a frying pan as I walk into the kitchen one morning.

"Morning." I kiss her cheek and take the frying pan from her pan. "What're you making?"

"Just scrambled eggs so don't get too excited. Or too scared." She jokes, whisking the eggs as I set the pan on the stove.

I lean back against the island, crossing my feet at the ankles and watch her. She's really been trying to cook more lately and it's adorable. Mainly because I know she's doing it for me, because she wants to do something for me. It's sweet and thoughtful and makes me not even care that the food isn't particularly good. I just like knowing she cares about me.

"What time are you heading in today?" she asks me.

"Not until later. Sal asked me if I can close today so I don't have to be in until one."

"Sweet. Want to come register for a pre-natal class with me?"

"A pre-natal class? Is that the one where you learn how to breathe?"

She giggles. "I doubt it. I think I'm already breathing okay on my own."

"Quit it. You know what I mean."

She pours the eggs into the pan and nods, "Yeah, I know what you mean. I don't think so. It's one of those classes where you learn about labor, what to expect, coping techniques. And other stuff too, like how to change a diaper, give the baby a bath, swaddle them."

"What's a swaddle?" I ask, confused as hell. Was having a kid always this complicated?

"It's the way your wrap them in their blanket when they're born."

"Why can't you just give them a blanket?" I pop some toast into the toaster.

Sierra shrugs, running a spatula over the eggs. "I don't know. You're supposed to swaddle them so their arms are tucked next to their sides. It's supposed to make them feel safe and help with their startle reflex."

A startle reflex? "Baby, you lost me. But yeah, I want to register with you and learn all this stuff because I don't know what any of it means."

Sierra turns to me, flipping her long hair over her shoulder and grinning, "Good thing you have a few months to learn it all then."

"Good thing." I agree, swatting her ass and pulling her in for a kiss...or five.

"Baby, I can't burn another meal." She says seriously against my mouth and I chuckle.

"That's true. How much time do we have between breakfast and registration?"

She lifts an eyebrow at me before adding the eggs to two plates. "If we eat quickly, we have enough time."

I carry the plates to the table and pull out her chair. "You better start chewing."

She snorts, walking over to the table and passing me a glass of orange juice. "For hydration."

I chuckle, taking a large gulp of the juice. Tucking a piece of hair behind Sierra's ear, I take the seat across from her and eat my breakfast. The entire time, my body is on edge, waiting for her to finish so I can have her to myself for at least a little while. Or longer if I'm lucky.

NOVEMBER

19

SIERRA

"Hi Tota, it's me, Sierra," I say when my grandmother's warm voice fills the line.

"Sierra? Oh, hello. How are you, dear?"

"I'm well, thanks. How are you doing?"

"I've been thinking of you," she says, her voice holding a note of excitement. "I'm sorry I haven't called you back but I keep thinking you have something to tell me."

"I've been thinking of you, too." I smile, biting my bottom lip, wondering if she's going to tell me I'm expecting or if she's waiting for me to spill the beans.

"I believe you are in a time of new beginnings, of excitement, and wonderment. Perhaps a bit of uncertainty and anxiety as well, but that's natural. Are you?"

I laugh now, enjoying her indirect way of asking. "Yes, Tota. I'm having a baby."

"I knew it!" she exclaims, and the happiness in her voice is genuine. "I told your father just last week, something is going on with Sierra. I can feel it. I've been having dreams about you for months, my dear, and in the beginning, they were a bit disturbing. You were lost, unsure, confused. But little by little, you began to find your way, and a month or two ago, I started getting the inkling that it wasn't just you anymore, but you and another tiny heartbeat."

"I'm due in May."

"That's wonderful news, Sierra."

"Thanks, Tota. Is my father there, by any chance?"

She whooshes out a deep breath, and I can hear the disappointment in it. "No, dear. I'm sorry; he's not. I promise to tell him you called."

"Thanks, Tota. I'm not sure when I'll be able to visit again but—"

"Oh, don't you worry about that. Take care of yourself. And your baby. And that dashing man who I believe is taking care of you?"

I smile again, not even surprised that she seems to know my life better than I do. "He is."

"That's the type of man you need, Sierra. A man who will be beside you and support you when you need it without you having to ask."

I nod, agreeing with her words, realizing that Denver is doing all of those things without my prodding. "You're right."

"I know I am."

I snort, shaking my head.

“He's a good man, isn't he?”

“He is. A very good man.”

“Good. Sometimes, we are bogged down, really affected by our past that it makes it difficult to move on, find peace in the present and in the future. I worry about your own father sometimes, and the relationship he had with his father. I wonder if his father had been more of a role model, would he have been a better father to you and Lachlan? A better husband to your mother? It's a difficult thing to admit when you have failed as a parent and in many ways, I failed your father.”

“Oh, Tota, don't say that. It's not –”

"It is true, dear. But he is to blame, too. He never tried to work past his issues. It's important to embrace the present for all the wonder it offers, Sierra. Not to continually live in or compare the now to the past."

I nod, thinking over her words. Does Denver still have unfinished business with his father? How could he not? Is that what Tota's hinting at?

"You'll be a wonderful mother, Sierra. I know it. Take care of yourself, dear. And call soon."

"'I will. Bye, Tota." I click off, leaning back against the couch cushions.

Picking up the TV remote, I flip through channels randomly, but my head is lost in thought. Is Denver still haunted by parts of his past that will complicate his future with me and the peanut? Should he address them now? Is he still trying to clear his name?

When the door opens around dinnertime and his large frame fills the space, I'm so relieved to see him after my thoughts have been tangled up, spinning in circles for hours, that I practically tackle him.

"Whoa." He takes a step back, catching me in his arms. "What's that for? You okay?"

I nod. "Yeah, sorry."

"What's going on?" His eyebrows draw together in concern and I trace my finger over them, smoothing out the lines.

"I spoke to Tota today."

"That's great, right? Wait, is she okay?" He places me on the ground and walks us over to the couch.

"Yeah," I collapse on the couch, angling my body to face him and hooking my legs over his knees. "She's great. She just, she said some things that made me think."

"What kind of things?"

"Just about my dad and his relationship with his dad. And not comparing the present to the past. I don't know. I've just been thinking of so many things and we haven't talked lately about you wanting to clear your name. About the stuff with your dad. Do you want to see him? Maybe get some closure? Are you still trying to clear your name?"

Denver sits still, a frown marring his perfect features as he chews the corner of his mouth thoughtfully.

"I didn't mean to upset you." I rush to explain, placing a hand on his forearm.

He shakes his head, turning to look at me. "You didn't upset me. It's a good point and fair questions. Honestly, I've been so wrapped up in the move here and working that clearing my name has been placed on the back burner. But I still want to do it and you're right, maybe I do need to close the door with my dad."

"You don't have to close the door. That doesn't have to be the only way to seek closure with him."

Denver's eyes narrow. "With Darren it is. And I want that door locked up before the peanut arrives."

I sigh, settling back against the cushions. "Maybe you should visit him, then?"

"In prison?"

I shrug.

"Maybe." He agrees. "Let me talk to my brothers and sister. There's a few things I still need to wrap up in Georgia too, so the timing would work out. I just, I don't want you to be on your own."

I wave a hand. "It's fine. Honestly. My mom is dying to come out to visit since I told her about the baby. She's having such a tough time not spilling the beans to my brothers but her and James are really happy. Mom adores babies. And I miss her. A lot. It's strange but now that I'm pregnant I feel like I understand her so much more. We've always been close but now we message or talk almost every day. It would be good for me too."

"You sure?"

I nod. "Take care of your family stuff. And then come back to me."

"I'll only be gone two or three days."

"That sounds perfect." I agree, shifting my weight to crawl onto his lap. Straddling him, I wind my arms around his neck and shiver as his large hands slide up from my waist to the center of my back.

"Miss me today?" he asks, dipping his lips to mine.

"Always." I admit, closing my eyes and letting his kiss consume me.

* * *

Later that night, I call Mom who is ecstatic to jump on a plane and visit with me for a few days. She is already talking about nursery shopping and items the baby will need when he or she is born. Her excitement is contagious and I find myself online shopping, spending an absurd amount of time on Pottery Barn Kids alone. Why does all of their stuff have to be so damn cute?

Denver calls his siblings and books a flight to Georgia. He's off tomorrow and the weekend so the timing is perfect.

In the morning, we lose track of time having one last romp in our bed. Denver kisses me hurriedly over a cup of coffee and rushes out of the apartment, unsure if he's going to make his flight. We can't stop laughing the entire time and I'm relieved when he messages me from the plane that he made it.

While I eat breakfast, Daisy and I chat and she tries to convince me to fly down with Denver for Thanksgiving. I plan to talk to Denver about that. Maybe we can have Daisy visit us instead?

After that, I disappear into my studio to paint for a few hours until Mom's plane arrives. Losing myself to the colors, the scent of Denver still hugging my body, I can't stop smiling. I don't know if I've ever been happier.

20

DENVER

When Carter pulls into the driveway of our family home, it's strange. It feels different now, not exactly like home, which is insane considering I've lived here most of my life. Already, I want to get back to Sierra and our little peanut. I hate that I'm missing the first prenatal class but she assured me it's fine and that her mom is going to go with her.

"You okay, man?" Carter asks, staring at me as I sit in the passenger seat and stare at the house.

"Yeah, sorry."

"You miss her?"

"It's stupid, right?"

"Not at all." Carter shifts his weight and faces me. "I hate being away from Taylor. Even when she's only gone for a night or two for a photo shoot, I hate it. I mean, I'm happy for her and proud of her but I hate being away from her."

"How do you like living together?"

He grins, letting out a low whistle. "It's really good, man. I want to go to sleep at night just so I can wake up next to her."

I snort, shaking my head at him. If anyone else said that, I'd make fun of them for being whipped but with Carter, it's different. I'm just happy he's finally found a woman who makes him so happy.

"Come on. Daisy is waiting for us. There's something we want to talk to you about."

I raise my eyebrows.

"It's good. I swear."

"Alright." I agree, opening the car door and swinging my duffle bag over my shoulder. Following Carter inside the house, I catch my sister in a hug and we retreat to the kitchen.

"Y'all ordered pizza?" I ask, eyeing the boxes.

"Yep. Are you hungry?" Daisy asks, sliding a slice onto a plate.

"Starving." I admit.

We sit down at the table and bite into our pizza and a calmness settles over the kitchen. Over our family.

"I wish Jax was here." Daisy says after a few minutes.

"Yeah." Carter agrees. "FaceTime him in Daisy. He wants to see Denver's expression when we tell him the news."

"What news?" I ask, suddenly anxious.

"Oh, relax. You're going to love this." My sister reassures me.

And really, nothing could prepare me for what comes out of her mouth next. But man, does it make me love my family. I'm lucky as hell to have them. And so is Sierra. And, of course, the peanut.

* * *

The cool wind blowing through my open windows clears some of the fog in my brain and makes the drive more therapeutic than I imagined. I'm halfway to Montgomery, Alabama and the throbbing in my temples is beginning to dim, the stress flowing from my body. Using this time to make overdue calls to the lawyers Taylor connected me with, to touch base with my brothers, and to check in on Sierra, it seems like I'm taking an important step forward for my future.

My cell rings again, and I press the small Bluetooth device in my ear to answer it. One of these days, I'm going to be able to afford a vehicle with a built in Bluetooth system.

"Hey," I answer.

"How's the drive?" Jax asks.

"Slow but good."

"Clearing your head?"

"Something like that. How's Evie doing?"

"She's good. Worried about you going to talk to Dad."

I shake my head. Of course, she is. Evie Maywood is one of the most giving and selfless women I know. Jax is lucky to have won her heart back.

"I'm calling with some good news," he continues after I don't say anything.

I chuckle but it's nearly soundless. "This is turning into a theme these days. I'm not used to it. What's up?"

"I reached out to Kenny and a few Army buddies of mine. One of the guys, Migs, opened a new autobody shop doing some repairs, but mostly custom rebuilds, about a year and a half ago. He works with a pretty select client base and does a lot of American muscle cars."

I let out a low whistle. The guys and women doing custom rebuilds are like artists; it's way above my monkey-wrenching around.

"He's got an opening. Wants to take you on."

"Jax, man, that's really incredible. But I can't do that stuff. I'm a Mickey Mouse mechanic compared to the people who do custom rebuilds and—"

"He'll train you. Six months base pay. After that, if it works out, base plus commission. And you keep all the tips, which I hear are pretty generous."

I shake my head again, unable to process how something this good, an offer this sweet, could just fall in my lap. "You're kidding me, right? What's the catch?"

"No catch."

"It's too good to be true." I tell him after he fills me in on the salary and the types of tips I could expect after a few months. "It would mean working only one job."

Jax sighs. "You're too damn skeptical for your own good. Just trust me on this one, it's legit."

"What's the backstory?" I ask, because there has to be one. What business owner would take on a guy like me, a guy without the necessary skill set required to do the job, and train him out of the goodness of his own heart?

Jax is quiet for a moment before he mutters out a curse. "All right. Don't ever repeat this. It was during my second tour. There was an IED explosion near a Humvee. Me and my guys were the closest to the Humvee, and we took some fire locking down the area. Command said to wait for backup, but I knew the guys wouldn't make it if we waited that long, so I ignored the command, never radioed back to confirm I received the message, and me and my guys went in. One of the guys we pulled out was Migs. He was in rough shape, and everyone was doubtful that he would pull through. I kept my fingers on his artery until the medics arrived. He says I saved his life. I didn't. It was a team effort, and a lot of guys were involved, but he wants to help you out. So take the offer."

I chew the corner of my mouth, once again in awe of my brother, Jax. He doesn't talk much about his time in the Army, and while he had a rough transition back home and suffered from PTSD, it's always surprising to learn of all the things he achieved and accomplished while in the service. Not surprising because he did it, but surprising because he never wants to talk about it. He shies away from any kind of recognition and only shares stories about his friends and the pranks they pulled, never about the heroic deeds they did.

"Thanks man," I say finally, knowing if I comment on his story, he'll shut down.

"It's no problem. I'll text you his number. Give him a call when you're back from Alabama."

"Will do. Appreciate it."

"I know, Den. Drive safe."

"Tell Evie hello."

"I will. We'll talk to you soon."

I disconnect the call and check the time. Deciding I should eat something, I pull off at the next exit to grab a bite and a Coke and to process everything Jax just shared with me.

* * *

It's bright and sunny the next morning as I wait outside the prison in my SUV for visiting hours to begin. It's strange, the weather being so cheerful on a day I feel so much dread. I hate walking back into a prison. A slew of memories I wish I could forget, a tightness in my chest, and an edge of fear underlying every move I make assault me until the throbbing headache is back, and my fingers repeatedly clench into fists.

I take a gulp of water from the plastic bottle in the center console and lean my head against the headrest, closing my eyes. It's going to be fine. I can do this. Walk in there, confront my old man, and move forward with my life.

And now with Jax's friend's offer on the table, Taylor's lawyer friends helping me out, and Sierra waiting for me in New York, it looks like my life is finally changing for the better.

My phone rings, interrupting the silence and I grin at Sierra's name on the screen.

“Hey baby, how're you feeling?”

“Hi! Pretty good, thanks. The nausea is starting to slow down and I'm not as tired as I was a few weeks ago.”

“That's good news.”

“Yeah. I miss you.”

“Me too. I'll see you in two days though.”

"I know. I can't wait."

"How's your visit with your Mom?"

She laughs, the sound comforting as it washes over me. "She's already in that crazy grandma mode."

"Crazy grandma?"

"Just don't be alarmed by all of the shopping bags and deliveries arriving over the next few weeks."

"Oh, no. Is it that bad?" I ask, my eyes widening. For a family who has built-in ovens, who knows what they do for a baby's nursery?

I can hear Sierra's smile through the line. "It's pretty bad. In a good way. Our baby is going to be so spoiled. But mostly with love. Mom is just really excited; it's her first grandbaby."

I reach into my pocked and finger the small pouch with the gemstone that Carter and Daisy passed along to me last night. I wonder how my mom would react to the news of my having a baby? I can picture her sitting up at night, her knitting needles in hand, making the baby a blanket or hat. A pang hits my chest and I have to move the phone away from my mouth to regulate my breathing.

"She's coming with me to the gallery for a few hours this afternoon. She's also really excited to come to the prenatal class with me tonight so don't feel bad about that." Sierra continues to chatter and I pinch the bridge of my nose to refocus on the conversation with my girl.

"I'm glad y'all are spending some time together. I hope to meet your mom, and James, soon."

"You will, don't worry. Are you nervous about seeing your dad?"

I blow out a deep breath. "I guess so. I just want to get this over with and get back to you and our bed."

"It's cold without you." She says playfully and I cough, just the thought of her naked body splayed out across the sheets affecting me.

"I'll be there soon." I repeat and frown at how scratchy my voice sounds.

Sierra laughs, the sound carefree. "You better be. I'm over sleeping with all these boyfriend pillows."

I chuckle. "Hey, I have good news. Jax is connecting me with a guy he knows who has his own autobody shop doing custom rebuilds."

"Den! That's amazing! When's the interview?"

"It seems to be past that point already. Jax says he wants to take me on and train me. Six months base pay but if it works out than base plus commission. We could be in our own little place before Christmas."

"Wow! I'm so proud of you." She gushes and the craziest thing is, she means it.

My chest feels funny at her unwarranted praise and it makes me yearn for her even more.

"Baby, it's nearly eleven so I gotta go. Call you after, okay?"

"Yeah, call me. Good luck, Den."

"'Bye baby." I click off and store my cell in the center console, placing the pouch holding the gemstone beside it.

When eleven rolls around, I exit my SUV and walk the short distance to the main entrance of the prison. Darren is held in a maximum-security facility for drug and gun related charges. He's facing twenty years and has already served eight. I'm always waiting for the call that he's getting out early, which makes my blood gel in my veins, while also offering my mind a breath of relief I don't understand.

How can I have such conflicting feelings toward my father?

While I often hate him for setting me up to take his fall, for manipulating Carter, ignoring Jax, and dismissing Daisy, I can't erase the handful of happy memories from my childhood: of sitting on his lap as he read me bedtime stories, of him teaching me how to throw a football, of twisting Oreo cookies and eating the icing before the chocolate wafers just like he taught me. The entire thing is a mess in my mind and makes my feelings toward him a vortex of confusion and turmoil.

Stepping into the prison, I take in the yellow-beige walls and the no-nonsense officer sitting behind the check-in desk.

"Morning," I say, sliding her my driver's license for identification. After signing in, divulging my past record, and confirming that I am here to visit my father, Darren Kane, I'm led to another room to wait for the security check.

Sitting with a group of people of all ages, all ethnicities, and religions, with varied life experiences, it's funny how much we all have in common in this moment. Everyone wears an expression filled with nerves and anxiety, underlined by hope and a glimmer of longing to see their loved ones. Kids clutch colorful drawings on construction paper tightly in their fists. One man counts out his singles and quarters, probably to make sure he has enough change for the vending machine.

"Group B." An officer calls out, walking over to our section as we all stand, quietly forming a line as we're led to the metal detectors.

After we're all cleared, we remain in a cafeteria-style room to sit and wait for the inmates to arrive.

Within minutes, I spot him. His hands are cuffed in front of his waist and his hair shaved nearly to his scalp. His eyes are dark and humorless, like mine, and his expression is severe. I frown, wondering if this is what I'm going to look like in twenty-something years. God, I hope not.

"What're you doing here?" He practically sneers as he takes the chair across from me. He nods at the guard standing to his side, and the guard backs up a few feet, but his eyes never leave my father.

"How're you doing?" I ask instead.

"How do you think?"

I nod slowly, absorbing his shitty attitude and reminding myself that the man who once read me bedtime stories and schooled me in the proper way to dunk a cookie in a glass of milk no longer exists. The man before me, the hardened, selfish, hateful man in front of me is who my father is now.

"You're going to be a grandfather."

He snorts, the sound loud and harsh. "Who the fuck you knock up?"

"My girl. We're going to have a baby." I keep my voice quiet, but there's an edge to my tone that I know Darren hears as a small smile lifts the left side of his mouth, the same way Carter's does. As much as I want to punch Darren in the face for insinuating my girl is some trash I could care less about, I know what he wants more than anything is a reaction from me. I fight to keep my features neutral, my expression bored.

"Congratulations." His voice is dry and empty.

Around us, little kids squeal and family members exchange quick hugs and tearful reunions. But for Darren and me, this tense dance border-lining on a power struggle to maintain our cool is as good as it gets.

"I came to tell you that I've hired a team of lawyers. I'm going to clear my name, so my son or daughter doesn't have to live with having a parent with a record the same way Carter, Jax, Daisy, and I did."

A low, humorless laugh whooshes out of his nose as he shakes his head, knocking gently against the table. "You're pretty funny, Denver, you know that?"

I don't say anything, continuing to wait for him to get to his point.

"You think I don't know about you and Daisy's friend? I know everything." He points to his chest. "I have eyes everywhere. I'll hand it to you and Carter; y'all did good finding girls with money. But don't forget where you came from. You'll always be a bottom feeder, and your kid is half you, so that's not saying too much for his future, yeah?"

I bite down hard on my tongue to keep from lashing out.

"There's no evidence that links anyone but you to that robbery. You already served the time. What the fuck does it matter now?"

"I'm innocent."

He snorts again. "You're anything but innocent, Den."

"I just came to give you a head's up."

He gives a slow nod, his eyes narrowing at me once he realizes I'm not dropping this. "All right." He glances at the clock, as if he has somewhere to be. "You do this, go against me, go against the Club, and it's not gonna end good for you. Or Sierra Begay."

I stiffen the moment her name leaves his mouth and he laughs, this time with more humor.

"A New York painter, isn't she? Lives in a penthouse on Park?"

I swallow thickly, a lump forming in my throat, unsure of what to say next. I hate that my father always seems to be one step ahead of me, but I shouldn't be surprised. He's a sneaky fucker, and he has been for a long, long time.

"Drop this bullshit, leave the past in the past, and I'm sure my grandson will be born healthy and without any complications," he says quietly, leaning forward to catch my eyes with his.

The dark depths of his black eyes are bottomless, devoid of any real emotion except hatred.

"You should let her go. I hear Scotland is a beautiful country. Not that I'll ever see it, but I'm sure Sierra and the kid will be better off without you. What the hell are you, a guy with no degree, no skills, and no future, going to provide for a girl who could hold the world in her hand?" He raises his eyebrows. "How are you going to support a kid? On what salary? With what future?" He smiles at me, a frightening expression on him. "You're a lot more like me than you think, Den. Why do you think I tried to train you? To bring you into Club life? You could have been someone, done something with your life. Something your kid could be proud of. But now," says, his smile widening, "now you're nothing. And deep down, you know it. So drop this stupid idea.

Let your girl and kid go; let them have a real shot at life. And keep doing whatever the hell it is you do all day."

I lean closer to my father, making sure our eyes are connected so he can see all the hatred I feel for him when I tell him my next words. "Fuck you, Darren." I say quietly, my voice hard as steel. "Don't ever speak about my girl or kid again. In fact, I never want to hear her name come out of your mouth again. Don't forget, you're in here." I gesture to our surroundings. "The real world is out there. And this Club you speak so highly of doesn't need you anymore. You're not worth anything to them. Get the fuck off your pedestal and remember that I can make your life in here a lot more difficult than it is now. And I will if I have to." I stand, my limbs shaky from the rage radiating through me, beating in my blood like lava.

"Have a nice life, Darren. I hope you only see the inside of this building for the rest of it." I rap my knuckles twice against the table to signal the end of our conversation, and then I turn around to leave.

"Denver." His voice rasps out and I stop, not bothering to turn around and face him. "I take it back. I don't care what you do or don't do regarding your record. Just know I'll have eyes on your girl and the baby either way. I guess we'll see what the future holds."

I see red at his words and more than anything, I want to turn around and knock his teeth down his throat until he chokes on them. But knowing I can't do that, especially in here, I force myself to walk steadily out of the prison. It isn't until I'm back in my car that I take in the shaking of my hands, the anger thrumming through my veins, causing my body to vibrate. It takes me three attempts to shove the key into the ignition and another five minutes to pull out of the parking lot and point the SUV in the direction of Georgia.

But the entire drive back to Ashby County, Darren's words play like a loop in my mind.

Could he hurt Sierra and our baby? Does he have eyes on her right now?

My blood turns to ice at the thought. And then the ice cracks because deep down, I know he's capable of it. He's capable of anything.

How could Sierra and our baby not be better off without me?

21

SIERRA

I haven't heard from Denver since we talked before he went to see his dad. It's been one day and I'm starting to worry. He's supposed to fly back home tomorrow and I'm questioning if he's still coming.

I've texted him several times and left a voicemail but still...silence. My nerves are starting to get the best of me, anxiety spiking in my chest. Did something happen to him? Is he okay? Did something happen with his dad?

I don't know much about Darren Kane, other than he's a thorn in the side of all the Kane kids. He's hurt them, repeatedly, and he makes my absent father look like a saint. Knowing all the hurt I feel by my own dad's rejection, I can't imagine how Denver or Daisy feel when trying to build fences with their father.

But still, I should have heard something, anything, from Denver by now.

Mom left this morning and I'm relieved she's not here to see me like this. My fingers are twitchy, and my head is all over the place. I hate the worry snagging my heart, the constant loop of questions and doubts playing in my mind on repeat.

Something is wrong. I don't know what, but I know that something is definitely wrong. Women have an intuition about these things. That cold chill that settles in your chest and seeps through your bones, making you question everything, recount all your past conversations and actions, looking for a sign to explain the sudden radio silence from your person. It all points to them pulling away, putting space between you and him, pushing you into a corner.

It all means something bad is coming.

Huffing, I slide my laptop off the couch and onto the coffee table. I need to get out of the apartment, clear my head, quiet my mind. Lacing up a pair of sneakers, I decide to go for a walk, an aimless stroll that will allow me time to window shop, grab a hot chocolate, and distract myself from staring at the time on my phone.

* * *

"Hi. How's the mama-to-be?" Daisy answers on the first ring and I breathe out some of the panic coursing through my veins at the sound of her voice.

"Dais."

"What's wrong?" Her tone changes immediately and I try to keep my stupid tears from slipping out.

"Is Denver okay? Is he home?"

"Yeah, he's fine. He got back yesterday. Why?"

"I haven't—he hasn't, called me." I admit, wincing at how stupid the words sound once they're out in the open. Like I'm Denver's keeper and he has to share every detail of his life with me now that we're a couple and having a baby.

But Daisy's silence lets me know that she sees the issue in this scenario.

"Has he reached out at all? A text?"

"Nothing." I almost-wail.

"That idiot!"

"Did something happen?"

"He's been in a foul mood since he got home, but I just assumed it was from seeing Darren. I don't know him that well, but it seems dear old dad can piss anyone off."

"But he's okay?"

"Yeah. Physically, he's fine."

"I just, I feel like something's wrong. Something shifted and now, I don't know, I'm worried. And it's not the crazy pregnancy hormones; it's real. He's avoiding me and I don't know why."

"Okay, okay. Let me talk to him. I'll call you back. Sierra," she sighs, her voice wavering slightly, "whatever happens, you're my best friend, okay?"

I nod, squeezing my eyes shut tight as the tears threaten to fall. Whatever happens? Does she think Denver's trying to cut me loose? Forget all about the plan to be in New York and raise our baby? Is he having second thoughts?

"I'll call you later, okay?" Daisy's voice is gentle, and I know that she knows I hear her and just can't speak. "Love you."

"Yeah," I manage to squeak out. I hang up the phone and let the tears come.

Cradling my growing belly, I take comfort in the tiny fluttering of my little peanut.

No matter what happens, I'm going to be the best mama I can for my baby.

At least I know that much.

* * *

The night is long and dark, and time seems to stall as I sit and stare out the window. Little by little, night fades and the sky lightens. I haven't heard back from Daisy. I also haven't heard anything from Denver.

I can't sleep. I can't eat. I can't do much of anything but sit and worry. And think. My mind jumps from one thought to the next with a million different scenarios and explanations.

Around dawn, my brother texts to remind me that my window on James's offer is closing, and I need to decide one way or the other. He also says he's happy to hear about my visit with Mom and the art gallery and he understands that I've been busy but he misses me. His words make my eyes well with tears as I realize how much I miss him too. I really need to tell him about the peanut.

I sigh, suddenly wondering if Denver and I should move to Scotland? At least there, we'll be surrounded by family. Now that Mom is gone and Lachlan is messaging me and Denver is being weird, I feel a wave of homesickness that I can't shake. Being alone in New York right now seems hard, lonely, and while I trust Denver, the past forty-eight hours have shaken my confidence in my ability to rely on him.

My eyes grow heavy and sleep beckons when the shrill ringing of my cell phone startles me awake. I grab it quickly and relief floods my bones when Denver's name appears on the screen.

"Hello," I answer quickly.

"Sierra." His voice is quiet, gruff, and distant in a way I can't explain. It's just...he sounds off.

"Are you okay?" I ask, concerned for him, relieved that he's finally calling.

He clears his throat, mumbles a few colorful curse words. "I went to see my dad."

"I know. You were supposed to call me when you got back."

"Yeah, well, I've had a lot on my mind."

I roll my eyes. Like I haven't? I've just wasted two whole days sitting here and worrying about him and his conversation with his father. And how whatever the heck happened is going to affect his flying up tomorrow and coming home to me.

"I don't think I'm going to be able to clear my name," he admits, an edge to his voice.

"Why not?"

"It's just not going to happen."

"Is that what the lawyers said?" I wait for him to offer me concrete reasons why this is no longer an option.

He's quiet for several seconds before he says words that turn my life upside down and rip apart the future I've been envisioning for us. "I think you should take the job offer in Scotland. And go home."

My heart stops in my chest for a full beat before galloping to a start again. "What?" I hiss, anger and frustration getting the best of me. My temper flares as I wait for him to give me something, anything, to fight back against. A real reason.

"It's for the best. I'd just hold you back."

"Denver, you're not making any goddamn sense. I don't even know what you're saying right now. We're in this together. Me and You. I love you. We're having a baby. And now what? You have one conversation with a man you haven't talked to in years, and you're suddenly questioning everything? But you can't give me one good reason why you're questioning us?"

He's silent, and his lack of a response fuels my fire.

"You're being a coward!" I shout at him. "If you don't want to be with me, just tell me that. Don't cut yourself out of our baby's life because of it. Don't make me promises one day and then renege on them all the next. Talk to me! Tell me what the hell is going on," I practically beg him, my voice pleading and whiny and not like my voice at all.

But instead of his angry and emotional response, he sighs heavily, as if it's a massive burden to have to answer my questions. "This is for the best. I'm removing myself from the picture for you. For the baby. You just have to trust me."

I laugh, loud and obnoxious and sarcastic. "Trust you? That's rich. How the hell am I supposed to manage that when you tell me you're coming back in three days and then you don't come home? When you register for prenatal classes with me and then just decide not to show up for any of them? What just happened to the future we were figuring out together?"

"I just, I can't do it. I won't do this to you."

"Do what?"

"Take the job, Sierra. You'll be better off. So will the baby. And maybe one day, you'll understand that. Take care."

Take care?

He hangs up the phone.

Hangs up on *me*.

I sit in shock and stare at my phone screen for several long seconds before tossing it on the coffee table. Looking around the apartment wildly, as if it's going to magically provide me with some answers, I drag myself off the couch and take a long, hot shower. I run through all of my conversations with Denver, think about our past few weeks together, desperate for a clue or sign that would explain how this happened. That would show me he was unhappy, that I should have seen this coming. But there are none. I can't come up with one freaking reason to explain why he's doing this to me. To us.

I cry. A lot. Ugly crying with sobbing and shaking shoulders and hiccups.

And when I'm done, I swipe my hand across the steamy mirror and stare at my puffy eyes and the bags underneath them. But then my eyes snag on the slight swell of my lower abdomen, and I know I can't dwell on this, can't dwell on him. I need to make smart choices, sound decisions because it's not just me anymore. It's me and peanut.

And I don't need Denver Kane.

I don't need anyone except myself.

Around eight in the morning, my hair twisted in a towel, my body clad in a bathrobe, I finally succumb to sleep. And I'm grateful that it drags me under like quicksand. I don't dream or think or wonder. I sleep, deep and soundly, until four the following afternoon.

When my eyes finally open and the throb in my chest is a duller version of yesterday, I pick up my phone, scan my messages and missed calls, and begin forming a plan for my own future. Without Denver Kane.

22

DENVER

"What the hell is wrong with you?" Daisy's voice is furious as she storms into the kitchen, the swinging door bouncing hard off the wall.

I look up slowly from my bowl of Cheerios. I shove the spoon into my mouth and continue to watch her as she paces next to the kitchen island.

"I knew this would happen!" She throws her hands in the air. "I knew you would hurt her. I never imagined you'd be this stupid or selfish about it, but I knew you would let her down."

Daisy's words pierce my heart as she confirms everything Darren said the other day. I'd never be good enough for Sierra and our baby. I'd just let them down. Better now than in five or ten years, right? This way, my kid doesn't even have the chance to grow attached to me, to feel the void when I mess up in the future. It's better this way.

"Is it about Mom's gemstone? Are you scared of committing? Are you even listening to me?" Daisy slaps an open palm on the butcher block next to my cereal bowl.

I look up and her eyes narrow. "You look like shit," she says.

I nod, taking another bite of my cereal. I feel like shit.

Complete and total shit. What the hell am I doing? Am I becoming the man I swore I'd never be like?

"You're ruining everything." Daisy's voice drops, her eyes swirling with anger and bewilderment and...questions I can't—won't—answer. "You're ruining everything, and when you wake the hell up and realize that, you'll only have yourself to blame."

I nod again, her voice ringing with truths I already know.

"Stop nodding at me and say something. Den, please, help me understand why you're shutting Sierra out. Why are you pushing her away? What happened with Dad?"

I wince at the mention of our father, and I know Daisy catches the movement because her eyes widen with a flare of understanding. "He got to you, didn't he?"

"Just drop it, Dais. None of this concerns you. It's not your problem."

"Doesn't concern me? Not my problem?" she repeats, her tone incredulous. "You're breaking my best friend's heart. You're walking away from the best woman you're ever going to meet. From your child. Your kid, Denver, and for what? A few stupid thoughts and words from our sperm donor?"

I wince at her expression "sperm donor." She said it because Darren was never present in her life, just like I'll never be present in my kid's life if I keep this up.

I fix Daisy with one last look, pleading with her to let it go, before I cut around her and storm out the back door to the porch.

It's been raining on and off all day, and the musty air and heavy pressure hanging around me is both soothing and stifling. Staring out over the back yard, I scrub my hand down my face and try to even out my breathing.

On some level, I know Daisy is right. I am breaking Sierra's heart, and that cuts deep, to the bone. But Darren's threat was clear; he'll go after her, after them, if I don't let them go. Isn't that what parents are supposed to do? Make decisions in the best interest of their child?

Despite the fact that Darren was right, that I can never give Sierra or our baby the life they deserve, despite all the doubts and questions he filled my head with, he also served a blatant threat.

And as much as I don't want to believe him, I do. I know he'll have someone go after Sierra. After the baby. And I'll be powerless to stop him.

Then what? How will I deal with the fact that my own baby and girl are hurt because of me? Because of my father? Because of my last name?

"Fuck!" I yell out into the wind, slamming my fist down on the railing of the porch.

No matter what I do, I lose. But I'll be damned if Sierra loses our baby because of me.

It's better this way.

It has to be.

* * *

"What the hell are you doing?" The anger in Jax's voice is barely contained when he calls me the next day. "I vouched for you. Called in a favor for your benefit, and Migs tells me he hasn't heard from you."

I sigh, pinching the bridge of my nose, the pressure in my head lifting for a nanosecond.

"And then Daisy tells me you're ending things with Sierra? One minute, you're planning on a future. The next, you're breaking her heart. What the hell did Darren say to you?"

"I didn't mean to mess things up between you and your buddy."

"The hell with that, Den. What's going on with you? Three days ago, you were all about creating a family, building a future, and now, you're acting like a deadbeat, like a coward, like our father."

I groan at his words but don't fight back. He's looking for a battle, and I'm not willing to give him one. He wouldn't understand unless I told him the whole truth, and I can't do that because he'd try to convince me we can find another solution. That we could somehow beat Darren at his own game.

But we can't. No one can. You can't beat a man who has nothing to lose. I know that because I've been that man, once. I'm not anymore, and I have too damn much to lose to risk it.

"Get your head out of your ass. I'm giving you twenty-four hours before I blow my small savings account on a flight home to knock sense into you." He hangs up and I curse, the pounding back in my head.

I know it will only get worse when Carter shows up.

* * *

He kicks my feet hard and I start, banging my head against the undercarriage of the truck I'm working on. I'm relieved Dean flipped it to me to work on for the next two days just so I can keep my hands busy, my mind occupied. Dean didn't say anything to me about telling Sal I needed to take some time off, he didn't say anything about anything. Just took one look at my face, sighed, and offered me the truck to work on.

"Fuck, Carter!" I yell out, the wrench I'm holding clattering to the ground and just missing my eye.

"What the hell is wrong with you?" My brother's voice is low but filled with venom.

I slide out from under the car and peer up at him. "I could have lost an eye."

"You're going to lose a lot more than that if you don't cut this shit and grow up."

"Grow up? Are you kidding me right now?" I finally lash out, the hours of pent-up aggression and silence bursting out of me.

"No, I'm dead serious. I know you, Denver. And I know

Darren, almost as well as you. He's playing you—that much is obvious. What isn't, is the reason why? So what is going on?"

"Nothing. Nothing is going on."

"Bullshit." Carter paces in front of me, pinching the bridge of his nose the way he does when he's agitated. "He's got something on you. He has to; that's how he operates." he says slowly, talking to himself, trying to sort out my mess on his own. The way he always does.

"This has nothing to do with you, Carter."

He stops suddenly, his neck snapping to me. "Oh really? I'm supposed to just cut off my nephew or niece because their father is acting like an asshole?"

I glare at him, wanting nothing more than to tackle my brother to the ground and get one good punch in just to release some of the anger I feel at being manipulated by Darren and not doing anything about it. My head is all over the place, and I don't know how to sort out the jumbled thoughts ricocheting in my brain, but I do know how to fight until exhaustion finally claims my body.

"Denver, man, just tell me what's going on." Carter finally stops moving, his body sagging against the wall of the garage, as if all the frustration just leaked out of him. He crouches down in front of me, so we're practically at eye level. "I've been where you are. Manipulated and desperate because of Darren. I get it. I really do. But I can't help you if you don't let me in."

"Oh, just like you've let me in all these years?" I throw back in his face, still itching for that fight.

His face contorts, grief-stricken for a moment before it hardens. "I knew you were still pissed about that. Look, I didn't want you to get bogged down in my mess."

I raise my eyebrows at him; he basically just proved my own position.

"But this isn't the same thing. This affects your child, a baby that needs your love and protection. Can't you see that, Den?"

I sigh, leaning back until my head hits the truck door. "Carter, I can't do this right now. I need to finish this job, and my head's all over the place."

My brother nods once. "I'm calling off Jax's ridiculous solution of flying here to make you see reason. I'll back off for now, but just know that the more time that passes, the harder it's going to be for Sierra to forgive your sorry ass. If she even decides to."

He gives me one last look before he leaves the garage, and I hit my head back against the truck, hard. Why doesn't anyone trust that I'm making the right decision? Why can't they understand that I'm doing this for Sierra and the baby?

Because you're being stupid. The unbidden thought appears in my mind, pissing me off even more. *You had an opportunity, a chance, and you're throwing it away for a man who already jeopardized your future once.*

Scrubbing my hand over my face, I lean back and slide under the truck once more. I need to finish this job and clear my head. I need...an image of Sierra fills my mind, and I squeeze my eyes shut tight.

More than anything, I want to reach out and hold her and feel her in my arms.

Am I risking everything, or am I protecting her and the baby?

I don't know anymore, and the confusion eats at me almost as much as the guilt riding in my stomach.

I don't know how to make sense of any of the thoughts in my head. I don't know how to explain myself. I never did.

Except this time, my entire future could depend on it.

23

SIERRA

It's been one week since Denver and I broke up, or whatever you want to call it. While I've been hurting, suffering even, each morning I wake up without a message from him hurts less than the day before.

I throw myself into my painting. Creating canvas after canvas of dark colors and swirling lines, my paintings take on an abstract element that is out of character for me but soothing in this moment in time.

I reach out to my father again, not at all surprised when my call goes unanswered. For some reason, the usual sting that accompanies his rejection isn't as sharp.

I suppose I have Denver to thank for that. His sudden and unexpected dismissal of me has toughened me up in a way I never anticipated. It's shifted my priorities, and now I'm focusing solely on my peanut.

And myself.

I emailed Lachlan and Callum and let them know I'm ready to discuss the job next week. Immediately, Lachlan blew up my cell, but I sent his call to voicemail, not yet ready to deal with all of the questions.

I've taken more control of my life and my future in the past seven days than I have since the moment I found out I was expecting. Always thinking of Denver and our future and his role in our baby's life halted me from making any decisive plans for myself. But now that he's out of the picture, it's been easier to forge ahead and make the choices I should have been focused on over the past several months.

I sigh, placing my paintbrush down and tilting my head as I study my latest painting.

Daisy called earlier and asked again about my Thanksgiving plans. She offered to come up and spend the holiday with me. I ended up crying, not able to commit one way or the other. Just get through today. Keep moving forward. By next week, I vow to have a solid plan for at least the next year of my life. Knowing that I'm making decisions settles some of the uncertainty in my stomach, and finally I manage to crack a smile.

* * *

The cramp is sharp and intense, waking me from my sleep. I curl into a ball, my hands automatically flying to my belly as I take a deep breath. It's probably just round ligament pain. I've been experiencing pulls and twinges for weeks now, and Dr. Leona assured me that it's just my ligaments stretching to accommodate the growing baby.

It happens again, sharper this time, and I cry out, my voice echoing in the darkness of the penthouse. I reach out next to me in the empty bed, knowing Denver will never claim the pillow next to mine, but wishing he were here anyway.

Shuffling to the bathroom, I sit on the toilet and squeeze my eyes shut tight, already knowing what I'm going to see but desperately hoping I'm wrong.

Except when I look down, blood fills my underwear, streaking my inner thighs.

Oh God.

I'm bleeding.

A panic I've never experienced before claws at me, turning me into a useless heap as I sit and try to think of what to do next.

Do I call 9-1-1?

Page Dr. Leona?

Uber to the nearest ER?

I don't know what to do.

The tears swell unbidden, dropping over my lower lashes and tracking my cheeks. Fear and anxiety and uncertainty flood me, locking down my limbs, even while my mind continues to race.

I sit for several seconds. Think, Sierra. Oh, my God. My baby! The thought finally breaks to the forefront of all the confusion swirling in my mind, and I jump into action. Stripping down, I grab a pair of clean underwear and slap a sanitary pad inside. Pulling on a bra and T-shirt, I slip into a pair of leggings. Running around my room, I notice the bright red blood staining my bedsheets and comforter. Unable to deal with it at the moment, I leave everything the way it is and slide into a pair of sneakers before grabbing my coat, purse, and keys and frantically hitting the button for the elevator.

The second my feet hit the lobby I call out for Tom, the doorman, to hail me a cab.

Moments later, I'm zooming down Park Avenue toward Lenox Hill Hospital.

My hands clench and unclench, my heart pounds, and adrenaline spikes in my blood stream. Dear God, please, please just let my baby be okay.

Oh, my God. I never told Denver. Should I tell him? Would he even care?

Pulling my phone from my purse, I tap on his name, and my thumb hovers above the call button. Shaking my head, I scroll up to Daisy and call her instead.

The phone rings and rings, and I'm about to hang up when I hear, "Sierra?" Her voice is thick with sleep.

"Daisy." It's all I say, and yet I hear the sharp intake of breath on the other end of the line.

"What's wrong? Are you okay?"

I swallow back the tears that surge forward at the sound of her voice, at the concern in it. I take a fortifying breath, about to tell her what happened.

"Sierra? What's going on?"

"I'm bleeding."

"What do you mean? Why?"

"I don't know, Dais. But it's kinda a lot. I'm, God, I'm so scared. I wish my mom were here. Or Denver."

"Where are you?"

"In a cab on my way to the hospital."

"A cab? Like a freaking taxi?"

"Yes, I'm almost there."

"What hospital?"

"Lenox Hill."

"Are you okay? What do you need from me in this moment?" I hear noises in the background that I can't completely decipher, but it sounds like she's pulling open her dresser drawers and banging them shut again.

"I think so." My voice sounds small, and I close my eyes, wishing I was brave and independent instead of yearning that Denver was here with me. Or Daisy. Or my mom. Anyone really so I wouldn't have to do this alone.

My hands cup my stomach, and I remember I'm not alone. I have my little peanut with me. God, please, let the baby be all right.

"I'm on my way," Daisy says, and I hear a door slam.

"What? Now?"

"Head to the ER, Sierra. Demand whatever you need from the hospital staff. I'll be on the next flight to New York. You're not alone. I'm coming. You can do this. You're the strongest person I know, and you can do this. Okay?"

"Okay." I yawn, suddenly feeling completely fatigued, like I could doze off any moment.

The insides of my thighs are sticky, and when I touch my pants, my fingertips are stained red.

Shit.

"Dais, I'm really bleeding," I say, shock lacing my words, even though I don't feel much of anything at the moment. Just tired. And cold. "I'm cold."

"You're okay, Sierra. Everything is going to be fine. Just get to the hospital. Just get there and let the doctors take over. Everything is fine."

"Miss? We're here," the driver says.

I nod, pushing a bunch of cash toward the driver.

"Are you okay?" the driver asks, turning in his seat to look at me.

"I need help," I admit.

"Sierra!" Daisy calls through the line. "Stay on the phone."

But at that moment, I drop the phone and forget what we were even talking about.

I hear the frantic voice of the driver and a rush of cold air skates over my skin as he pulls the back door of the car open.

The lights outside the hospital blur, and black spots appear before my eyes. Tiredness weighs down my arms and legs, and coldness seeps into my bones. I'm supposed to do something now. I just can't seem to remember what it is. I can't seem to remember anything at all.

24

DENVER

"Wake up," Daisy demands, shaking my shoulder hard.

I squint up at her and sit straight up in bed when I take in the seriousness of her expression, the barely concealed panic on her face.

"What's going on?"

"It's Sierra. She's bleeding. Badly."

"What?" I jump out of bed, falling forward and just catching myself against my dresser as my legs tangle in the bedsheets. "Motherfucking hell," I roar.

"Get your stuff together. We need to get to the airport. Like now."

"How do you know this?" I glance at my phone. Did I miss Sierra's call?

"She called me."

"Why didn't she call me?" I ask, dread working its way through my body as the realization of my actions over the past week slams into me. She doesn't trust me. I pushed her away, and now she doesn't need me. At all. Not even if our baby's life is in danger will she reach out to me. I swallow past the guilt and shame in my own throat, as Daisy stares at me with wide eyes.

"Is that a real question?" Daisy throws my duffle bag at me and pulls a handful of T-shirts out of my dresser drawer.

I frantically pull on a pair of jeans and throw another pair in my duffle bag. I look around my room, waiting for the things I need to pack to magically appear in my hand.

My sister sighs and I look at her, knowing I need her. I need her help. I need her advice. I need her to pack my bag, book my plane ticket, and make sense of everything happening. Oh Jesus, what did I do?

Did I cause this?

Was it too much for Sierra? Did I place too much stress on her?

"Denver, pack some underwear and a sweatshirt. Socks. Your toothbrush. Everything else we can grab in New York." My sister's voice is calm and steady, and I'm so relieved that she's here with me in this moment.

Until I realize that Sierra is all on her own. All by herself in a hospital in New York, and guilt mixed with fear practically chokes me as I breathe heavily, my head spinning.

"I already called Carter. He's booking our tickets and on his way to get us. Our flight is in an hour and a half; we should land in New York around six am. Finish packing and meet me by the front door."

"Okay." I take a deep breath, my scattered mind focusing on the task at hand.

I finish packing quickly and curse as I trip down the stairs, stubbing the hell out of my toe.

Daisy looks up at me, a flash of sympathy crossing her face. Outside, Carter honks the horn.

Grabbing the water bottle Daisy hands me, I hike my duffle bag higher on my shoulder and grab my sister's small traveling suitcase. We fly out of the house and down the steps to Carter's SUV. I slide into the passenger seat and drop my head against the headrest, my eyes closing. Around me, Carter and Daisy sort out logistics and speak in some type of code I'm too overwhelmed to sort out at the moment.

Is Sierra okay?

Is the baby okay?

What happened?

Jesus. Please let the baby be okay. Please, please let the baby and Sierra both be okay.

She shouldn't be on her own. I never should have left her in New York alone. I never should have pushed her away, hurt her. I broke her heart and now she's bleeding. Not even a parent and I already failed them both. What if the baby doesn't survive? What if Sierra never forgives me? Why would she? I've cost her too much.

A dull throb starts in the base of my neck, working its way up until my temples are ringing, and my head is engulfed in a fog. I drink some water, hoping the cool liquid will bring some clarity to my frame of mind.

Carter breathes out a sigh and hands Daisy his cell phone. "What hospital is she at?"

"Lenox Hill," Daisy responds, tapping on the phone screen as she places a call, speaking in hushed tones. "She's okay," Daisy finally says from behind me, squeezing my shoulder as she leans forward from the back seat of the car.

"You don't know that."

"I do. I called the hospital. Said I was her sister, and I'm on my way."

She called the hospital. Why the hell didn't I think to call the hospital? Relief and guilt swell equally in my stomach, churning until my gut aches as much as my head. Jesus, I need to get it together. What is wrong with me?

"What happened? Is the baby okay? What caused the bleeding?" I trip over my words, desperate to get them out.

Daisy's fingers dig into the material of my sweatshirt. "I don't know. They wouldn't give a lot of info. Just said she is recovering and on bed rest."

"We need to get to that fucking hospital." I throw out to no one in particular.

Carter accelerates, and I close my eyes again, desperate and anxious and on edge. I feel cagey and agitated, knowing at any moment, my temper, the one I work so hard to control, could completely unravel. I need to keep it together.

I am not my father. The thought pops into my head unbidden.

I will never be him.

But as we approach the airport, I'm scared out of my mind for Sierra and our baby. And I've never felt more like my dad in my life for all the pain and hurt I've caused.

* * *

I have no idea how I manage the flight to New York. My knee jerks up and down in agitation while my fingers tap out a restless beat on the armrest. Daisy reaches over and places her hand over mine, causing me to jump. I cut her a sharp gaze, and she raises her eyebrows at me.

Sighing, I turn to look out the window. But I also flip my hand over and squeeze her fingers in mine, grateful for the reassurance. Grateful that my brother and sister are doing this with me, even if I can't voice my appreciation, especially when I don't deserve their support, not after the way I treated them, pushed them away. Not after I hurt Sierra. I don't deserve anyone's kindness, and yet Daisy and Carter have rallied behind me the way they always do.

When the wheels touch down in New York, I feel like a caged lion—restless and desperate. I barrel off the plane and beeline for the taxi stand, Carter and Daisy close on my heels. Thank God we all packed in quick carry-ons, and there's no need to wait at baggage claim. I couldn't spend one more minute in the airport without completely losing it.

"Lenox Hill Hospital," I bark at the taxi driver who meets my eyes in the rearview mirror. For one moment, I see recognition flicker in his eyes, a look of compassion that grounds me almost as much as it heaps more guilt on my conscience. I'm not worthy of anyone's understanding, not even strangers.

He pulls into the New York morning traffic, and I watch each passing block with anxiety and nerves flooding my limbs. At last, we make it to the hospital, and I sprint out of the car, jogging to the wide double doors, my head swinging for reception.

Carter must handle the cab fare, as Daisy is close behind me, colliding into my back when I stop suddenly in front of the receptionist.

"Welcome to Lenox Hill Hospital. How may I assist you?"

"Sierra Begay. She's my...my girlfriend. She's pregnant with our baby. She came in last night for bleeding. I need to see her."

The woman types on her computer before looking up, a frown marring her features. "Ms. Begay is in room 384." She looks at my sister and brother behind me. "But only family is welcome at this time. As the baby's father, you can visit."

"That's fine. We're her sister and brother. I called earlier," Daisy cuts in smoothly.

For the first time in my life, I'm grateful that none of my siblings look like me. While they all favor my mother, blondish hair and light eyes, I'm all my father. Dark hair, black eyes, olive skin. Miserable and stupid and a failure.

She glances at them curiously before handing them each a visitor pass.

"Take the elevators to the third floor." She gestures toward the elevator bay and we take off.

The elevator opens the moment Carter pushes the button, and the three of us step inside, hitting the third floor. I hold my breath, suddenly nervous. What if Sierra doesn't want to see me?

What if she hates me and won't let me be part of the baby's life? What if something happened to the baby? What if she blames me for causing this? My guilt surges forward with unrivaled intensity, stabbing just below my ribs and stealing my breath.

The elevator announces our arrival to the third floor, and we make our way to Sierra's room, a heavy silence stretching between us. I pause outside the door and look at my brother and sister.

"Thanks for coming with me."

"Get in there." Carter tilts his head toward the door.

Daisy offers me a tight smile. "We're going to grab some food for you guys and be back in a few."

I blow out a long exhale and rap my knuckle against the door twice before pushing in.

25

SIERRA

I look up, startled when Denver's hulking frame, enters my hospital room.

"Den?" I ask, positive I'm seeing things. What a roller coaster of emotions the last eight hours have been. Now, I have to add hallucinating to the long list of crazy I'm dealing with.

"Sierra." He's at my side in three strides, sinking to his knees, his hand folding over mine. "Are you okay? How's the," his says, eyes darting to my abdomen covered by a stark white sheet, "how's our peanut?"

I soften slightly toward him at the concern, edging on panic, in his voice. His eyes are too dark to read, but his expression is tight, his features exhausted.

"We're okay."

His eyes glaze over, moisture collecting in the corners, as he drops his head to where his hand covers mine. His breathing accelerates and he nods once, at a complete loss for words. "I...I didn't know what to think."

"Me either," I admit. I still don't know what to think. The baby is okay, thank God. Everything is okay with my physically. But

Denver shattered me, devastated me in ways I never thought possible.

Except now that he's here, I'm relieved, even though I want to be angry. Carrying around the fear and uncertainty and anxiety for the past eight hours on my own, without having him to share it with, took more of a toll on me than I anticipated. Lifting my free hand, I run my fingers over his head, latching onto this moment in case I never get another one. Once my nails snag on the band securing his man bun, he shifts back, his eyes swinging up to mine, searching.

I avoid his gaze and free my hand from his. Untying his hair, I let it fall down. It nearly hits his shoulders. Dark and wavy, black and chocolate and chestnut, his hair is thick and beautiful. "I never see you with your hair down," I tell him quietly. "I always wonder..."

One side of his mouth lifts up. "I don't usually wear it down."

"It's...you're beautiful."

He snorts under his breath, his hand reaching up to cup the side of my face. His thumb swipes up my cheekbone. "I've never been more scared in my life. "

"I can't believe you're here."

"I never should have left."

"No, you had to go see your dad. I understand that. What I don't get is everything that happened afterwards. You never should have pushed me away."

He winces, shaking his head. "I know. You're right. I'm so sorry, Sierra. So unbelievably sorry for everything I put you through. You were right; I was being a coward."

I don't say anything, waiting for him to continue.

"I'm not leaving you again."

"You mean the baby."

"I mean you."

I smile at him sadly. "I don't know if I can trust that, Denver. And that's okay. I really want you to be present in our baby's life, whether that happens from Georgia or New York or Scotland. But me and you," I say, shaking my head, "I'm not sure if that's realistic anymore."

He swallows, and I watch his Adam's apple bob up and down. "Please, Sierra. I know I was stupid and desperate, and I let you down. I hurt you, badly. And I hate myself for that. But I thought I was doing the right thing. I thought I was protecting you."

My eyelids grow heavy, and I know it's because of the lack of sleep and blood loss. And, in some strange way, the comfort that someone is here, and I can finally rest.

"Please forgive me, Sierra. Let me make it up to you. I promise, I won't let you or our baby down again. I swear I'm all in, and I'll explain everything, answer any questions you have." His voice is low and gruff, tugging on my heart. His thumb brushes against my cheekbone again. "I'm not giving up on us." His gaze moves to my stomach as his hand settles there. "I'm not going anywhere. I'm going to prove to you that you can trust me, Sierra. And we're going to figure it all out. We have to."

My eyes drift shut, emotions clogging my throat, but I'm not ready to have this conversation right now. I'm not sure I can trust Denver, and I'm too tired to wade through my murky emotions.

"Tell me about the baby."

I smile at the mention of my peanut. Snuggling deeper against my pillows, my eyes crack open, watching Denver as he stares at my belly, his fingers drawing lazy patterns.

"The baby is okay. That machine there," I say, pointing to one of the stands at my side, "is tracking the baby's heartbeat, and it's strong and steady. About one-hundred-forty-eight beats per minute."

Denver's shoulders relax, and he tips his head toward my stomach. "Can I?"

I nod, and he rests his cheek against my baby bump, as if listening to the baby's heartbeat himself.

"Why did you start bleeding?" He nuzzles his ear against my abdomen.

I sigh and Denver straightens, his concerned eyes swinging back to mine. I offer him a pinched smile, and his eyebrows pull together.

"What is it?" he asks.

"It's called placenta previa. It's when the placenta, the part that gives the baby all of the nutrients, covers the opening of the woman's cervix," I explain.

"You have that?"

"Partially. The placenta is covering part of my cervix, and that's what caused the bleeding. The hope is that as the baby grows and my uterus stretches, the placenta will move farther away from my cervix. I will have more frequent ultrasounds now. If it does, great. If not, I'll need a C-section."

"That's okay, right? I mean, having a C-section."

I nod. "It's fine. Whatever the baby needs."

"What do you need?"

I wrinkle my nose. "I've been put on pelvic rest and bed rest."

Denver's eyebrows drop again, a confused expression on his face.

"It basically means no sex."

His teeth rake over his lower lip as he watches me carefully.

"And not a great deal of physical activity. A lot of lounging in bed and watching Netflix."

His expression turns thoughtful as he considers this.

"I think the sooner I move to Scotland, the better."

He visibly starts at my words. "Please don't take the job offer. I know I told you to, but it was stupid of me. I didn't mean it. I want to be here for you, for the baby, and if you give me a second chance, I'll make it work. I promise."

I frown at his words. "You've been making a lot of promises you haven't followed through on. And I need a support system I can count on. At least in Scotland, I have my mom, James, my brother Liam, and my cousins Aaron and Finn."

His eyes widen, an undercurrent of panic flashing through the blackness. I've never seen Denver unsettled before, but I honestly can't concern myself with his rollercoaster of emotions. I have my peanut and my health to consider, and while my heart still yearns for Denver, my head needs to be smart about my future decisions.

"Please, Sierra. Don't move away. Don't take our peanut away from me. I'll move here to New York, or Scotland if you're that set on going, but please don't shut me out."

"Like how you shut me out?"

He curses under his breath. "I know I messed up, but I'm going to fix this. All of it. Please just give me the opportunity to do right by you. And the baby."

I breathe a heavy sigh, resting my eyes again. "Denver, I'm having a child. I'm on bed rest, and my pregnancy is substantially more high-risk than it was yesterday. I need someone I can count on, someone who is reliable and present, and not going to get scared and push me away for reasons I don't understand."

"He threatened you."

"What? Who?" I ask, confused but more awake than I was a few minutes ago.

"Darren. My...dad. He knew all about you. About the baby. Where you lived and what you do. He threatened to hurt you, to hurt you while you were pregnant, if I didn't drop the investigation to clear my name. After I told him to go fuck himself, he threatened you no matter what. As if you're connection to me was going to result in you and the baby being harmed."

My eyes widen in response, and while the story would be far-fetched if anyone else said it, the small amount I know of Darren Kane, coupled with the severe expression on Denver's face, convinces me he's telling the truth.

"I know I hurt you, but I honestly thought I was protecting

you. Seeing him again, having him plant all of this doubt about the type of father I could possibly be along with his threat, it scared me. More than I admitted to myself. And it was stupid, the way I hurt you, and I hate that I did that. But at the moment, I really thought I was doing what was best for you and the baby."

"And now?"

"Now, I realize what an idiot I was. And how anything can happen at any time, with or without Darren. I don't want to miss our baby growing in your belly." His fingers twitch on my abdomen, his expression so serious and sincere, my breath catches in my throat. "I don't want to miss out on the chance of proving to you that I can be the man you need. That I want to be that man, for you and for our baby. Please, just one chance. I swear on everything, I won't mess it up. I'm not saying I won't make mistakes, but they'll be the small kind, like leaving the toilet seat up or getting your coffee order wrong."

I snort, biting my lower lip as I watch him.

"I can't keep putting my and the baby's life and future on hold while you work through whatever's in your head," I tell him seriously.

"I'm in, Sierra. I'm all in. If you'll have me."

I blink, my heart hammering in my chest at his words, but my hope refusing to soar too high in case it crashes and burns again. "We'll take it slow."

He nods. "I'm coming back to you, to New York. I'll rent a place and come to you every single day if you don't want me in the apartment again. I won't miss another prenatal class and I'll be at every appointment. Please, I want to build the crib and pain the nursery and set up all the things your mom bought for the baby. I'll cook our dinners and bring you ice cream at three am."

"If you're really committed to this, I'm going to need you to move back into the apartment with me. I'm going to be on bed rest, so I can hire someone or—"

"I'm there. Whatever you want. We can still move into a new place or—"

"It's okay. Really. We can stay at James's apartment for now. I don't want to move while I'm on bed rest. I'm comfortable where I am. I have my studio and my painting and I'm close to work. If—"

Denver holds his hands up. "As long as James and your Mom don't mind that I'm there."

I release a big breath. "They'll be fine with it. Especially once they learn about this pregnancy scare. I need to tell my brothers I'm pregnant. I've kept this from them for way too long and Mom says they're all starting to worry about me. She's had to talk them out of flying here several times already."

"Okay. We'll do whatever is best for you and the baby."

"Will you get me a bell to ring when I need you?"

He snorts again, some life coming back into his face. "Now, you're pushing it."

A knock on the door causes both of us to turn just as Daisy's head peeks in.

"You're here!" I shriek, giving Denver a look, as if to ask, *why the hell didn't you tell me*?

He shrugs.

"You got me, too," Carter announces, stepping into the room behind Daisy, holding a bouquet of flowers.

Daisy's by my side in an instant, wrapping her arms around me tightly. "You okay?"

I nod into her shoulder, squeezing her back, so unbelievably grateful that she's here. I didn't realize until this moment how much I miss my best friend, how much I need her to be by my side, have my back, while I'm going through the most important and significant change of my life.

"Thanks for the flowers," I tell Carter once Daisy pulls back.

"Really? You're not helping my case. At all." Den narrows his eyes at Carter.

I pull out the card attached to flowers and read aloud, "It says here, 'love Denver.'"

Denver grumbles, shaking his head. "Thanks."

Carter and Daisy laugh, easing some of the tension. Carter presses a quick kiss to the top of my head and settles into a chair at my bedside. "So, what's going on? What happened?"

Denver and Daisy also take seat, Denver's hand finds its way to mine, and I don't pull away when he laces our fingers together. If this is going to work, I need to be open about forgiving him. I'll never forget what happened, but for the sake of our peanut, I'm willing to give him one more chance. Slowly. He'll need to earn back the trust he dashed. But the fact that he's here is a good starting point.

Turning my attention to Daisy and Carter, I fill them in on the situation and most of what transpired between Denver and I, leaving out the parts about his dad.

"So, you're moving back?" Daisy asks Denver when I finish, a hesitant smile on her mouth.

He never takes his eyes off of me as he nods. "For good." But it's the smile on his face that convinces me he wants to be here.

And that's another step in the right direction.

* * *

The morning surrounded by Denver, Daisy, and Carter passes quickly, mainly because they keep my mind off of everything happening. In some ways, it's easy, especially the sisterhood between Daisy and I and the friendship between Carter and me. In other ways, it's comfortable yet unnerving, like how Denver can't keep his eyes from wandering to mine, the way he reaches over from time to time to squeeze my knee or brush the hair out of my eyes. His gestures are sweet and thoughtful, and I desperately want to lean into his touch, get lost in his searing kisses, and for things to go back to the way they were just two weeks ago. But

I can't help the hesitation I feel and instead of leaning into his touch, I don't react, keeping my expressions neutral.

In the early afternoon, after I sweep another game of Texas Hold 'Em, Daisy and Carter offer to grab some lunch, so we can have a decent meal and so Den and I can spend some one-on-one time together. After they leave, Den leans forward and tucks a stray piece of hair behind my ear.

"I'm just going to use the bathroom really quick, and then there's some things I think we should talk about."

"All right," I agree, settling back against my pillows, both nervous and excited for whatever new ground Denver wants to cover. It's like now that he told me the truth about his dad and I agreed to stay in New York and see where things between us go, he's desperate to hammer out all the details. As if he's nervous that if we don't, I'll disappear and head to Scotland. I can understand his fear since it's the same way I felt when he gave me the cold shoulder, but now that I've made up mind, I know in my heart of hearts that I'd never forgive myself if I didn't give Denver one more chance. For the sake of my peanut. And for myself.

The bathroom door locks just as the door to my room swings open, Lachlan and Callum shadowing the doorway, their faces a mixture of anger and pain, their eyes wide with worry.

"What are you guys doing here?" I ask, bolting straight up in my bed.

The bathroom door slams open and Denver strides out, a scowl on his face as he takes in my expression. He immediately positions himself between my brothers and me, which is probably not a great move, considering that my brothers' eyes narrow, their faces both taking on aggressive expressions.

"Who the hell are you?" Denver asks them, placing his outstretched hand behind him, warning me to stay back.

As if I could go somewhere.

"This the guy?" Callum bites out, his Scottish brogue stronger than I've ever heard it, his voice injected with venom.

Before I can respond one way or the other, Lach swings at Denver, catching him off guard, his fist glancing off Den's cheek.

Den falters but catches himself. Swiping the back of his hand against his cheek, he stares at Lachlan and chuckles, the sound low and dangerous. He widens his stance and tilts his head, studying my brothers. And while I can't read the expression on his face because his back is to me, the way Lachlan shuffles tells me everything I need to know. Denver Kane is fierce as hell. And no one, really no one, should cross him.

"Come at me again," Den says finally, his voice low and slow, as if he's bored. "Come at me again and I promise you, you'll be laid up in the room next door. Now, who the hell are you, and why are you bothering my girl?"

Both of my brothers open their mouths, but Den raises his hand, cutting them off. Turning to me, Denver asks, "You okay?"

I nod.

"You want them here, or you want me to make them leave?"

Callum mutters a string of profanities under his breath that Denver ignores.

"They can stay. They're my brothers," I say, my voice smaller than I'd like it to be. I'm trembling and not at all from fear, but from the overwhelming feeling of everything that has happened in the past twenty-four hours. Why are my brothers here? How did they know where to find me? I never even told them I'm pregnant. Did Mom finally spill the beans?

"Brothers, huh?" Denver turns back around, his posture casual and his voice flat. "You're her brothers? Why the hell are you stressing her out? She's on goddamn bed rest; she doesn't need this."

I roll my eyes at that. Like Denver should be talking about my stress levels. Still, it's good to see that he has my back, especially after everything that's happened recently.

Callum's eyes widen as Lach strides to my side, his shoulder brushing against Denver's in a way to check him without actually checking him. A male pissing contest. How ridiculous.

"What happened, Sisi?" Lachlan asks quietly, sitting on the edge of my bed. His eyes are wide with concern, swimming with worry and sadness and hurt. *How could you not tell me?* His eyes accuse me, but his words are kind.

"I'm fifteen weeks pregnant," I admit aloud for the first time to my brothers.

Callum draws in a sharp breath as Lachlan's eyes close as if in pain.

"Last night, I started bleeding and came here, to the ER. I have placenta previa, which means that the placenta is partially blocking my cervix. While nothing is wrong with the baby, my doctor has recommended moderate bed rest."

"Are you okay? Is...is the baby all right?" Callum asks, his brogue thick, his voice shakier than I've ever heard it. He's standing behind Lachlan now, his eyes glued to my abdomen.

"Yes. We're fine."

"You scared the shit out of us," Lachlan admits, his eyes studying me. "We flew in this morning. I don't know; I knew something was off. You sent me that email about taking the job and then radio silence. Mom tried to talk us out of it, saying you're just busy and stressed with work but you've been weird for weeks now. We got to James's and shit, there's blood all over your sheets, in your bathroom," he pauses, steadying the shake in his voice. "I thought you were, I don't know what the fuck I thought. Taken? Attacked? I—God, we called every freaking hospital."

"That's why we came in here so aggressively. We were relieved we found you and that you're relatively okay," Callum continues.

"I'm fine. I didn't know you were coming. I didn't know."

"We know, Sisi. We didn't even know we were coming." Callum smiles at me gently. "We're just glad you're all right."

"Y'all really didn't know that Sierra's pregnant?" Den's voice interrupts from behind my brothers, and they both turn to glare at him.

"Had no idea." Lachlan's voice is sharp, partially out of concern for me and partially because his punch barely caused Denver to wince.

Den nods, as if processing this new information. "I'm Denver," he says finally, holding out a hand to Lachlan and Callum. "Denver Kane."

Callum shakes his hand first, smoothing the way for Lachlan. They both introduce themselves.

"Wait a minute," Lachlan says after a moment. "Kane? Are you related to Daisy Kane?"

"She's my sister."

Lach regards Denver curiously, his head tilted to the side. "Sorry I hit you, man. But then again, not really because I didn't even know you and my sister were dating."

Denver nods, “Understandable.” He says as if being punched in the face is water under the bridge.

At that moment, the door to my room swings open. And, God, I've never been more relieved to see Daisy and Carter in my life.

Or the bags of food in their hands.

"Hey y'all," Daisy greets my brothers brightly.

I settle back against my pillows, knowing she's about to handle this...and all the boys present.

26

DENVER

I could kiss my sister for choosing this moment in time to walk back into Sierra's hospital room and crack the tension with her easy smile and drawl.

"I didn't know y'all were coming, or we would have grabbed more lunch. But there should be plenty." She holds up the brown paper bags with a sandwich shop emblazoned across the side.

Callum steps forward to take the bags from my sister and shakes Carter's hand, introducing himself. He smiles down at Daisy with an easy affection and presses a kiss to her cheek. "It's good to see you, Dais."

"You too, Cal. Hey Lach." Daisy steps around Callum, kissing Lachlan.

It's weird to see my sister controlling the situation, making sense of a scenario that is straight up crazy at this moment.

"Hey," Lachlan says back, his eyes accusing as they pierce Daisy with the same hurt they looked at Sierra with.

Daisy shrugs, offering him a gentle smile, as though interpreting the look.

"Why don't we sit down, have some lunch, and talk?" she says to the room at large.

Everyone glances to Sierra, who has been extremely quiet since Daisy and Carter entered the room.

"I'd like that," Sierra announces, smiling at my sister with such warmth and gratitude that I want to hug the both of them.

"Great," Daisy says as if it's settled, even though no one else has spoken.

But within seconds, we all spring into action, rearranging chairs, unpacking lunch bags, and passing out sodas.

Once we're all settled and seated around Sierra's bed, the steady beeps of her monitors serving as background noise, Daisy whispers something to Sierra, who nods and looks at each of us. Addressing the room, she says, "So, Denver and I are having a baby."

Carter chuckles, Lachlan shoots me a glare, and Callum mumbles a "congratulations." I take Sierra's hand in mine and look at her brothers.

"So, I know y'all don't know me. Or what you do know about me is probably crap. But Sierra and I are in this together, all of it. And while we didn't expect this to happen, it did. And we're really happy about it. We're together, we're having a baby, and we're going to be parents. Understand?" I say this with a confidence and bravado I don't feel, given my shitty behavior toward Sierra this past week. Still, I need her brothers to know I'm serious about my role as a dad, about taking care of their sister, even as Sierra and I work through our own issues.

Lachlan's jaw tightens and Callum's eyes narrow, as they both look me over. Their eyes catch on my long hair, several days worth of scruff, and bright ink. They take in my appearance, and I know what they're thinking—he's trash, he's beneath you, what were you thinking? But when I turn to Sierra, her eyes are wide and shimmering, dark orbs of black diamonds. Her lips curl upwards at the ends, and she offers me the first true smile since I screwed everything up between us. And right now, that's all that matters.

I don't need approval or permission from Sierra's brothers to watch out for this girl, to love my baby. I don't need them at all. I'm not saying it wouldn't be nice to be on good terms, but it's not a necessity.

"All right, so let me get this straight," Lachlan finally speaks, his accent a strange American-British hybrid. It's weird because Sierra doesn't have an accent at all and sounds completely American. "You and my sister are together and having a baby that you plan to raise together?"

"Yes," Sierra and I say in unison, our voices unwavering.

"Then why have we never heard about you?" Lachlan asks, his voice hard. He stares at me, but I don't see any hate in his eyes, just concern for his sister.

"It's still new." Sierra offers. "I didn't anticipate getting pregnant and things with Denver and I sort of developed from there. I wasn't ready to tell you, Lach. I'm sorry." Sierra's voice shakes at the end and I can tell she and her brother are really close. Crap. That means I have to make more of an effort to be on good terms with him.

"But you're for real?" He asks again, directing his question to me.

"One-hundred percent." I say, feeling Sierra's gaze swing to my profile. "I'm for real. I'm in love with Sierra. Even though I have a stupid way of showing it, and I nearly messed the whole thing up." I look at her. "It's us. Me and you and our baby and that's the end of it."

Daisy turns to me, her eyes wide with excitement, before her gaze darts back to Sierra.

I squeeze Sierra's fingers and look right into her wide, chocolate eyes. "I love you, Sierra Grace Begay. I'm in love with you. And I'm not letting you go. I'm not letting our baby go. We're in this together, and I mean for all of it. Feel me?"

She nods, her eyes shimmering with unshed tears and her skin glowing. She laughs, the sound sweet and feminine, before tilting forward and catching my lips with hers. She tastes like cherry Chapstick and hope. She tastes like home, and I know now that all the stupid shit of my past doesn't even matter because it led me to right now; it brought me to her. And I'm never letting go.

Because let's be honest, guys like me don't get chances like this too often. And this girl is willing to give me a do-over after I messed it all up once.

Carter slow claps from behind me, and I flip him the bird. He chuckles in his easygoing manner. I pull away from Sierra, our noses touching for a brief moment before I press one last kiss to her forehead.

Daisy is practically squealing. "Now, we're going to be sisters for real!" She jumps way ahead, clasping her hands together in front of her face, dreamlike. Carter's chuckle turns into a full-blown laugh as a brief moment of panic flickers through me. And it's not because I can't imagine or don't want to be married to the beautiful girl sitting next to me, it's because I can't remember what I did with Mom's gemstone. Carter gives me a knowing look and I relax instantly.

"All right then." Lachlan nods, holding out a hand to me. "It's good to meet you, Denver."

Huh? I shake his hand, eyeing him skeptically. What the hell caused this change in behavior? My suspicions rise as I study his relaxed posture and almost smile.

"It's going to take us some time to find our footing," he says finally. "But if you love my sister and are really going to be here for her and the baby, then who the hell am I to judge you for being a man who takes care of your family? I wanted to make sure you were for real."

Carter snorts again behind my back, and I can picture him texting a play-by-play to Taylor to fill her in on all that's going down in this hospital room. I swear the two of them together are worse than a gaggle of old ladies at a hair salon.

"I understand," I say instead to Lachlan because I do get it. If Daisy were Sierra, I'd be pinning the guy down with my nastiest glare until I figured out his intentions. No one wants their sister to make a life mistake. And good guys look out for their girls. Sisters included.

"Congratulations, man," Callum says, his grip not quite as hard as Lachlan's, his expression less severe, his accent full blown Scottish. "We'll have to grab beers sometime and get to know each other."

"That'd be cool," I agree, knowing that while I don't care one way or the other if Sierra's brothers like me, she does. And man, I also know I'd do pretty much anything for this girl.

It's funny, really, how one moment, one situation, one blink, can change everything. I knew I had feelings for Sierra. Hell, I've had them for years. But from the moment she called me to tell me she was expecting, I knew my feelings for her were more serious than I ever admitted to myself. I wanted to be here for the baby, my baby, no doubt. But I also wanted to be here, to show up, for her.

My conversation with Darren made me question myself, made me question everything. I hate that I let him have some control. His threat, whether it's for real or not, rattled me. It made me react the way he wanted without thinking things through logically. That, right there, is another indication that my feelings for Sierra are for real. I've never been really rattled by Darren, not the way Carter has. And yet, I was willing to throw my whole relationship, my whole future, with Sierra away because of some bullshit Darren Kane spewed?

And then last night, Jesus, was it just last night? Having Daisy shake me awake and tell me that Sierra was bleeding and on the way to the hospital literally made my world stop. It stopped, and the only thing I could think about was getting to her. She became my everything. And while I've known it for a while, I'm ready to admit it to the whole freaking world. I'm in love with Sierra Begay. And we're having a baby.

Now I just need for her to agree to marry me. But I need to take that slow, earn back her trust, show her she can't count on me. That I'm one-hundred-percent in. Forever.

Daisy's arms wrap around me, and she presses a kiss to my cheek. "I'm proud of you," she says it quietly, so only I can hear her, and it warms me from the inside out. Because I've never been much to be proud of, not for a long, long time. And now, I'm having a baby. And I want to be worthy of him or her. I want to be worthy for my family.

I want to be enough.

And I will be.

27

SIERRA

It's late when I'm dismissed from the hospital. My brothers and Daisy and Carter went to dinner about an hour ago, so Denver could help me get discharged from the hospital and settled in at home without a bunch of people hovering around.

It's quiet between the two of us, but it's comfortable, natural. He speaks to all my doctors, asks a string of relative questions, and even taps some notes out on his phone. Once he has a bag filled with prenatal vitamins, pamphlets on bed rest, and books with Sudoku and crossword puzzles, he hails a taxi to take me home.

Sitting in the back of the taxi with him just twenty-four hours after I called Daisy in a panic from the back of another taxi is a bit like my life coming full circle. Last night, I thought I was about to lose everything. And while this pregnancy was completely unplanned, I don't know how I'd get through losing my baby. In such a short amount of time, barely four months, this little peanut growing inside of me has become my whole world, and I am so in love with him or her. It's unreal and unlike anything I've ever experienced or expected to experience. I guess becoming a mom is really one of those situations that you can't understand until you're doing it.

Denver reaches out and places his hand on my thigh. I nuzzle closer to him and rest my head on his shoulder.

"How you doing?" he asks.

"Relieved," I admit. "I've never been more scared in my life. I thought...I thought I was losing the baby."

His fingers grip my thigh, and I know he felt the same fear, the same hopelessness and desperation that I did.

"I'm glad I'm going home."

He turns to brush a kiss across my lips and his scruff tickles my cheek. “We need to call your parents.”

"We?"

"Me and you, babe. In it together, remember?"

"Yeah." I smile to myself, wrapping my arms around his bicep. "I think that's my favorite thing you've ever said to me. Not counting I love you."

"I do." His voice is low, his breath fluttering over the shell of my ear, causing goosebumps to break out along my arms. "I love you, Sierra. And I intend to show you just how much."

I kiss his shoulder before pulling back, so I can see his eyes when I tell him. "I love you, too. I think I've been a little bit in love with you since the first time I saw you."

His eyebrows spike. "Really?"

I nod, snorting at myself. "But you were so..."

"Unapproachable?"

"Yes."

"It was to keep you away."

"Well, I can see that now."

"I guess we have our little miracle to thank for bringing us together, huh?" He places his hand on my abdomen, patting it gently.

"Yes. We do."

"Do you want to find out the gender?"

"I think so," I say, after thinking it over for a moment. While I love surprises, all of these life changes happening in such quick succession have filled my quota. I think I'd like to know if the baby is a boy or girl, so I can at least pretend I have some control moving forward. Plus, there's decorating a nursery. Ooh, I can't wait to Pinterest with Daisy. "Do you?"

"I want to do whatever you want, babe."

"Let's find out."

Denver laughs, and it's easy and uninhibited and sounds like my Denver again. "All right. We'll find out."

I lean back against his shoulder and let my eyes close, soaking in this moment, soaking in his warmth, and drift off to sleep.

* * *

"You ready?" I ask him as we sit in front of my laptop.

"Ready." He smiles back at me, not an ounce of nerves in his expression.

I FaceTime my mom and I'm relieved when she answers on the first ring.

"Sisi, I'm so glad you called."

"Hi Mom."

"Your brothers flew to see you. Did they get ahold of you yet? I tried to talk them out of it but you know how persistent they can be."

"They found me." I admit.

She offers me a sympathetic glance. "I'm sorry, love. How'd they take the news?" She asks, her eyes snagging on Denver as the edge of his face enters the frame. "Oh, I didn't know Denver was back." Mom's eyes find mine, widening slightly. Even though we've talked about Denver a lot, she's never actually met him.

I grin. "Is James home?"

"Uh, yes, he's somewhere. James?" Mom calls out over her shoulder. "Sierra's on FaceTime. Can you come say hello?"

A moment later, James enters the screen as he takes a seat next to Mom. "Sierra, I'm so glad to finally see you. How are you feeling, sweetheart? Your brothers told me you're accepting the position. Are you sure that's —"

"Actually, there's been a change in plans."

James frowns as Mom's forehead wrinkles in concern. "What's going on?" Mom asks.

Underneath the table, Denver laces his fingers with mine and gives my hand a reassuring squeeze.

"This is Denver." I tug him gently into the frame.

"Hello." Denver manages a small smile.

Mom's expression softens immediately as she sees Denver. "Hello Denver. It's nice to finally meet you. And congratulations."

James nods and says hello but isn't quite as warm as Mom. It takes him longer to open up. In this moment, I'm relieved that I never confided in Mom about last week or she'd never be this kind to Denver.

"I had a scare last night," I admit, and her eyes flash with worry.

"What happened?" she asks, her composure regained.

As I fill my mom and James in on everything that's happened over the last two days, they both sit and stare and listen intently. Mom's eyes fill with tears on several occasions, and James studies Denver thoughtfully.

"I want you to both stay in the apartment indefinitely," James says when Mom allows him a word in.

Denver chews the corner of his mouth. "Sir, I don't want to take advantage of your—"

James holds a hand up, cutting Denver off. "Please. I know Sierra is comfortable there, she has her painting, and I'm not sure how much work she's going to be getting done at the art gallery if she's on bedrest but –"

"I can work from home for the time being." I interject.

He nods. "That's good. But if you did have to go into the office, at least you're not too far. I think your and the baby's comfort is the most important thing at the moment. It's no problem for you and Denver to live there for the time being. We can discuss alternate plans once the baby is born."

Denver nods, his expression neutral. "Thank you, sir. I appreciate it."

"Call me James."

"All right. Thank you, James."

"We're going to find out the gender," I share, taking the attention off of Denver.

"Oh, you are," Mom breathes out, her hands clasped under her chin. "Are you going to do a reveal party? My friends' kids are all doing that in the States. You guys should have a party. It's so fun. We'll fly out."

James turns to Mom questioningly, but her eyes are glued to me, her smile widening the more I fill her in on all things baby-related.

I laugh. "We haven't talked about that but if we do decide on a party, you'll be the first to know."

"All right," Mom agrees, her smile falling a bit.

I yawn and Denver's hand comes down on my knee, squeezing lightly. "I'm going to turn in. I'm pretty beat."

"Oh, yes, you need your rest. I remember when I was pregnant with you, I napped every day," Mom says.

I snort, unable to imagine my Mom, the Energizer bunny, ever napping.

"I'm serious. Those hormones are no joke. Call me this weekend and tell me how Denver does at his first prenatal class." Her eyes move to Denver and she smiles. "I'm sure you'll be great but a new dad's reaction to these things is always great fun for us women to talk about."

Denver chuckles and nods. "I'm sure Sierra will have plenty of stories to keep you entertained then."

Mom laughs, nodding her approval of Denver to me.

"I love you, Sisi. I'm so relieved you and the baby are okay. Get some rest and if you need anything, anything at all, I'm there. Just call me." Mom reminds me as she does every time we talk on the phone. She stares at me, her eyes filling with tears again.

"I love you, too, Mom. I will. Thank you. And thank you, James." I look at my stepdad.

"Goodnight Jenni. James." Denver looks at Mom and James and offers a small smile.

"Goodnight," James says, his voice stiff but polite.

I love how excited my Mom, and even James, are for the baby to arrive. A sudden pang aches in my chest, and I wish I could call my own father. I wish he would answer, and I could share my pregnancy news, and he would be...happy for me.

Once FaceTime is disconnected, Denver turns to me and his hands reach up to frame my face.

"How're you feeling?" His thumbs brush over my cheekbones, his eyes intent on mine.

"Not too bad," I admit.

"Tired?"

"Exhausted."

"Bedtime?"

I nod, laughing as Denver pulls me into his arms and against his chest and carries me to bed, the door closing behind us.

28

DENVER

The next morning, once I'm sure Sierra is okay and being looked after by Daisy and Carter and her brothers, I track down Jax's friend Migs at his auto body shop.

"Can I help you?" A guy looks up when I enter, his eyes giving me a quick once over.

"I'd like to speak with Miguel Sanchez."

"That's me," he says, eyeing me curiously.

"I'm Denver." I hold out my hand. "Denver Kane."

Recognition flickers across his face. "Jax's brother?" he asks as he shakes my hand.

I nod. "Yeah."

"Good to meet you, man." He regards me warily, his voice cooler than I would have hoped. But I get it. He thinks I'm flaky and with good reason. Jesus, when I make a mess of things, I go full disaster mode.

"I'm sure you think I'm flaky. Unreliable. And I don't blame you. But I'm really not. I'm usually dependable and punctual. A hard worker and a fast learner. I moved to New York to be with my girl. We're having a baby."

Migs's eyes narrow as he sizes me up.

"The past week was not my finest but my priorities literally changed overnight. My girlfriend had a scare two nights ago, and it sort of shifted everything for me. I want to work for you, man. I want this job. I'll do whatever you need me to do, and I'll prove that I deserve this opportunity. If it's still on the table."

Migs sighs and nods slowly. "I need to know I can count on you, man. This place," he says, gesturing to the photos of custom design jobs on the walls, "it's growing and business is picking up faster than I can turn out the jobs. This is for real. I'm willing to take you on, to train you, all of it. But I have to know you're for real. I talked to your brother over two weeks ago, and this is the first I hear from you."

A vice squeezes in my throat, and I hate how many people I've let down in such a short amount of time. "You're right. I flaked, but I'm here now, and I'm one-hundred-percent serious. I'm your guy."

He nods once. "All right. I'm doing this as a favor to your brother. I owe Jax my life. But if you mess up just one time, one shift skipped, coming in late, bad attitude, any of it, you're out."

"That's fair."

Migs watches me for another beat before extending his hand again. "Welcome to Custom Carz."

"Thanks for the chance, man. I really appreciate it."

"You start training tomorrow. Be here at seven sharp."

"I'll see you then." I turn on my heel and leave the shop, but I can't stop the massive grin splitting my face. On my way back to Sierra, I stop and pick her up a bouquet of flowers. They're not fancy or anything special, just a simple bouquet from a corner store.

But when I arrive home and hand them to her, her whole face lights up, brightening my world.

I know how lucky I am to have this second chance.

And I want to savor each moment of it.

* * *

Training begins bright and early the next morning. I'm outside Custom Carz at ten 'til seven, finishing up a bacon and egg bagel sandwich and a cup of coffee.

Migs's eyes widen slightly in surprise when he walks up to the shop five minutes later, but he doesn't say anything except a mumbled good morning. Unlocking the door and holding it open for me, we begin with him walking me through opening up the shop.

Once we make it into the garage, he explains the process of Custom Carz to me from the moment a client calls to receiving final payment for a completed job. I'm given my own computer login info and handed a packet of designs and interior selections to study and learn about. He asks questions of my knowledge on American muscle cars, on technical issues, on interior. I answer as honestly as I can and have no clue how the hell I'm doing.

By the time Migs dismisses me for my lunch break, my head is swimming with information. Still, as I inhale a slice of pizza, I gotta admit it feels good to be challenged. To be learning and acquiring a new skill set. To actually be doing something with my life.

Migs shows me some of the jobs that are in various phases of completion and introduces me to the rest of the team in the afternoon. At four, he nods at me sharply. "All right, Denver. I like you, and I'm willing to give you a real shot. Come on in tomorrow, and we'll go through some of our current jobs. Thursday is Thanksgiving, and we're closed until Monday. That's when we'll begin your real training." He holds out his hand and I shake it, relief and a tiny swell of pride growing in my chest.

"Thanks, Migs."

"See you tomorrow."

I'm exhausted when I arrive back at Sierra's. It's been a long time since I've had to learn anything, and today was a lot of information in a short amount of time. But I'm excited and happy and feeling a sense of purpose that I haven't experienced in years.

"All good, man?" Carter asks me when I walk through the door.

I take in his appearance, his duffle bag slung across his shoulder. "All good. You heading out."

He nods, a grin working its way across his mouth. "Yeah, man. I gotta get home. Taylor and I leave for St. Maarten with her parents tomorrow for Thanksgiving."

"That's right! I can't believe I forgot all about that."

"You've had a lot on your mind."

"Thanks for coming with me. For everything."

Carter pulls me forward into a brotherly hug, slapping my back harder than necessary. "Don't mention it. Just take care of your girl. I'll touch base with you when I'm back. Happy Thanksgiving, Brother."

I snort. "Happy Thanksgiving, Carter. Have fun on your trip and tell Taylor hello."

Carter nods once. "See you soon."

And then he's gone, and I look around Sierra's living room. She's snoozing on the sofa, Daisy sitting on the other half of the couch, watching a movie. Callum and Lachlan are sitting at the dining table, their laptops open in front of them, their earbuds plugged in.

I'll admit this is the strangest Thanksgiving I've ever had, but I've also never been more thankful for anything in my life than I am for right now.

* * *

I wake up at dawn on the morning of Thanksgiving, knowing how much food needs to be prepped so we can all sit down for a nice meal together. I hit the markets as soon as they open, while the rest of the house is still sleeping, and buy everything I need.

My turkey is awesome. I even add bacon strips and it's just dirty. I also make a mean stuffing. Not trying to brag or anything, but there's only a handful of things I do well...and Thanksgiving dinner is one of them. I learned from my mom when I was a kid, and it's one of the only traditions the Kane kids have kept alive—a proper meal on Thanksgiving and decorating the tree for Christmas. After picking up my ingredients, I also grab a basket of apples, as Daisy wants to make an apple pie. Once I'm loaded up with everything, I struggle to make it back to Sierra's.

"Happy Thanksgiving y'all," I call out as I enter the door, slipping the two kids who helped me carry all my bags a few bills.

"Thank God you're here." My sister comes around the corner, nearly colliding into me. "They want to order out," she hisses, her eyes rolling to the living room where I imagine Sierra and her brothers are hanging out.

"Take-out?" I ask, confused.

Daisy gives a vigorous nod. We stare at each other for a long moment before we both burst out laughing. I mean, I'm laughing for real. I can't remember the last time I laughed so hard in my life. Daisy's pointing at me, one hand over her mouth, her eyebrows raising at the sudden outburst. And the louder I laugh, the harder she cracks up, until we're both leaning against the door, wiping tears from our eyes.

"Oh, my God. That was hysterical. I can't remember the last time... oh yeah, wait. I was a kid and Carter farted on your old girlfriend, Dahlia or Deana or something."

"Dina." I nod, remembering the night well. We were playing Uno and Carter was in a prankster mood. That was the beginning of the end for Dina and me.

"Whatever. The point is you really need to laugh more."

I nod in agreement, still feeling the bubbles of laughter floating around my body.

"What's so funny out there?" Sierra calls out to us. "I don't think I've ever heard Denver laugh that hard. Unless, of course,

I'm the one making him laugh. But now I realize I need to come up with better jokes."

"It only happens about once a decade, so be grateful you were here today," Daisy calls back as we walk into the living room, the grocery bags still on the floor by the door.

"Okay." Callum looks up at us. "We've narrowed it down to three restaurants that do Thanksgiving dinner. Even though it's so last minute, I'm sure if we pay double, they'll squeeze us in."

Daisy and I exchange another look.

"What?" Lachlan asks.

"Y'all, I'm cooking Thanksgiving dinner."

"Kane tradition," Daisy adds. "And if you tell me ordering takeout is your family tradition, I'm just going to feel sorry for y'all. You haven't lived until you've tasted Denver's bacon wrapped turkey on Thanksgiving."

"You're overselling it." I nudge my sister.

"Bacon?" Callum looks up from his phone.

"Yep. And stuffing. Daisy makes an apple pie."

"And pumpkin." My sister smiles as she captures Lachlan's attention.

"You're sure it's not too much trouble?" Callum asks politely.

"Are you kidding? It's one of our favorite days of the year." Daisy waves her hand. "But y'all gotta help. That's Mama's rule. Everyone helps out on Thanksgiving."

I bite down on the corner of my mouth. Daisy was so small when Mom passed, I sometimes wonder if she has any memories of her at all. Carter, Jax, and I tried to keep Mom alive for Daisy by doing a bunch of her traditions. I've always made Thanksgiving dinner. Jax makes these sandwiches with potato chips in them the way Mom did when we were kids. Carter kills at Christmas. Although Daisy repeats Mom's rule easily—and that was one of Mom's rules—I don't know if it's second nature to her because she remembers Mom insisting on all of us in the kitchen with her on Thanksgiving, or because Carter and I say it every single year.

Either way, I can tell that last bit convinced the Begay-Anderson family that take-out isn't happening this year.

Instead, we're doing Thanksgiving Kane-style.

* * *

It's hours later by the time we sit down at the table. I will say that Sierra and her family know how to nail a table presentation. That is an area I completely fail at. The table is set with gold place-mats, cream dishes, and rolled linen napkins tied with some type of orange flower mixed with red berries on a branch. Flowers and candles are set in clusters in the center of the table, and various colored leaves decorate the space between them.

"Wow," Daisy breathes out, looking at Sierra. "It's so pretty."

Sierra shrugs. "I can't boil water, but I can do this part."

I nod. Sierra really can't cook. The one night she tried to make me dinner, she overcooked the pasta. It was straight-up mush. I kissed her hard anyway, as her attempt was thoughtful, but after that I've been doing all the cooking except for breakfast which she does fairly well.

Daisy brings in several plates of appetizers and side dishes: stuffed mushrooms, candied yams, sweet potato pie, cornbread, and collard greens with bacon for Callum. I set the carved turkey on the table, and we all sit around.

"Okay." Daisy looks up and smiles. "Before we start—"

"Are you going to make us say grace?" Lachlan interrupts, his eyes widening. "Cause we're not super religious. I mean, Sierra's got a better chance of worshipping a tree than—"

"We're going to say one thing we're thankful for this year." Daisy sticks her tongue out at Lachlan.

It's nice to see my sister relaxed and playful. She's been stressing this job search for the past several months and has been spinning her wheels. I've always known she was best friends with Sierra, but I never realized how close she was with Lachlan and Callum. Although it makes sense, given how close Sierra is to Carter. They've all spent a lot of time together over the years, and the Begay-Andersons have taken Daisy on several of their family vacations.

"I'm thankful for bacon," Callum starts, his mouth watering as his eyes dart between the bacon in the collard greens to the bacon strips wrapping the turkey.

"I'm thankful for my sister's happiness," Lachlan says, looking at Sierra with heartfelt warmth.

"Seriously? You had to show me up like that? I said bacon." Callum glares at Lachlan.

Lach shrugs, and Sierra reaches over and squeezes his hand.

"I'm thankful to be sharing this meal with y'all," Daisy continues.

"I'm thankful for my peanut." Sierra looks down at her belly and rubs just above her belly button.

Everyone looks to me and I swallow, an emotion I can't name coming over me. I wonder if this is how Mom felt when she sat down and listened to all of us say what we were most thankful for. This simple moment filled with love and pride for the people sitting with you.

"For today," I say simply, grinning at Sierra. I'll always be thankful for the new life she's given me.

DECEMBER

29

SIERRA

"So, I need to talk to you about something." I bump my shoulder against Daisy's. It's been a week since Thanksgiving and I loved having so many of my favorite people visiting for so long. Lachlan and Callum flew home yesterday, and Daisy is going back to Georgia. But right now, I'm soaking up some much-needed girl time with my best friend. We're lying in my bed, reruns of *Grey's Anatomy* playing in the background.

"Uh-oh. I don't know where this is going." Daisy turns to me, collecting her hair at the nape of her neck and twisting it into a bun. "

"I think you do." I widen my eyes at her.

"Just tell me. I hate this guessing game."

"Okay. I'm going to lay it all out there for you. I've seen you these past few months, struggling with your job search but not wanting to accept help or support from anyone which I respect, honestly, but I don't entirely understand. Everyone knows you get jobs through who you know. And I know people!"

Daisy rolls her eyes but a small smirk shadows her lips.

"I backed off after you told me you didn't want to relocate but it's been several months, Dais. And you'd be great working in the UK. It would be a new adventure for you, a new experience, and you'd learn a ton in a field you're really interested in. Now, give me one good reason why I can't pass your CV along to my brothers? I mean, even my Mom is asking me when you're moving out there. You have a support network, my family loves you, and you'd be doing a job you enjoy and getting paid good money for it."

Daisy sighs but doesn't shut me down right away which I take as a good sign. "I never thought it would take me this long to find a job. I've had a few leads and even an offer, but I can't support myself on what the salary was. Especially because I'd have to relocate to Alabama."

"Alabama?" I wrinkle my nose.

She nods. "Honestly, I didn't want to take a handout from you because I didn't want your family to feel obligated to hire me."

"It's not a handout. And trust me, Lachlan wouldn't hire you if he didn't think you could do the job. I'm just talking about passing along your CV. What happens from there is up to him. And you. But are you open to relocating to the UK? It could be London or Edinburgh or Dublin."

She nods. "Yes, I am now. I'd move anywhere for a job, for a chance to begin my life and start properly supporting myself. But it has to be enough money to live on. I could always work a second job. But the Alabama offer wasn't even in my field. Is that stupid?" She wrinkles her nose. "I turned down a job because—"

"Because it's not what you want to do, and you're way too young and talented to give up your dreams for the first chance that comes your way." I sit up, eyeing her seriously.

She nods, miserable. "I'm working at Cork's, you know, that wine bar Carter used to serve at?"

I nod, remembering how just this past summer, Carter waited tables, bussed, bartended, anything to make money legitimately.

"It's a fun environment, but I don't want to do it forever. I've been saving as much money as I can, and I'm open to relocating, even to the UK, but I can't ask my brothers for anything."

I open my mouth to refute this, but Daisy talks over me.

"I won't ask them. They have all sacrificed so much for me, especially Carter. And now, Carter's finally with a great woman and starting a life. Jax and Evie are planning their future. You and Denver are having a baby. Come on! For me, it's just me. I should be able to support myself."

"Are you dating anyone?" I ask, wondering why she isn't jumping at the chance for me to pass her information along.

But her eyes close, and she shakes her head. "No one. It's so hard being back home after so many years away. Everyone I run into, I've known forever. There's nothing there between us, you know?"

I make a sympathetic sound and link our arms together, settling back against the pillows with Daisy.

"Okay. Just so we're clear, there is nothing holding you back from making this move. And nothing stopping you from going after this opportunity."

"Nothing except ruining our friendship if your family hires me and I screw it all up."

"Oh please. You couldn't ruin our friendship if you tried and you'd have to work really hard at screwing everything up when my brothers and cousins have already done that several times. Each. It's called a learning curve and it's all good as long as you learn from the mistakes."

Daisy turns to me then, a genuine smile crossing her face, her eyes brighter than they were a few minutes ago. "You really think I have a chance? You really don't mind passing along my resume?'

"Daisy! I've been saying this for months. Of course you have a chance and I want to pass along your resume."

"All right, all right. Do it." She grins at me and I smile back, hugging her closer.

“That was a really good pep talk by the way. You’re going to be an incredible mother.”

I squeeze her harder and snort. “Stop it or you’ll make me cry.”

"It isn’t too hard to do these days.” She jokes.

“Tell me about it.”

“God, I can't believe you're going to be a mom. Or that Denver is going to be a dad!"

I laugh. "It's pretty crazy, huh?"

"Totally. But it's also great. You guys are going to be amazing parents. Denver's like a totally different guy with you. It's just, I don't know, real for him now, you know? I know it's only been a few months, but I've never seen him like this before. He's really excited to be a dad."

I feel tears sting the backs of my eyes at Daisy's words. Ugh. What else is new? These preggo hormones are seriously intense. But I love knowing that Denver's different with me. Especially from his sister who has obviously seen him date and have relationships with other women.

"And you're different, too." she continues.

"What do you mean?"

"You're...happier. More relaxed but more focused. You seem really wrapped up in the life you're creating with Denver, with your baby, with your art, and that's, it's really good, Sierra."

I chew my lower lip, considering her thoughts. I understand what she's saying. I have changed, and while it may seem sudden to an outsider's perspective, to me it was the most natural thing in the world. My priorities literally shifted overnight. As soon as I learned I was expecting, all the things I thought were important seemed silly. Suddenly, my health, getting enough sleep, the well-being of my peanut became more important. Getting to know Denver, allowing our relationship the time and space to grow, was at the forefront of my mind. And after the bleeding scare, my peanut is the single most important person and priority in my life.

"I am happy." I smile at Daisy.

She pats my hand with hers. "I know. And I'm happy to see you so...in love with life."

“If you move to the UK, I’m going to miss you.”

“Are you kidding me? I bet you’re there all the time. There’s no way your mom is going to let you keep the baby in the States without constant visits to the motherland.”

I snort. There is that.

* * *

"Sisi, everything okay?" My brother picks up on the first ring. I think I scarred my entire family with my pregnancy news and bleeding scare. Every time I call one of them, they answer immediately inquiring about my health.

"Everything's great," I reassure him. "I'm calling because I have the greatest idea on the planet."

Lachlan snorts. "I find that hard to believe. I don't recall you ever having any ideas that didn't involve a keg or a boat party or a—"

"Hire Daisy Kane."

"What?"

"Daisy, my best friend."

"Yes, I'm familiar with her."

"Anderson PR and Marketing should hire her. She's—"

"Sierra, you know how dangerous it can be to mix friendships and business," he interjects, probably remembering how he hooked his best mate from boarding school up with a position after graduation, and the guy ended up messing up a string of deals, causing damage to the company’s reputation, and ruining his friendship with Lachlan.

I roll my eyes. "Daisy isn't Bradley-whatever-his-name-was.

She's smart and loyal and dedicated. She was a marketing major at ASU and graduated much, much closer to the top of our class than I did. She's job searching like crazy and willing to relocate anywhere and she'd be perfect. I know she would; she just needs a chance."

"You already talked to her, didn't you?"

"Yeah but not like how you're thinking. I didn't offer her a job or anything. I just said I'd pass her CV along to you. Lachlan, you have to give her a shot. I'm going to send you her resume, look at it. Treat it like you would any candidate. If you think she could be a good fit, and I'm confident that you will, give her a call. Feel her out; interview her without interviewing her. Take it from there," I propose the idea, realizing while I'm talking that my ideas just keep getting better and better.

Lachlan sighs. "All right. You really haven't promised her a job?"

"No. I told her I'd make the connection and the next part is up to you and her."

"Send over her resume."

"Yay!" I open my laptop and hit send on the email I had already prepared. "Sent."

My brother laughs, the sound rich and warm. "I'll take a look. But no promises."

"Sounds great."

"How are you and the peanut doing?"

"Really good. I love feeling the little flutters. We're going for one of those 3D sonograms soon. I'll send you photos."

"You better. He or she is my best nephew or niece, you know?"

"He or she is your only nephew or niece."

"And Uncle Lach is going to spoil the crap out of your kid."

"I have no doubt of that."

"All right, Sisi, take care of yourself. I'll call you about Daisy, one way or the other."

"Thanks. Love you."

"You too. 'Bye."

I hang up my phone and rest against the pillows in my bed, feeling quite satisfied with my work this morning.

30

DENVER

Now that I'm working at Custom Carz and earning a stable salary that's better than anything I've ever earned, my schedule is completely different. In fact, it's better. So much so that New York City is starting to grow on me. I work normal hours, am home each night in time to cook Sierra and me dinner, and get to explore the city on the weekends.

Sierra and I fall back into the routine we had going in October but it's easier now. I'm home at night and on the weekends and she's busy pursuing her art as well as working for the art gallery. It's incredible that she's able to do both from home so when she is feeling tired, she can rest. Once a week, we go on a date and once a week, we attend a prenatal class. It's a different life than I ever thought I'd be living but after everything that's happened in the past few months, I'm loving every second of it.

I'm still listening around for any chatter surrounding my dad but so far, I haven't heard anything. Of course, his threat makes me worry constantly about Sierra and the baby but being here with them in New York, knowing I can look after them the way I want to, eases that stress a little bit.

Punching out of work for the day, I holler a quick goodbye to some of the guys and sling my workbag, an old duffle bag with a spare change of clothes, over my arm. Walking to the subway, my phone buzzes in my pocket, and my heart stops the way it always does, as my mind immediately thinks something is wrong with Sierra or the peanut.

Pulling out my phone, my heart rate only increases as Callum's name flashes across the screen.

"Hello? Is she okay?" I answer, unable to keep the panic from my voice.

"Hey. Who? Sisi?"

"Yeah."

"Oh, yeah, mate. She's fine. I'm calling to speak with you." His Scottish brogue sounds thicker on the phone and I shake my head, still not used to the sound.

"Oh. Okay. What's up?" I ask, trying to connect the dots as to why Sierra's brother would be calling me to chat. Although we're no longer at each other's throats, actually that was really only Lachlan, we're not friends, either.

"I'm dropping into town with my cousin Finlay for a few days. Want to grab a bite and some beers one night?" Callum says this as if it's the most natural thing in the world.

"Sure," I agree easily, confused and skeptical, but also not about to turn down an invitation to hang out with anyone in Sierra's family. She adores her family, and I know she'll be so happy to hear that I'm spending time with her brother and cousin.

"Okay. I'll message you the details once it's sorted."

"Sounds good. Thanks man," I mutter.

"Take care then, Denver." He clicks off.

I stare at the phone for a second, shaking my head. Weird.

But in the next beat, I'm popping into a supermarket to pick up eggplant, zucchini, and spaghetti squash for tonight's dinner.

I move through the shop quickly, anxious to get home and be with my girl.

* * *

"You look very handsome." Sierra smiles at me from her perch on her bed.

"I look ridiculous," I respond, grimacing at my reflection in the mirror. I'm going to meet Callum and Finlay at a pub for beers and wings.

And Sierra, in consultation with my sister, has taken it upon herself to order me a new...wardrobe.

That's right.

Clothes.

As if they both don't know that I only wear jeans, white, black, or grey T-shirts, and my leather jacket with boots. I'm a simple guy. Simple guys like simple things. One of those things is not having to make a bunch of decisions first thing in the morning about what the hell to put on and how it looks. Especially when there are other important things to consider. Like breakfast.

"I really like that color on you," Sierra continues, her eyes bright, her skin glowing.

The color she's referring to is...cranberry. I didn't even know how the hell to explain it until Sierra helpfully pointed out that cranberry is more than just a fruit. It's a color. Jesus. I'm wearing a cranberry wool sweater with jeans that have tears and rips throughout the knees, and not from use, but because she bought them like this! That's right. She literally spent money on pants with holes in them.

Thank God I'm still rocking my own boots and jacket.

I nearly lost it when Sierra tried to wind a scarf around my neck. It's not that I can't wear a scarf to keep myself warm. It's that this scarf serves no purpose. It's not warm. At all. It's an "accessory." Another term I learned from Sierra.

She walks over to me and stands on her tippy toes to press a kiss to my cheek.

I turn to glare at her but when my eyes connect with hers, any annoyance I'm experiencing dies. Literally goes out like a flame. She's happy. Her eyes are wide and excited, the smile on her face genuine. She looks like a younger version of herself for a moment. Of the plotting and mischievous Sierra who was always organizing pranks with Daisy, walking around without a care in the world, and laughing wildly over anything that brought her joy.

And, Jesus, am I really going to deny her a moment of carefree contentment because she was thoughtful enough to pick out stylish clothes that are meant to help me fit into my new life in New York?

She spends the whole day working from a chair or resting for the benefit of our peanut. And lately, the packages arriving at the front desk have tripled in quantity, but Sierra is so happy to be decorating a nursery and buying me little presents that I don't have the heart to tell her that we shouldn't be spending money on these things when we could be saving more for our future rent.

"It's growing on me," I tell her instead, kissing the tip of her nose.

"Let me just take a quick picture for Daisy."

"What? No!"

"Hold still. Say cheese." She holds her phone up, and I give her a look. She snaps the photo.

"It's so...you." She snorts, turning the phone so I can see a photo of myself, dressed in cranberry, sulking.

"It's genuine," I tell her instead.

She laughs, pressing another kiss to my cheek. "Have fun with the boys."

"Are you sure you'll be all right on your own?" I ask, worried about leaving her.

"Den, I'm alone all day."

"I know, but it just feels different when I'm going out for a beer and not to work."

"I'll be fine."

"I'll bring you a burger."

"Ah, finally a man who gets me."

I swat at her ass, steering her to the living room. "What are you going to do all night?"

"Paint." She smiles up at me as if working is the greatest thing in the world.

"Don't overdo it," I remind her. She's been working so much lately. Painting, photographing her work, posting on social media. Working on the business side of things. Plus managing all the digital content for the gallery. It's been a lot, and I can't help but worry she's pushing herself too hard.

"I won't. I'm just putting in extra hours now, so I can take more time when the peanut comes."

"I know. Which reminds me, we really need to start discussing baby names."

Sierra wrinkles her nose. "I feel like that's going to be an interesting conversation. One we shouldn't start now."

I chuckle, leaning over to kiss her. A kiss that could go on for a lot longer if I don't force myself to pull away. "All right. Call me if you need anything."

"Drink a lot of beers."

"I'll see you later, baby."

"Have fun!"

I nod, waving without turning around as I exit the apartment and wait for the elevator to deliver me to the street.

* * *

The pub is noisy and boisterous when I enter, and the environment immediately puts me at ease. I don't know Sierra's family that well, but I do know that they can wine and dine with the best of them. I prefer the simplicity of a rickety bar stool and a cold beer, and I have a feeling that Sam's Pub will be more my speed than the fancy, uppity restaurants on Park Avenue that Sierra frequents.

"Denver!"

I turn and see Callum holding up his arm in a booth.

I start heading in his direction, my eyes scanning the guy next to him. Finlay. Even their names sound wealthy.

"Hey. I'm Denver," I introduce myself to Finlay as I approach the booth.

He stands, his height impressive, as he's almost—almost—taller than I am. And that's saying something because I'm six foot three.

"Good to meet you, mate. Finlay Anderson."

I nod, shaking hands with Callum and sliding into the booth next to him.

"We ordered a few pitchers and wings," Callum explains, picking up an empty pint glass and pitcher of beer, eyeing me to make sure that's good.

Not one to let my guard down, especially with guys I don't know that well, I'll admit that the beer and wings definitely put me at ease. "Sounds good."

Callum hands me a pint and raises his glass to mine. "Cheers, mate."

"Cheers." I raise my glass to the two of them and take a gulp of beer, the taste hitting the back of my throat relaxes me further. Jesus, I needed this: a cold beer, a plate of wings, and the comfort of a pub.

In some ways, Sam's Pub reminds me of Raf's, the hole-in-the-wall bar and grill from back home. It always smells of stale beer and peanuts, and the memory takes root in my chest, causing a wave of homesickness to wash over me. Of course, I'm happy to be in New York with Sierra and the peanut, but it's been a lot of changes in a short amount of time.

Luckily, we're heading back to Georgia for Christmas.

Right now, it's nice to just sit and sip on a beer.

"How long are y'all in town for?" I ask the guys, leaning back in the booth.

"Just a few days. We're working with a New York based athletic company on their marketing campaign. It's contract based, but we're hoping to expand our reach a bit and the States is a new frontier for us," Callum explains.

I nod. "You both do advertising?"

Finlay laughs, shaking his head. "No, no. Just Callum, Lach, and my brother Aaron are interested in fonts and images and whatever the hell else they do."

"Finlay's a lawyer. In-house," Callum explains, tipping his chin to his cousin. "And he's an arrogant arse about it."

Finlay laughs again, a chuckle that says he's used to being called out.

I find myself cracking a smile, their easy banter reminding me of my brothers. And damn, I miss them, too.

"Help yourself to some wings." Callum pulls a plate of wings closer to my seat and I grab a few, starting to get antsy. Why the hell did they ask me to meet with them?

"Listen, Denver, I'm sure you're wondering why we asked you to meet up," Finlay says, as if reading my mind.

I nod, biting into a wing and chewing slowly to give him time to explain.

"Daisy explained a bit of your past."

My eyebrows shoot up at this. My sister told Sierra's family about me? About the jail time and Darren and—

"Very little," Finlay continues, reading the anger brewing in my expression.

"Look, I'll be straight with you. Daisy told us you have something that could use legal assistance, and given how busy you've been with the move, the baby, and taking care of Sierra, you haven't had the time to follow-up with the lawyers you were feeling out in Georgia. We don't know any of the details other than it involves a past incident that requires legal counsel." He tips his head to Finlay. "Finlay's a lawyer in-house, but he's also registered to practice in the state of New York and California."

"I went to law school in the States," Finlay throws out in explanation.

I nod slowly, mulling this over. Eyeing them with wariness, I can't get a read if they know all about my past, or if Daisy really did just reach out so they could help me. Do I even want help from Sierra's family? And why did Daisy reach out and not Sierra? Probably because Sierra is a better secret-keeper than my sister, and Daisy wonders why we never told her things when she was growing up.

Jesus, there's probably nobody better than a member of Sierra's family to help with this. But still...

"You don't have to go this route. I just wanted to throw it out there in case you're interested," Finlay finally says, biting into a wing, giving me time to figure out what the hell I want to do.

Sighing, I scrub my hand over my face. "I did two years in Jackson Penitentiary for a robbery at a gas station. The clerk was assaulted."

Finlay shifts in his seat, peering at me with curiosity burning in his eyes. Callum's reaction isn't as measured, as his mouth literally drops open and hangs as he regards me...warily. Well, I guess that clarifies that they really didn't know the details.

"All right," Finlay says, his Scottish brogue intensifying.

"I didn't do it. I've maintained my innocence from the start. My father set me up."

At this, Callum's head swings to stare at me as Finlay coughs into his hand, trying not to laugh at his cousin. "Your father?" Callum repeats, incredulous.

I nod.

"Best work on that poker face, Cal," Finlay says to Callum who tries to tame his expression.

"It's all right." I wave them away. "I would be concerned if you didn't react like that. Especially given my involvement with Sierra."

"There is that," Callum recovers, and I crack a grin.

"There is. That's what started all this. I need to clear my name. I can't have our baby carrying around that weight. The negative that drags on the Kane name."

Finlay nods in understanding. "All right, how do you know it was your father who set you up?"

"Him and Griller told me. They were behind the string of robberies taking place at that time."

"Griller?"

"My dad is an officer in the Devil's Shadows Motorcycle Club. Griller is the president."

Finlay lets out a low whistle as Callum's mouth drops wide open again.

"We'll never take him to Vegas with us," Finlay says to me, shooting his cousin another look. "Damn, I didn't know we'd be going up against an MC."

"We?"

"I'm going to reach out to some connections I have here, if that's alright with you? With DNA testing, several names were cleared in recent years after the people did time."

"They also paid off witnesses. And the video surveillance went missing."

Finlay is quiet for several moments, thinking. Finally, he looks up at me, “Well we definitely have something to work with at least. Can you tell us a bit more?”

I nod, taking a long pull on my beer before repeating the past to Callum and Finlay.

Finlay smacks the table with his open palm. "We can work with that. Are you cool with me digging around?"

"Yeah," I agree, after a moment. At this point, what do I really have to lose? I'm in New York with Sierra. I have eyes on her and the baby if Darren tries any of his stupid bullshit.

"Great. We'll see what we can do." He lifts his pint for another pull, and I do the same.

Only Callum continues to sit and stare like he can't believe the turn of events.

31

DENVER

"Are y'all ready?" I call out, carrying in a box of colorful cupcakes and placing them on the massive island in the penthouse.

Looking around at all of our family, I can't even believe they're all here. Carter, Taylor, Daisy, Callum, Lachlan, Sierra's mom Jenni and stepdad James, her younger brother Liam, and cousins Finlay and Aaron. Jax and Evie are FaceTimed in on a laptop with a view of the entire kitchen.

"Hurry up already!" Jax yells out, a massive grin splitting his face. "Evie's about to have a heart attack with all this anticipation. I swear, Den, she's been on Pottery Barn Kids nonstop looking at nursery items. Get ready for a massive shipment of things to your place. And to foot the bill once Evie fails this semester."

"Oh, stop it. I'm not failing. I'm just a little distracted. And can you even blame me?" Evie's voice rings out before her face pops into the frame. "I really am so excited, y'all!" she gushes, her accent thicker with her escalating excitement.

Sierra laughs and blows her a kiss. "Give us two minutes to set everything up, and then we'll have the big reveal."

A gender reveal. I'm participating in a freaking gender reveal.

I always poked fun at the people who did these parties to reveal the gender of their baby and then plastered photos all over social media like the rest of the world is supposed to care. It's ridiculous, really. Except now I'm swept up in the excitement, and while I made Sierra promise not to post a ton of photos on her Instagram account, I also can't deny that I'm stupidly excited and happy that our family is here to share this moment with us.

"Bubbly?" James hands a champagne flute to Daisy who accepts it gratefully. James keeps passing out champagne, handing a flute with sparkling water, blueberries, and raspberries bobbing at the top to Sierra. "For a boy or a girl." He shrugs, a sheepish smile on his face, and I can tell that he's excited, too.

We all are, which given how this baby was brought into our lives, is really incredible. Our little peanut is already loved so much by so many people that he or she really is a miracle. And has smoothed so many tense and awkward moments between our families over without even trying. Or knowing. How wild is that?

"Denver." Jenni beams at me, handing me a plate with a blue and pink cupcake on top.

"I'm more nervous than I was writing my final exams." Liam laughs, running his finger through the icing on his cupcake and sucking it off with a loud pop.

"Wait for Sierra and Denver," Jenni scolds him, and he rolls his eyes.

"Wait. We need to restate our gender before we dig in. For the bets." Finlay holds up a hand, quieting the general buzz in the kitchen. "Who's team blue and who's team pink?"

"Blue!" Taylor raises her hand, holding up a sign that says, "It's a boy!"

"I'm going girl," Carter disagrees with Taylor who sticks her tongue out at him.

"Girl," Daisy calls out.

Finlay looks up at her, his eyes lingering a moment longer

than necessary, and she seems to freeze under his gaze, her cheeks coloring.

Finlay mumbles something under his breath that I don't catch, as he jots down the guesses on a piece of paper.

"Team boy," Callum throws out.

"It's a girl," Jenni says confidently, beaming at her daughter.

"Do you think so? I really think it's a boy," Sierra says.

"I'm with you, Sisi," James agrees.

"Nope, it's definitely a girl. Look how she's carrying," Jenni says to James, pointing at Sierra's baby bump.

"Girl! Please, a girl. I'm with Jenni all the way," Evie calls out from the laptop screen, desperate to be included.

Jax's laugh follows as he manages to elbow his way onto the screen. "Blue."

"Aaron?" Finlay asks his brother.

"Boy."

"Den?" Finlay looks up at me.

Shit. I have no freaking clue. I mean, either way I have a fifty percent chance of getting it right, right? "Boy," I say, because how the hell would I raise a girl? The thought makes me shudder with anxiety.

"See, the parents know best." Sierra slips her hand in mine, beaming at me.

"Liam?"

"Pink." He points to his pink polo. "Real men wear it."

"You're such a doofus." Callum launches a punch, hitting Liam's shoulder.

Liam shrugs off Callum's hand. "Doofus? Showing your age, Cal."

"Quit it." James fixes the guys with a look, and even though they are both grown men, they quiet down.

I bite the inside of my cheek to keep from chuckling but Carter laughs easily.

"I'm going with boy," Finlay says. "That's all of us. All right, losers are each throwing down a hundred bucks for the peanut's college fund. Or twenty-first birthday bash in Vegas? Which is it?"

"Vegas!" Everyone except Jenni and Sierra, who both opt for college, call out.

"Eat your cupcakes, already," Evie's bossy voice chides us again.

"Okay, let's do this." Sierra says, dropping my hand and lifting her cupcake to her mouth. "On three. One, two, three!"

We all take gigantic bites into our cupcakes. Dropping half of my cupcake onto the plate, my eyes nearly fall out of my head. Pink. The center of my cupcake is filled with pink icing.

I look up at Sierra who's laughing, tears pricking the corners of her eyes, as she drops her half-eaten cupcake. I pull her toward me and kiss her hard, icing smearing on both of our faces.

"We're having a girl," she yells out.

A girl. We're having a baby girl!

"I told you," Jenni laughs, coming around to envelop both of us in a hug.

"See Den," Liam says, clasping a hand on my shoulder, "real men wear pink. And real men have daughters." He laughs, shooting a look at his father who clearly had all boys.

James rolls his eyes, laughing at his youngest son's antics.

"Woo! I knew it. I knew it. Okay, I need to shop," Evie calls out from the computer screen.

Daisy and Taylor fold Sierra in a hug, the three of them holding hands and jumping up and down. Tears track my sister's and Sierra's faces as Taylor says something, her hands gesturing wildly, pink icing sticking to the ends of her long, blonde hair.

"Congratulations, bro." Carter tells me, pulling me into a hug and slapping my back harder than necessary. Pulling away, his eyes look a little watery, and I know mine are the same way.

I'm having a daughter.

"Congrats, man." Lachlan extends his hand to me and I shake it, a look of understanding passing between us.

In the next minute, James pulls Sierra and me aside. Jenni comes up, placing a hand on James's back and smiling at us.

"Okay, kids, here's the thing," James begins, his eyes crinkling at the corners as he smiles at us. In such a short amount of time, James has really warmed up to me. Sierra says it's because he knows I'm working hard and taking such great care of her. I don't know what the reason is; I'm just relieved he's accepting me into his family. "We know you didn't expect this." He gestures toward Sierra's growing belly and we all laugh. "But this baby is loved so much. Your mom and I wanted to do something special for you. I know you're not going to move back to the UK and accept a job with Anderson PR," James says to Sierra.

Sierra rushes to explain, "It's not that I'm not grateful or—"

James holds up a hand, stopping her. "I know that, honey. But you have different priorities now." His eyes shift to her bump, then to me. "As you should. We're going to miss you."

"And I'm going to be making a ton of more trips," Jenni adds.

Sierra grins at her mom.

"We'd like for you to stay here after the baby comes," James says.

Now, it's my turn to open my mouth and rush to explain how I can't continue living in a penthouse I can't afford. I need to be able to take care of my family, to provide for them, not live off of Sierra's stepdad.

Once again, James holds up a hand before I can get any words out. "I know what you're going to say, Denver. And I understand where you're coming from. When Gayle, my first wife and I married, her father was financially successful, and I felt like I was always trying to prove myself to him. I don't want you to feel like you have to do that. Gayle's parents and my parents both helped us get started once we began having kids. It's a grandparent thing. So I'm going to rent the penthouse to you."

I continue to stare at him, my mind racing as to how to

explain to him that I could work for the next year and not afford a monthly payment.

"Three hundred dollars a month," he says seriously. "And you promise to take care of our girls and to come visit the UK twice a year. And you and Sierra pursue the types of careers that make you happy and work for your growing family. I'm not offering as a favor, Denver. I'm offering because I want to and because I can. And because I know your past, and men like you deserve a second chance. So take it, get on your feet, and pay me back by creating a beautiful family that you're actually present for. I ruined my first marriage by never being around, always working. I missed out on most of Callum's childhood. I won't make that mistake with Jenni, and I didn't miss a moment with Liam. Learn from my mistakes and accept the support, because families support each other. And you're family now."

Sierra glances at me from the corner of her eye as I stare at her parents in complete awe. These are the types of families I'd see on TV, but I didn't know they existed in real life. I mean, he's handing us the keys to his penthouse for a measly three hundred dollars a month and the promise to visit his family?

It's too much.

He's offering me a fresh start, a do-over.

"Thank you, sir." I stick out a hand and he shakes it.

"It's my pleasure, son."

Son. Jesus. How different it is to have a man like James to look up to.

And that's who I'm going to be to our daughter. The type of man she can look up to and be proud of. The type of man she's proud to call Daddy.

32

SIERRA

Pinks and peaches and creams and golds are taking over my life. I sit in the studio for hours now, my brush knowing exactly what to do against the canvas. It all started last week when I spent hours lost in my studio, Ed Sheeran on the Sonos, a cup of decaf tea on my side table.

My hand arced wide, brush stroke after brush stroke of soft curves and gentle movement. Light pinks, peaches, creams, and golds. Dashes of white for lightening and black for shadowing. And then, the emergence of a mother, her graceful neck bent lovingly, her gaze intent on the sweet baby cradled in her arms. Her swollen belly was visible under her dress, pieces of her hair falling forward and shadowing her jawline. The bundle in her arms stretching one arm up sweetly to touch her face in a moment so pure, so true, it brings tears to my eyes, and I can hardly believe that I created a moment of such simple grace.

But since the creation of this canvas, they've all been similar. Tender moments of love, sweet snapshots of family, minutes that are gone in the blink of an eye now frozen in time. Mothers and babies, fathers and newborns, brothers and sisters, families. So much love, so much caring, so much...everything.

Looking around my gallery, I decide to spend the morning taking photos of my work and preparing social media posts. I choose five recently completed canvases and clear some space where the natural light is best to take pictures from various angles. Once I'm satisfied with the results, I close up the studio and retreat to my usual place on the living room couch to work on my laptop. Bed rest is seriously the most boring thing ever, but I am getting a ridiculous amount of work done now that I have hours and hours to work without any social plans distracting me.

Each work I complete is simple and sweet and...heartfelt. Abstract, with a family-centric vibe, my painting has moved in an entirely new direction from the portraits and landscapes. And I've never had more fun with it in my life.

Updating all of my social media accounts before lunch, I sit down to take a break and eat some of the leftovers from the gender reveal party.

The buzzing of my phone causes me to place my sandwich on my plate and pick up my cell. A New York number I don't recognize flashes across the screen.

"Hello?"

"May I please speak to Sierra Begay?" a woman's voice, friendly but professional, asks.

"Speaking."

"Sierra, hello. My name is Judy Crantz. I own and run a small art gallery on—"

"Sway Gallery. That's you! Oh, my God, I'm so sorry I interrupted you," I trip over my words, shocked and excited that Judy Crantz, the Judy Crantz, is calling me!

She laughs warmly. "You're familiar with us, then?"

"Oh, yes. I love your space and the art you showcase, and I spent way too much time walking around your gallery."

"That's excellent to hear because I'd love to show some of your new pieces."

My blood stops and so does my heart. And my ability to

speak. I can't even breathe. I take a moment to collect myself and wish my voice wasn't shaky when I say, "Really?"

Judy laughs again. "Really. I've been following your Instagram for a while now, and I really love the new work that you're doing. Your older paintings were beautiful, but this new style, the abstract and the shading, even the blending of colors, it caught my attention. Especially the paintings you posted this morning."

"I'd be honored."

"Excellent. Shall we have lunch next week to discuss the particulars?"

"Absolutely."

We make plans to meet for lunch, and then I nearly swoon onto the couch, giddy happiness filling me up. The peanut and I have an impromptu dance party as I sway around the living room, belting out an old Mariah Carey song my mom used to love.

Oh, my God! I'm an artist. A real one!

My hands tremble. I pick up my phone, about to call Daisy, since she's been my go-to for the past four years. But before I can call her, my finger hits Denver's name, and I hold the phone to my ear.

"Sierra. You okay?" he answers immediately, and my heart swells at how much he worries about me.

"I'm an artist."

"Sorry?"

"I got a call. Judy Crantz. Freaking Judy Crantz from a gallery that I'm obsessed with. She wants to showcase my work. In her gallery!"

"Wow," Denver exclaims. That's right, he exclaimed something. True story. "Sierra, that's, wow, that's incredible. Congratulations, baby! I'm proud of you."

"I'm losing my freaking mind over here. Can you believe that?"

Den chuckles, the sound low and sexy, and I wish he were

here with me right now. "I can definitely believe it. You're all talent, babe. Let's celebrate tonight. I'll cook—"

"Let's go out. Please, Den. I feel really good today. I know whatever you make will be a million times better, but let's just go out."

"All right," he agrees easily. "I'll pick you up for our date at six."

"That sounds great."

"See you later, babe." He clicks off and I squeal again.

Resuming my dance party, I shimmy all the way to my closet for...wait a minute, this news deserves a new outfit, doesn't it?

Stuffing my feet into a pair of boots and shrugging into a winter coat, I leave the apartment and head to Rosie Pope and Seraphine. This girl needs to do some serious shopping.

At six a knock sounds on the door and I laugh, knowing it's Denver and loving that we're playing this as a proper date. Dressed in sheer black tights, they're kind of creepy because of the giant belly built into them, a simple cream cashmere knit sweater dress with a massive roll neck, and sweet boots, I feel like myself again. I can't believe how long it's been since I dressed up. My hair is curled at the ends, hanging down my back. I'm wearing makeup. And perfume. And I'm so excited for tonight.

"Hi." I open the door, smiling at Denver.

His eyes widen the moment he sees me and my smile grows.

"Hey. You look," he swallows, "beautiful. Really beautiful." His eyes meet mine, and a ghost of a grin touches his full lips. He holds out a bouquet of flowers for me, and I lean forward to kiss his cheek.

Taking the flowers, I hold open the door, and we walk inside while I add the flowers to a vase. "Thank you. They're lovely," I tell him, my fingers fluttering over the petals of the winter bouquet: amaryllis, silver brunia, dusty miller, pine cones, and berries. It's really exquisite.

"You're lovely." Denver watches me, his dark eyes molten.

"Where are we going?"

He waggles his eyebrows playfully and I giggle. This is a side of Denver I rarely see and I love it. "Wouldn't you like to know?"

"A surprise!"

"It's not that exciting, but yes, a surprise." He holds out his hand to me. "Ready?"

"Ready." I place my hand in his, and we leave the apartment, the door closing behind us.

Walking outside, soft flurries swirl around us, the air biting cold, and the wind whipping my hair back. But inside, I feel toasty and warm.

Grinning up at Denver, he chuckles at my expression and dips his head to capture my lips. Nipping his lip lightly, I close my eyes and breathe in this moment. I could stay in it forever.

33

DENVER

Having no idea how to plan a special date or where to take Sierra on such short notice, I debate if I should call Callum or Lachlan. But then, what do they know? They spend all of their time in fancy restaurants and trendy nightclubs. I want my date with Sierra to be a celebration for her huge accomplishment today. To be able to spend some real time with her, hear her over the music in the background, and have an actual conversation.

"Hey Migs." I turn to the only guy I know in New York who can point me in the right direction.

"Yeah, man?"

"If I was going to take my girl out tonight, someplace fun and laidback but nice. Good food. Good music. She had a big day today. Where would I go?"

Without even blinking, he rattles off three restaurants. I opt for the Mexican cuisine and he nods. "Good choice. I'll make a call and get you a reservation."

"Thank you," I tell him sincerely, and he waves a hand at me.

"You're doing good here, Denver. You should go out and celebrate your big day, too."

I chuckle, not really understanding what he's talking about. But then he hands me a folder. "This is a new client that came up. Here's the proposal I'm thinking about. We start on Monday. You're in. Hands on, all of it."

I open the folder and whistle low under my breath at the 1967 Shelby Mustang inside. "You sure?" I ask him.

"I don't know. Are you?"

"Yeah, man. I definitely want in on this."

"See you Monday."

After clocking out, I begin to walk toward the subway when I pass a florist. A real one, not just a bunch of flowers outside a bodega. Popping in, I chat with the florist as she creates a bouquet to bring home to Sierra. I know it's simple and not really original, but I hope she appreciates the thought.

The truth is, she's pretty much all I think about these days.

* * *

When I knock on the door to the penthouse and Sierra answers, my eyes almost fall out of my head. Not because of how beautiful she is, but because of how happy she looks.

She's wearing a dress I want to slide my hands under and boots I wish she'd wrap around my hips. Her dark hair is curled at the ends and hangs down her spine like a waterfall. Her chocolate eyes are bright, and her cheeks are rosy. She's just...breathtaking.

Once she's placed the flowers in a vase and we're on our way to the restaurant, our fingers laced together and our breaths mingling in the cold air, I realize how excited I am to be taking my girl out on a date and how incredibly proud of her I am.

"You cold?" I ask her as she snuggles into me.

"I'm good." She says, her eyes twinkling.

"The place we're going, it's not fancy or anything."

"I'm sure it's perfect."

"I hope you like it." I'm suddenly nervous. Should I have planned something different? Something better? Isn't dinner what everyone does on a date?

"I'm sure I'll love it. Honestly, I don't care where we go. I'm just happy to be spending time with you, out of the house, and doing something different.

I nod. I guess for us going out to dinner is different since most nights I cook, and we eat together before Sierra nods off.

We make a right and she shimmies a little, her laughter uninhibited and genuine, as we walk closer to the Mexican restaurant. The music flows out onto the street, and inside the tables seem lively, the atmosphere fun, and the entire vibe chill but cool.

"We're here." I extend a hand for her to walk in front of me through the door.

"This is awesome!" she squeals as she dances to the hostess.

I chuckle because really, how is everything with her so much damn fun?

Once we're seated, Sierra smiles at me over the candles on the table and I can't stop staring at her. Reaching out to hold her hand, I enjoy that I can still make her blush. This pelvic rest has been a lot harder than I thought it would be but tonight, tonight it seems impossible to keep my hands off of her.

We order guacamole and chips to start. I ask for a Corona and Sierra orders a fancy mocktail. When our drinks arrive, we cheers to her success and spend our date, and the rest of the night, completely wrapped up in each other.

And it's perfect.

34

SIERRA

"This was your doing, wasn't it?" Daisy calls me early the next morning, shouting the second I answer the phone.

"What are you going on and on about?" I ask, biting back my smile. Lachlan emailed me a few days earlier with one sentence. *You were right.*

I'm always right.

And I love Daisy's reaction.

"Your brother called me. He offered me a job. As a senior marketing associate. Senior! To work in Scotland. Did you hear that? I'm moving to Edinburgh. To work. I have a job. I am a gainfully employed real person with a real life!"

I laugh, leaning back against the throw pillows on the couch. "You've always been real, Dais."

"I'm so freaking excited. Thank you, Sierra. Thank you!"

"I didn't do anything. You did. Trust me, Lach wouldn't have offered you the job if he didn't think you were qualified for the position."

"I move in January. I'm going to be working for your cousin, Aaron."

"You'll love working with him. He's the marketing guru in the

Edinburgh office. And I'm sure you'll see Finlay a lot too since he's the in-house lawyer. Don't be afraid to reach out to either of them if you need anything."

"I can't even believe this is happening to me."

"Believe it, sister. You've got a job and a new life!"

"Really, thank you. I...I don't even know what to say."

"Say you'll have dinner with my Mom once a month since she's desperate for girl talk, being around the boys all the time."

"Done!"

"She'll be thrilled."

"I gotta tell my brothers. Call you later?"

"Of course. Love you."

"Love you more."

I hang up the phone, smiling at Daisy's obvious excitement and happiness. This is going to be great for her. She's going to love Edinburgh and her new position. Plus, she'll build some confidence after feeling down for so many months about not having any real job offers. While I know her brothers are going to be upset that she's moving to another country, she'll have my brothers and cousins and Mom and James. She won't be on her own; Mom would never allow it.

"What's that about?" Denver asks, collapsing on the couch next to me.

I run my fingers through his hair, playing with it. "You'll find out in about ten seconds."

He peers up at me curiously. "What're you up to now?"

I shake my head just as his phone rings.

"Dais," he answers.

I hear the screaming and squealing on the other side of the line and watch as Denver's mouth curls into a large grin.

"That's incredible, Dais. Congratulations. Scotland, huh?" His eyes shoot to me, narrowing slightly.

I shrug.

"All right, yeah. Go call Jax. Proud of you," he says gruffly and I snort.

"You've got my sister moving to Scotland?" he asks me when he hangs up but he's grinning.

I bat my eyelashes. "Now, you'll be more willing to go for all of our family visits."

He laughs, the sound carefree. "You're always up to something, Begay. You're sneaky."

"Only where you're concerned," I manage to admit before Denver's on top of me, his lips pressing against mine.

* * *

"Okay, tell me everything," Daisy answers the phone, as if she was sitting by it waiting for me to call.

"She was wonderful. Just like I imagined her to be," I gush, hardcore fangirling over the Judy Crantz. We just wrapped up lunch in Soho, and I'm barely a block away before I call Daisy.

"She must be so fabulous. What was she wearing?"

"A simple cream sweater, cowl neck, with Citizens jeans and the hottest Louboutin boots I've ever seen. Her purse was Chloe."

"Sigh, gasp, obsessed," Daisy gushes with me. "I hope I'm like her when I'm fifty-whatever."

"I hope I'm like her when I'm thirty."

"True story. So, tell me about your paintings."

I grin, just remembering the offer. "She offered me a show!"

"Stop it."

"I know, right? It's so wild. An actual show. At a real gallery. And not just any gallery, but one I swoon over."

"Congratulations, Sierra. That's amazing. When is it?"

"I'm not sure yet. Either before the baby or way after. Usually, it would be afterwards to give us enough time to prepare everything, but since I have a variety of completed works that haven't been shown elsewhere, Judy thinks we may be able to arrange everything before. Since you know, after could be..."

"Interesting?"

"Nice word choice."

Daisy laughs, the sound giddy with excitement, mirroring my own happiness.

"We're going to sit down after the holidays and sort everything out. But honestly, I wasn't expecting that. At all. She blew me away. We talked about my art and the trajectory of where my painting is heading. What my vision is for the future and the types of works I'd like to create, the different materials I'm looking to incorporate moving forward. It was a really inspiring conversation. And honest. I really like that about her. She's super honest and straightforward, which is refreshing."

"That's awesome. Your first show. I bet your whole family flies in."

I roll my eyes but I'm cheesing. Hard. Because I'm sure they will, too.

"And of course, I'll be there. Have you told Denver yet?"

"No, not yet. I texted him but haven't heard back yet. We're supposed to meet at Bryant Park in a little bit, so I'm going to tell him then."

"He's going to be so proud of you."

"I'm just so excited, you know?"

"You should be. Things are definitely looking up, Sierra."

She's right. They really are.

35

DENVER

"Hey, mate. How's Sisi holding up?" Finlay asks as soon as I pick up the phone.

"Hey. Yeah, she's doing all right. Really busy with her painting."

"I heard. It's great she's doing that. I know we all tried to push her into joining us at the family business, but the truth is it was never for her."

"Yeah," I agree. "How are you?"

"Well, well. I'm calling because I have some news about your dad."

"Oh?" I swallow, sitting down on the nearest chair in the break room at Custom Carz. My heart gallops in my chest, my palms suddenly growing sweaty. This is it. Whatever falls out of Finlay's mouth can either make or break my future.

"There've been new techniques that have been used in recent years regarding DNA sampling. I know you maintained your innocence but still served the time. If we can link the DNA from the scene of the crime to your father or Griller, we can clear your name."

"Yeah, but what DNA? My dad and Griller are professional cons; they wouldn't leave any incriminating evidence behind."

"Except they did. And the video surveillance resurfaced."

* * *

I'm still reeling from Finn's news as I walk to Bryant Park to meet Sierra at the Winter Village. It's a quaint set-up with hot chocolate, dessert stations, and various winter items that make good Christmas gifts. For people who live in the cold, I guess.

And it's serving another purpose today as the backdrop of one of the most important moments of my life.

"Denver!" Sierra calls out when she spots me, waving me over, her hands covered in warm gloves.

"Hey baby." I smile at her, pulling her into my arms and kissing her like I haven't seen her in weeks when it's really only been a few hours. The gentlest swell of her stomach presses into me and I hold her closer, loving the way she looks and feels with her growing belly.

"How's your day?" she asks sweetly when I pull back.

I lace our fingers together and walk us closer to the ice-skating rink, wishing we could join the skaters but knowing I'd never take that risk with Sierra pregnant. "I just got amazing news from your cousin, Finlay. Things are definitely looking up and we're on the right track to clearing my name."

"Oh my God! Baby, that's amazing." Sierra squeezes my hand and beams up at me.

"Yeah. I'm still processing the news. What about you? How was lunch with that Judy lady?"

Sierra smiles, stopping in her tracks to face me. "She offered me a show!"

"What? Like an art show?"

She nods, squealing loudly.

"Wow, Sierra. That's amazing. I'm so freaking proud of you,

baby." I pull her in for a hug, squeezing her before cupping her cheeks and kissing her lips. I can't help myself. I'm in awe of every single thing this woman does. "When is it?"

"I'm not sure yet. We're still working out the logistics. Either before the baby arrives or way, way after."

"Well, whenever it is, it will be perfect. I'm really in awe of you."

"I love you, Den." She looks up at me, her sweet face vibrant and happy.

"I love you more. In fact, I love you so much that I want to make some changes."

Her brow furrows as she glances up at me. "What do you mean?"

"I want to talk to you about something. It's important. And afterwards, I thought we could grab some hot chocolate."

"Okay. What's going on?" Her eyes darken with concern.

Before she can panic too much, I ease her onto a park bench and get down on one knee in front of her.

She gasps, her eyes widening, and watches me intently.

"Sierra Grace Begay, I've been into you for a long, long time. And I've fallen for you and for our little girl, hard. I don't care what my future looks like as long as I get to share it with you and our baby. I want to make you happy, to create a family with you, and to grow old with you by my side. Please, will you marry me?" I pull out the ring I had fashioned from my mother's alexandrite gemstone from my pocket and present it to her.

Tears dot the corners of her eyes as she nods, her gaze never dropping to the ring, her hands cupping my cheeks as she pulls me in for a kiss. Around us, cheers and whistles ring out and Sierra laughs against my lips. "Yes, yes. Of course I'll marry you."

After we break apart, I slip the ring onto her finger and feel my chest swell with emotion at the perfect fit. "This was my mother's stone. It's alexandrite." I explain, running a finger over the teardrop gemstone that I had made into a ring with tiny diamonds bunched on each side.

Sierra gasps. "This isn't the gemstone that Carter was saving for Daisy, is it?"

I look up at her, moving from my knee to the spot next to her on the bench. "You know about that?"

She nods.

"It is. It was a pendant that I had made into a ring for you. When I went back to Georgia the last time, Carter and Daisy and Jax, via FaceTime, explained to me how Taylor's dad was recently able to buy the gemstone back for Carter. They all agreed that I should have it, to give to you. Daisy said you're her sister and she wants us to have something that belonged to Mom as we begin our new life and new family together."

"It's beautiful." Sierra says, glancing down at her finger, tears spilling onto her cheeks. "And I'm honored to wear it."

"Good. Because I'm honored to marry you." I tell her before capturing her lips once more with mine.

36

SIERRA

"Mom! I'm engaged!" I hold my finger up to the laptop screen and laugh when my mom gasps.

"Oh my gosh! Wow! Congratulations! You too, Denver!" She exclaims, waving as Denver's face joins mine in the frame.

"Thank you, Jenni. I'm just relieved Sierra said yes."

"Of course she said yes. She's been pining for you since she was nineteen." Mom announces and I feel my cheeks redden.

"Thanks Mom."

"Oh, honey, please. You're having a baby together. You'll be sharing a lot more embarrassing moments than this one during labor."

"And she just keeps going." I joke, looking up at Den to gage his reaction at my mother's embarrassing over-sharing.

But he just shrugs, laughing at us.

"That ring is stunning. Show me again." Mom commands, calling out for James and Liam. Unbeknownst to me, Lach and Callum are both visiting so we get the whole family, with all the shouting and exclaiming and excitement.

Denver is smiling harder than I've ever seen and I can't help but wish we were with my family in Scotland, about to go out for a big celebration. The consolation is that we're flying to Georgia for Christmas tomorrow and we will celebrate with his family in person.

"When's the wedding?"

"Better question, where's the wedding?"

"Is the baby going to be involved at all?"

My family tosses out question after question but Denver and I just look at each other and laugh. "Guys, we just, just got engaged. As soon as we have more information, I promise to let you know."

"Like for real let us know or wait a ton of months?" Liam asks and I stick my tongue out at him as my other brothers laugh.

"For real let you know."

"Alright, alright but we're waiting." He replies.

We chat with my family for several more minutes before we disconnect. I fix us some mugs of hot chocolate, tossing some marshmallows on top, and we snuggle on the couch.

"I can't believe we're getting married." I admit, smiling at Den over the rim of my mug.

"I can't wait to marry you."

"Do you think we should do it before or after the baby?"

"Whatever you want. If we do it before, it will be rushed and I don't want you taking on all of that extra stress so we'll have to keep it simple with the planning." He raises his eyebrows at me and I try to keep my face a mask of innocence. "But, if we do it after, it may be tough with all the new baby stuff going on."

I nod, agreeing. "Can we wait a little bit to decide?"

"We can wait as long as you want." He pulls my legs into his lap.

"I am so in love with my ring. I need to get a manicure." I look down at my hand again, my breath catching in my throat every time I see the shifting color of the alexandrite.

Denver laughs and places his mug on a side table before doing the same with mine. "I'm glad you love it. My mom would have loved you and it makes me happy to see you wearing something that belonged to her." He admits, moving closer until he's hovering over me.

"Me too." I smile up at him, winding my arms around his neck and pulling him closer. Closing my eyes, I breathe him in just as he settles between my legs and lowers his mouth to mine. Although we can't get carried away, we definitely push the pelvic rest envelope.

"Seriously, what is it with you and couches?" I ask him as he trails kisses down my ribcage.

Denver laughs, the sounds rich and warm, and I close my eyes, loving that I get to hear it for the rest of my life.

"Sierra, you have a package." Denver calls out the next morning as I'm frantically trying to squeeze everything into my suitcase before we head to the airport.

"Another one? Pottery Barn Kids is seriously taking over our lives." I call back, sitting on my suitcase and fighting with the zipper.

"I think you'll want to open this one." Denver comes into the room and hands me a small box.

I glance at the return address and forget all about my suitcase. Reaching out to take the package from his hand, I hold it to my chest. "It's from my dad."

Denver nods, his face thoughtful as he watches me.

Sitting on the end of our bed, Denver next to me, I open the package delicately, nervously. Unsure of what it contains and what it means, I unwrap the tissue paper gently, and tears spring to the corners of my eyes as I look down and see the small painting of a field of flowers—yellows and purples and oranges. Vibrant and lifelike, they are textured to appear as if they're growing out of the painting. And then, in the center, is a tiny string of hearts, the end of one beginning the top of the next. And I know, without him here to explain it to me, that it's his heart, my heart, and the peanut's heart. The first one is the largest and the third is the smallest, and it's a family tree of sorts. Of course, it's not accurate, but it's his way of giving me something, of showing that he does care, that I do matter.

"There's a note." Denver bends down to pick up the small card stock that fell out of the package.

"Dear Sierra, You're going to be a wonderful mother. I hope your daughter has your strength, your spirit, and most of all, your passion. Thinking of you." I read aloud, tears tracking my cheeks.

Denver wraps an arm around my shoulders and holds me close while I cry.

"Baby, don't cry. This is a good thing, right?"

I nod into his shoulder, trying to explain myself. "I'm not crying because I'm sad. I'm crying because I'm happy."

"Okay." He drawls, his expression unsure.

"I'm serious. This," I clutch the painting to my chest, "this is closure."

Den pulls me closer and I rest my head against his heart, hearing the rumble of his chuckle and laughing through my tears.

EPILOGUE

DENVER

"Wheels up." Sierra wrinkles her nose at me, and I reach over to clasp her hand in mine.

"We'll be there before you know it," I reassure her.

"I know. It's not even that I hate flying, I don't. It's just, things are different now." She looks down to our sweet peanut.

"I know what you mean," I say, my eyes locked on hers.

"Do we have a lot of plans while we're in Ashby County?"

"Besides telling everyone we're engaged?"

She smiles. "Besides that."

"Not much. Evie and Jax should be there by the time we get home. Taylor and Carter already have a tree at my family home set up, all ready to decorate. I know Daisy's been baking like crazy and had a stocking made for the peanut. Just, you know, a normal Christmas."

"Can we have hot chocolate and sing Christmas carols?"

"I'm sure that can be arranged."

"It's going to be strange without any snow."

"I'm definitely not missing winter." I look out the window, eager to get home, see my siblings, and share the news that Sierra and I are getting married. We called her family last night and the

Begay-Anderson reaction was overwhelming. I'm expecting something similar from the Kanes.

"Thank you." Sierra rests her head on my shoulder, her eyes glancing down at the alexandrite. "For moving to New York. For fighting for us."

I kiss the top of her head. "Thank you," I tell her quietly. I don't say the rest. About how grateful I am to have her and the peanut in my life, about how she's been a game changer for me. About how guys like me only dream about chances with women like her.

But the way she smiles up at me, her dark eyes sparkling, lets me know that she knows all of it anyway.

The thing I'm most excited about is starting the next chapter of my life with Sierra and our peanut.

This Christmas will be full of all the usual Kane family traditions, with a few new additions and twists.

And I can't freaking wait.

<<<<>>>>

DAISY'S STORY

Stay tuned for Daisy Kane's story - a hot and sweet workplace romance set in Edinburgh, Scotland - coming February 2018.

To celebrate Christmas with the Kane Brothers and learn more about Daisy and Finn, sign up for my newsletter for a FREE novella prequel!

THE LAST FIRST GAME

Have you read The Senior Semester Series yet? Dive into *The Last First Game*, a sweet New Adult sports romance, and learn how sparks fly between football God Cade Wilkins and medical intern Lila Avers. Now available on all platforms.

* * *

September
Chapter One
Cade

The airport is packed with the bustle of businessmen in crisp suits and compact luggage, weaving in between the slow gait of college students and their mother's tear-stained faces. It's the end of summer and back to school season is upon us. I shake my head with a laugh. I've been back at school since July. Our first game is in eight days against Arizona University. We've got to give 'em hell.

I sit down near my gate, checking my boarding pass to make sure I'm in the right place. Gate A24. Yep. I stretch my right leg out, flexing my knee. The soreness eases a bit as I rub the tender joint.

The weekend went by quickly, a lot faster than I anticipated. It was solid of Coach to even let me fly home for the weekend with the season opener so close. I close my eyes. I wish more than anything that I didn't have to come home for yesterday's memorial service. That this weekend didn't mark the one-year anniversary of his death. I dreaded each moment of being in the suffocating walls of my childhood home in New Jersey, struggling to breathe against the influx of memories that all center on him: tossing the pigskin in the backyard, washing down leftover cold pizza with flat beer on Sunday mornings, squeezing Mamma in between us in big sandwich hugs, helping Dad wash his car in the driveway during summer. Jared's death in Iraq last year—IED roadside explosion—was the worst day of my life.

His one-year memorial service was second.

I open my eyes and scan the airport. An old man bounces a baby, presumably his grandson, on his knee; two young girls huddle together on the floor, using the sticky blue seats as beds for their dolls; a young hipster pounds on the keys of his laptop, his eyes narrowed in thought.

And then, I see her.

A tall, thin blonde, struggling with two oversized shoulder bags. A Starbucks cup dangles from her fingers as she huffs loudly, the air blowing blond waves out of her eyes. She looks up and her gaze meets mine.

Her eyes are cornflower blue, the color of the sky on a clear summer's day. At the moment they glisten, as if she's struggling to hold back tears. Then she blinks and shrugs at me as she dumps her shoulder bags onto a chair several seats away and perches at the edge of the seat, taking a long sip of her coffee.

"Excuse me?" An airline representative approaches the girl.

She looks up in alarm, clutching her boarding pass and looking around to confirm that she is in the right place.

"Yes?"

"I'm sorry to interrupt you. It seems that this flight is overbooked. For customers willing to wait until the next flight to Los Angeles, which departs in three hours, we are offering a free round-trip ticket to be used within one year of today's date. Would you be willing to give up your seat on this flight and take the next flight?"

The girl looks startled, her eyes wide. She tilts her neck to the left, clearly assessing the offer, thinking over her options. After several moments a smile spreads across her full lips. "Sure. I think I can do that. Now this free flight, is it anywhere in the network or only JFK-LAX?"

I chuckle. Smart girl.

"JFK-LAX."

She shrugs. "Okay. That's fine."

The woman points to the desk near the gate. "My colleague will assist you at the desk. Thank you for your understanding and cooperation. And thank you for flying with us today."

The blond girl stands up and stretches her arms overhead. Her open cardigan is baggy and hangs to her knees, but the T-shirt she's wearing underneath rides up, showing a sliver of smooth, tanned skin. She yawns and looks at her bags in disgust before heaving them onto her shoulder and walking to the desk.

Suddenly, kicking it on the East Coast for a few more hours doesn't seem so terrible.

Not at all.

"Excuse me. Miss?" I call out to the representative.

She turns toward me and I break out my killer smile, the one I use to charm my way out of Biology quizzes and mandatory study halls. "Do you need any other customers to give up their seats?"

RESCUING BROKEN

Have you missed Book One in The Kane Brother's Series? Meet Evie and Jax in *Rescuing Broken*. Now Available on all platforms.

* * *

Chapter One

"I'm hurrying," I grumble to my ringing cell phone as I dash into my townhouse, kicking the door shut behind me. Turning around, I flip the locks and reach into my purse, searching for my cell. Of course, my fingers connect with the phone just as the ringing ceases.

"Shit." I already know I'm going to be late. I should probably cancel. I don't even feel like going out tonight.

The shrill ringing cuts the air again and I sigh. Dropping my purse on the console in the hallway, I head into my living room, collapsing onto the couch.

"Jenny," I answer, curling my feet up below me and resting my head back on the cushions. My eyes shut. "I'm not sure about tonight. I'm really not up for it and I've—"

"Save it. I don't care. You're coming. Miranda and I haven't seen you in forever, and I really need a night out. You owe me."

I smile in response to her tenacity, but refuse to give in that easily. "I don't know. It's been a really long—"

"Day, week, month for all of us, which is why we need to grab a drink. I know you're probably pouting on your couch at the moment, trying to think of an excuse to ditch us again, but I'm not having it. Get your butt up, hop in the shower, pull on a pair of jeans and a sexy halter, and maybe, just maybe, if you cut the resting bitch face and smile a little, you'll even get laid tonight."

I manage to choke out a chuckle while a shudder runs down my spine, my eyes snapping open. "With a guy I meet at Raf's? Come on. We're lucky we don't contract STDs just from entering the place."

Jenny laughs, a girlish giggle she's had since high school. "Or needing a Tetanus shot from the hazardous bar."

I join in her laughter now, forcing myself to stand up. "Fine. I'll meet you girls there in an hour."

"We'll be sitting at the bar."

"Duh."

"There will be a Cosmo with your name on it so don't be late."

"No. Lenny makes the worst Cosmos ever. Just order a whisky sour or a gin and tonic, or something he can't mess up."

"A shot then. He should be able to handle that."

"See you there." Ending the call, I walk into my bathroom and toss my cell on the vanity.

Pinning up my hair since I know I won't have enough time to dry it, I take a quick shower and towel off in front of the mirror. Taking a moment to study myself, I note how my shoulders curve inward, as if they're trying to kiss. I can count my ribs, my boobs are nonexistent, and my arms hang awkwardly at my sides. Dark smudges from too many sleepless nights glare from underneath my eyes, exaggerated by the paleness of my skin. I look sallow, dejected, and exhausted.

I look like me.

* * *

Fifty-four minutes after confirming I am, in fact, the most undesirable human on the planet, I slide onto a bar stool at Raf's Bar and Grill and hesitantly accept the shot of tequila and lime chaser Miranda pushes in front of me.

"You look like shit," she greets me matter-of-factly as Jenny comes up to stand beside me, throwing an arm around my shoulders in a half-hug.

"Bad day?" Jenny asks gently.

I wave to a girl I used to work with who is sitting across the bar at a high-top table. She left Morris last year to go to graduate school and do something with her life.

Turning toward my friends, I smile it off. "Nah, just the usual run-in with a couple of tough guys at work. Nothing I can't handle."

"The same guys that have been giving you trouble?" A frown twists Jenny's lips as she peers down at me.

I shrug.

"That's bullshit." Miranda shakes her head. "You work at a physical therapy center for the goddamn military. You think they'd be able to control their own with all their talk of discipline and service and blah, blah, blah."

"It's not that simple," I say, my voice quiet. I focus on my hands.

"It is," Miranda counters, nodding as if to agree with herself. "You need to tell someone, Evie. Tell your boss or superior or commanding lieutenant or whatever the guy is called. Tell him you're being harassed. We saw it that day in the parking lot. They were awful!"

"Miranda's right." Jenny squeezes my shoulder. "We're just worried about you. You've been avoiding us."

"I've been busy."

Miranda's eyes widen.

"I have been." I sit straighter on the bar stool, defensive to the core. I wish they never saw what happened in the parking lot two weeks ago.

"I know," Jenny soothes. "We just miss you and want you to be happy, Evie. That's all. You need to tell someone about what's been going on. It isn't right."

"I know. Thank you, guys. Look, I just, tonight, I just want to catch up with my best girlfriends and relax and have a good time, okay?" I gesture toward Lenny, who is walking toward us, a tray of shot glasses and mixed drinks balanced on his open palm. "Look, Lenny's bringing more shots."

Miranda's eyes brighten as Jenny nods. "Absolutely. We can definitely do that."

"Thank God." I smile at Lenny, accepting the gin and tonic he hands me and passing my shot glass off to Miranda.

"You're not going to have this?"

"It's all you, girl." I raise my gin and tonic in her direction. "Cheers, ladies!"

"To forgetting all the stupid things I do tonight." Jenny raises her shot.

"And forgetting whoever I do stupid things with," Miranda adds, a snort of laughter erupting from her nose as she clinks her shot against Jenny's.

I laugh along with them, taking a small sip of my G and T.

I wish it were that easy to forget.

I wish I could throw back a shot, dance in a crowd, and give myself just one moment to turn off my mind. Enjoy a night out with my girlfriends.

I wish a lot of things.

"I love this song," Jenny squeals, pulling Miranda off her barstool and swaying with her just to the left of where I sit.

"Dance with us." Miranda tries to pull my hand, but I shake my head, taking another tentative sip of my drink.

"I'm good. You girls are crazy." I sing along with the lyrics, trying to get into the good time mood. Trying.

"How've you been, Evie?" Lenny asks from across the bar, a welcome distraction from trying to fake having a good time with my friends.

"Same old, Lenny. What's going on by you?"

"Not too much. Kep's giving me more hours here, which is really helping. I'm hoping in another month or two, I'll be able to quit my job at the mini-mart and bartend here full time."

"No kidding? That's great, Len."

"I know. Then I can enroll back in school. I've only got one semester left 'til my BA, you know?"

I nod. I do know. I know because Lenny has always been focused on the future, even in high school. Even when things didn't work out the way he planned after graduation, he remained determined to get his college degree, to do more with his life than anyone else in his family.

I offer a smile because I'm proud of him, even as the reminder that I've yet to finish my own degree flashes through my mind. Taking courses on and off, in-person and online, has stretched my typical four-year degree into nearly eight years. If I take summer courses, I can complete my B.A. by July but then what? I'm studying Psychology. Who the hell would want me rooting around in their head?

Coming from a long line of accomplished, successful, determined soldiers, my family is all military. And I'm all sorts of disappointment.

"I hope it works out, Len."

"Thanks, Evie. You need anything?"

"Just water when you get a chance."

"You got it." He pulls a glass out from underneath the bar and fills it with water, setting it in front of me.

Once he's called away from the opposite side of the bar, I shift my focus back to my friends. Grinding against each other, giggling, throwing back their heads, they attract the attention of nearly every guy in Raf's.

I nurse my water and check my watch.

How long do I have to stay until it's acceptable to slip away? Closing my eyes, I think of my comfortable couch, the soft sleep pants I wear at night, and the oversized mug I like to drink my tea from.

Gah!

One night out won't kill me.

Plastering a bright smile on my face, I bop my head in beat with the music. I can do this. I'll be fine.

ACKNOWLEDGMENTS

So many thank you's for all the support and love shown to The Kane Brothers series! Hope you loved meeting Denver and Sierra in *Reclaiming Brave*.

Tony and my babies - thank you x a million for all of your love, encouragement, and constant cheering!

To my family and friends - your love and support means the world to me.

To Regina Wamba at Mae I Design - Thank you for creating the perfect cover for Denver and Sierra! I love it!

To Rebecca Jaycox - You are amazing!! Keep slaying those adverbs!

To Patrick Hodges - Thank you so much for all of the time and energy you spend on my books. And for catching all the typos.

To all the Bloggers, members of my ARC Team, and author friends (especially YAAR and the OP) - thank you for your advice, wisdom, and support. It's wonderful to be part of a community like ours.

To you, the reader, so much gratitude for sharing this experience with me and for loving my characters as much as I do.

Happy Reading!
Gina

ALSO BY GINA AZZI

Corner of Ocean and Bay

The Senior Semester Series:

The Last First Game (Lila's Story)

Kiss Me Goodnight in Rome (Mia's Story)

All the While (Maura's Story)

Me + You (Emma's Story)

The Senior Semester Series Box Set (All 4 Books)

The Kane Brothers Series:

Rescuing Broken (Jax's Story)

Recovering Beauty (Carter's Story)

Reclaiming Brave (Denver's Story)

Daisy's Story (coming February 2018)

To check out a prequel to Daisy's story and celebrate Christmas with the Kanes, sign up for my newsletter here!

ABOUT THE AUTHOR

Gina Azzi loved every moment of college – especially her study abroad experiences, internships, and travel adventures. She draws from these experiences to create the storylines for her new adult and contemporary romance books.

A passionate reader, frequent globetrotter, and aspiring baker, Gina resides in Canada with her family. Her new series, the Kane Brothers, releases in 2018.

For more information, connect with Gina at:

Email: ginaazziauthor@gmail.com
Twitter: @gina_azzi
Instagram: @gina_azzi
Facebook: https://www.facebook.com/ginaazziauthor
Website: www.ginaazzi.com

Or subscribe to her newsletter to receive book updates, bonus content, and more!

Made in the USA
Monee, IL
12 June 2022

97868813R00156